THE STRANGER IN THE MIRROR

"You know the intersection on Regent? Down by the stadium?" I asked her.

"Do you mean the star intersection? Where all those side roads meet and everybody's turning? Bike paths crossing? Yes, I know it. I'm surprised it's not blocked with accidents every day."

"Me too," I said. "I guess drivers are extra careful. Knowing the dangers, I mean. That's where this whole thing got started."

"At the intersection?" Andy Anderson asked. "When was this?"

"A little more than a week or so ago," I said. "That's when I saw her for the first time."

"Who, Tess?" Sally asked. "Who did you see for the first time?"

I looked at Anderson. His face was a stony mask. He'd heard my story and wasn't buying a word of it. I turned back to Sally. I could tell she already knew the answer. She just needed to hear it from me.

"I was in my car, waiting for traffic to move, when I saw her. She was coming out of Hotel Red." I took another sip of water. I knew what this sounded like.

"Who was coming out?" Sally asked.

"Me," I said. "I saw myself come out of the hotel, cross the street, and walk right on by."

THE WRONG SISTER

T. E. WOODS

KENSINGTON BOOKS
www.kensingtonbooks.com

KENSINGTON BOOKS are published by

Kensington Publishing Corp.
119 West 40th Street
New York, NY 10018

All Kensington titles, imprints, and distributed lines are available at special quantity discounts for bulk purchases for sales promotion, premiums, fund-raising, educational, or institutional use.

Special book excerpts or customized printings can also be created to fit specific needs. For details, write or phone the office of the Kensington Sales Manager: Kensington Publishing Corp., 119 West 40th Street, New York, NY 10018. Attn. Sales Department. Phone: 1-800-221-2647.

Kensington and the K logo Reg. U.S. Pat. & TM Off.

eISBN-13: 978-1-4967-1275-2
eISBN-10: 1-4967-1275-7
First Kensington Electronic Edition: March 2018

ISBN-13: 978-1-4967-1274-5
ISBN-10: 1-4967-1274-9
First Kensington Trade Paperback Printing: March 2018

10 9 8 7 6 5 4 3 2 1

Printed in the United States of America

This book, like everything I do,
is dedicated to my man.
He knows who he is.

Acknowledgments

I have endless gratitude for all those who've dedicated their time and talent to making this book a reality. Here's to you, Toni Streckert, for sharing wine; mulling ideas; and not chalking it up to merlot when we posited a woman, stalled in traffic, seeing herself walk out of a hotel. To Ron Webster, my favorite Madison cop, who schooled me on procedure and somehow got his points across despite my constant distraction by his stunning good looks. To my writing group, The Fictionistas. Your unerring insights and critiques are the lifeblood of every word I pen. To Barbie Simons and Judy Knoll. I should get you uniforms and pom-poms, so rapacious is your support. To my brilliant agent, Victoria Skurnick, whose take-no-prisoners honesty gives me guidance, courage, and confidence. To my editor, Wendy McCurdy. Where did you get that memory? That ear? That nose for sniffing out what stays and what goes? Can you share? Oh, wait . . . you do! A special toast to my family and friends, who tolerate my long disappearances into the writer's isolation. Thanks for welcoming me back into the fold each time I resurface. And finally, but never meagerly, here's to Lance. I'll never know what I've done to deserve the support, protection, and comfort you give me every, every, every day. It's faint reimbursement to tell you I acknowledge and appreciate all you are and all you do. I thought I loved you on our wedding day. Oh! What a tiny seed that feeling was. You are my person.

CHAPTER 1

I'd been in a police station before. When I was ten. I'd left my bike propped against a tree while I ran in to the neighborhood library to return some books. I figured it would take less than a minute and I didn't want the hassle of locking it up. But Mary Ann Dunnick was at the return desk, trying to impress the librarian by naming all the state capitals. Mary Ann sat next to me in Mrs. Asher's fifth-grade class. Always trying to get me in trouble passing notes or copying off my papers. She once made up a rumor that George Lyster kissed me on the spring field trip to Camp Randall Stadium. That was a stinking lie and she knew it. I remember being so angry I could have punched her right in that pearl-button nose she was so proud of. When I complained to my dad, he told me to rise above it. He says things like that a lot. I know what he meant by that now . . . what with my thirtieth birthday coming up fast . . . but back in fifth grade? When somebody said you kissed a boy? Well, there was no rising above that. That kind of wound sticks. From that day forward I've had to willfully remind myself that anything bad happening in the world . . . from Ebola outbreaks to that whole *Real Housewives* TV franchise . . . isn't *necessarily* the work of Mary Ann Dunnick.

Anyway, back to my earlier visit to a police station. Like I said, my in-and-out plans for dropping off the library books got thwarted by my smart-ass classmate showing off, so I took a detour to the library shelves holding all the biographies. I loved that section. Still do. Pick a person, any person, and there's their life, all laid out in four hundred or fewer annotated pages. I made like I was looking for a book, but I kept my eye on Mary Ann. She was taking her own sweet time. By the time she left and I got my books turned in, someone had helped themselves to my dented-up red Schwinn. After my dad got finished giving me the what-for for losing something he'd spent good money on, he made me go to the station with him to file the report. I remember the policeman being a whole lot nicer than my dad had been about it. He laid a big hand on top of my head and told me how sorry he was that my bike had gone missing. *It didn't go missing*, I remember thinking. *Someone took it. And if I were you, I'd go straight to Virginia Terrace and knock on Mary Ann Dunnick's door.* That was twenty years ago. I never did see that bike again. And I never again saw the inside of a police station, either. Until today. This time the policeman wasn't so nice. I guess you really can't expect that when he's asking you about a murder.

"I don't have time for long walks around complicated explanations." He said his name was Detective Andy Anderson. Why would somebody do that to their kid? He was skinny, in that way men who run marathons are. Like you can see the bones under their skin and all you want to do is run out and buy 'em a hamburger. Extra cheese and bacon with a double order of fries. He had a tight buzz cut. Maybe he figured he could shave a half second off his time if he wasn't burdened with hair. "We've got a dead body, and there are laws against wasting police time."

I'm not sure how long I'd been at the station, or what time it was earlier that day when I'd heard loud pounding on my front door. Remembering it is like trying to read a newspaper in the fog. Two policemen stood on my front stoop and asked if I'd allow them to drive me downtown. I wasn't sure what the reason was, and while the officers were polite, they gave me the impression that declining their invitation wasn't an option. When

I'd arrived and Detective Anderson had told me what they were investigating, my fog disappeared faster than you could say yikes. Murder isn't part of our regular doings here in Madison, Wisconsin. Around here, the biggest crime is offending someone's sensibilities.

When the officers first brought me in, three detectives sat me in this small room, asked a whole lot of questions, and listened to what I had to say while they scribbled notes on little pads. After they heard my story, I couldn't tell if they were disappointed or confused. Two of the detectives left, saying they'd check things out. Andy Anderson remained, telling me we'd both stay put until they "see what we're dealing with here."

After Anderson warned me about wasting police time, he left me all alone. I thought about getting up, heading home, and waiting to see if they'd come for me again, but I've seen enough television shows to know that someone was watching me behind the giant mirror on the far wall. So I sat there, getting to know every inch of that room.

About an hour later, the door opened and Anderson walked back in. This time with a woman. She didn't look much older than me. Midthirties, maybe. She wasn't as afraid of hair as Anderson. She had a whole head of unruly blond curls. She smiled and reached out to shake my hand when they sat down.

"Sally Normandy," she said. "Nice to meet you."

I liked her eyes. Blue. Clear. Like she was sincere but focused. Smart and not ashamed for you to know it. People used to tell me I was smart. But that was when I was a kid. Back when all you had to do was follow instructions, stand in line, and not do anything to piss off a teacher. Do that, and the next thing you know you're off to the Talented and Gifted program.

Things with me are different now. Folks in this town have lots of words for soon-to-be-thirty-year-old college dropouts. Smart isn't one of 'em.

"Tess Kincaid," I answered. I figured it was the polite thing to do, but I was sure she knew more than my name by the time she walked into that stuffy closet they called an interview room.

"I've already told Ms. Kincaid here we got a term for lying to the police. It's obstruction of justice." Andy Anderson shook his head to let both me and Sally Normandy know he wasn't going to let anybody pull the wool over his close-set brown eyes.

"I got a thumbnail sketch of your statement from the detectives you spoke to earlier," Sally said to me. "But I'd like to hear what happened, this time straight from you. Would that be okay?"

I nodded. She seemed nice enough. Besides, I was sitting in the downtown office of the Madison Police Department. Would anyone really have the right to say that talking about what got her here wasn't okay?

"Can I get you anything before we start?" she asked. "Some water, maybe some coffee? I could probably scare up a sandwich if you'd like."

I couldn't recall the last time I'd eaten. I looked up at the clock on the wall. It was behind a steel cage. That didn't make any sense to me. Who'd steal a government-issue wall clock from a police station?

"I'm not hungry." It was true, even though it was nearly eight o'clock at night. "But water would be great."

Less than a minute later someone knocked on the door. Andy Anderson opened it and an arm reached in, offering a glass. Probably delivered by those people behind the mirror. The ones watching and listening to what was going on in this humid little space. I thanked them both when Detective Anderson handed me my drink.

"Tell me what happened," Sally said. "From the beginning. Slowly. With as many specifics as you can. Details are very important. Start at the beginning and tell me like it happened yesterday."

I told her I didn't think that would be difficult since it was less than a dozen yesterdays ago that this whole mess got started. I took a drink and started in.

"Are you from here?" I asked her.

Sally's smile was easy and relaxed. "I was born in Ohio, but I think of this place as home. I came for school and never left."

Her answer reminded me of that old joke about Madison. The one about even the cab drivers having PhDs. I've lived here all my twenty-nine years, but native-borns aren't all that common. The majority of Madisonians came here to study and learned soon enough that this isthmus is a very difficult place to leave.

"You a west-sider?" I asked.

"Close enough." Sally turned to Anderson. "You too, right?"

Andy Anderson grunted a syllable that could have meant either yes or no. He didn't seem interested in chatting about Madison neighborhoods. I directed my conversation to Sally.

"You know the intersection on Regent? Down by the stadium?" I asked her.

"Do you mean the star intersection? Where all those side roads meet and everybody's turning? Bike paths crossing? Yes, I know it. I'm surprised it's not blocked with accidents every day."

"Me too," I said. "I guess drivers are extra careful. Knowing the dangers, I mean. That's where this whole thing got started."

"At the intersection?" Andy Anderson asked. "When was this?"

"A little more than a week or so ago," I said. "That's when I saw her for the first time."

"Who, Tess?" Sally asked. "Who did you see for the first time?"

I looked at Anderson. His face was a stony mask. He'd heard my story and wasn't buying a word of it. I turned back to Sally. I could tell she already knew the answer. She just needed to hear it from me.

"I was in my car, waiting for traffic to move, when I saw her. She was coming out of Hotel Red." I took another sip of water. I knew what this sounded like.

"Who was coming out?" Sally asked.

"Me," I said. "I saw myself come out of the hotel, cross the street, and walk right on by."

CHAPTER 2

I told them I had been on my way home after visiting my father. I stop by every few days after work. He doesn't get out much. Who am I kidding? If he leaves his house three times a month it's a real *Dear Diary* moment for the guy. I bring him groceries. Sometimes takeout from his favorite Thai noodle place. His liquor deliveries he arranges himself.

That Tuesday had been particularly hot and humid. Dog days of August. I thought he might get a kick out of something cold, so I swung by Michael's Frozen Custard on my way. I knocked on his door, but there was no answer. I kept knocking. Long enough that his across-the-hall neighbor poked her head out.

"I haven't seen him in two days," she said. "He didn't look none too healthy, if you ask me."

I thanked her and knocked again. The pint of custard was getting soft. I finally used my key and let myself in. I hate doing that. Bad karmic deposit. I wouldn't want anybody walking into my apartment unannounced. But then, he gave me the key for a reason and, like I said, I come by every couple of days.

His place was hot and smelled like dirty laundry, bacon grease, and seven-dollar-a-pint whiskey. I put the custard in the freezer, walked into his living room, and turned on the window air conditioner. The grinding sound of metal on metal warned

anybody listening that the unit was putting in its retirement notice. The fan alone was loud enough to wake him up when my
knocking hadn't.

"There she is." My father wiped a hand over his face. "I must
have dozed off. Heat and all."

"I brought you some Michael's," I said. "Death by Chocolate."

He struggled to bring his recliner to an upright position.
"What time is it?"

"Five-thirty." I picked up the mug and newspaper from the
table next to his chair. As I headed into the kitchen I collected a
half-dozen paper plates littered with tortilla chips and caked-on
salsa.

"Will you stay for dinner?"

He always asked me that. As though dinner was a scheduled
and respected event in his life instead of a grab-a-plate-of-what-
ever-is-handy-and-sit-in-front-of-the-television affair. When we
were living together, before I left for my ill-fated attempt at a
college education, I'd set the table and we'd talk. The meals
weren't fancy. I was never the cook my mother was. But I tried
to make it a special family time the way she always did.

"Not tonight." I threw the plates in the garbage, along with a
few empty cans of fruit cocktail—always the kind packed in
heavy syrup—and a flattened cereal box. "What did you do
today?" I pulled the garbage bag clear of the bin, tied it tight,
and carried it to the front door.

"I planned on walking over to Hilldale. Maybe see who's at
the coffee shop. But the day got away from me somehow. I
never seem to know where the time goes."

*It goes into that coffee mug you fill with booze first thing in
the morning,* I thought. *Followed by several more as you fry
your mind in front of morning talk shows.*

"Well, maybe tomorrow," I said. I got a packaged meat loaf
dinner from his freezer, stabbed a few holes into the plastic
cover, and popped it into the microwave. He asked me the same
questions about work he always does, and I gave the same an-

swers. Our conversation ended when the timer dinged four minutes later and I busied myself scooping the slice of ground beef,
dollop of mashed potatoes, and spoonful of green beans onto a
clean paper plate. "You want the gravy over just the potatoes or
the meat, too?"

"Let's live dangerously, Tess." He wiped his hand over his
face again, like he was trying to clear away the haze. "Gravy
über alles."

I set the plate on the table next to his recliner. I brought him
a fork and a glass of ice water. I knew he preferred a different
beverage, but I long ago stopped bringing that to him. The ice
water would be nothing more than a chaser for the fresh glass of
whiskey he'd pour the minute I left.

I kissed the top of his head and tasted his oily hair on my lips.
"Maybe you could take a shower tonight, Dad. Show off your
handsome side when you strut on over tomorrow for coffee
with the buds." I headed to the front door, collected the waiting
garbage bag, and told him I'd see him soon. "Don't forget the
custard in the freezer. It'll make a nice dessert."

He asked me to make sure the door was locked on my way out.

I was thinking about my father's life as I inched through traffic back to my place. He hadn't always been like this. I remember Sanford Kincaid coming home for supper when I was little.
Back when everything was different. He was a giant man with
shoulders as wide as any door he walked through. At least that's
what it looked like to my little girl eyes. He was always in a
hurry. A new professor at the university's law school didn't have
much time for family matters. But dinners were important to my
mother. She traveled a lot for her job. I remember she worked at
the university for some hotshot genetics guy, but when she was
home she made sure to carve special time for the three of us. He
always indulged her. I remember her saying, "We have seventy-
five minutes with your father. Let's make them count." She had
a way of making things festive. On nights my mother had to be
gone, my father wouldn't bother to come home for dinner at all.

Katya, a university student with acne so bad it scared me, would meet me after school and feed me canned soup or tuna sandwiches before sitting me down to concentrate on homework. But when my mother was home, her kitchen welcomed us with warm aromas of roasts or casseroles every night at precisely six o'clock. She'd still be wearing her good dress, the one she wore to work. I'd tell them what happened in school that day. Only the good things, Mother insisted. Things that would make my father proud. At precisely 7:15 he'd push away from the table, tousle my hair, kiss my mother's cheek, and head back to his office, where he would stay until long past my bedtime. Back in those days, even though it was my mother who traveled, I viewed my father as a visiting dignitary, granting us an abbreviated slice of his oh-so-important schedule before disappearing, leaving us grateful for the crumbs of time he'd dusted us with and filled with anticipation for our next encounter.

I remember begging him to teach me to ride a bike when I was six or seven. He always promised he would, but stacks of papers and piles of books kept him too busy to follow through. It had been my mother who took the training wheels off my bike one Saturday morning. We put that bike in the trunk of her car and drove to the empty parking lot behind the engineering building. In less than an hour I was confident enough to tell her to drive away, I'd bike myself home.

But my father did take great fun in letting me drive his car. It made my mother shiver in fear, but once or twice a week my father would come in, drop his briefcase by the door, and call out for my mother to hold dinner. *Just five minutes should do it, Audra,* he'd say. Then he'd wave for me to join him, let me crawl into his lap behind the wheel, and we'd go forward and back along our driveway. *Is D for Donuts?* he'd ask. I'd be very serious and tell him no, D was for *Drive.* He'd tell me how clever I was. *And R . . . I suppose that's for Rug Rats?* I'd shake my head, check my rearview mirror, and assure him I knew which gear was for reverse.

We started that ritual when I was eight years old. My legs

were too short to touch the pedals. We'd make five or six runs up and down the drive, then head in to hear my mother fuss that one day I'd plow right into the house.

"Or into the street and get hit by a truck," she'd say.

My father would give her that look. The one warning her not to say another word on the matter. Then he'd nod at me, closing the subject before taking his seat. No matter what my mother served, dinner always tasted better on those nights my father took me driving.

After my mother left us I tried my best, but running a house that big was too much for a preteen, no matter how grown up I thought I was. My father had to shop for groceries and take me to dentist appointments. He had to write checks, gas the car, and go to my school conferences. I convinced him I was old enough to stay home alone, even though it was scary rattling around those rooms all by myself. And there was a giant oak tree with a branch that liked to knock against my bedroom window when the wind was strong enough. Truth told, I was relieved when a concerned neighbor called CPS and my father gave up those evening working hours. But that didn't work out so well for my father. His students complained he wasn't available. He no longer had the time to devote to his research. He missed one important conference when I was sick with pneumonia and another when my wisdom teeth needed to come out. I'll never forget those weeks after the dean informed him he wasn't putting my dad's name forward for tenure. I'd just started middle school. He'd sacrificed his career to take care of me, and the look in his eyes told me he was wondering if I was worth it.

He'd been allowed to finish the year. They offered him a one-year extension as an instructor, but he declined. My grandparents died before I was born and left him a modest trust fund. It carried us for a while, but we had to sell the big old house on Lathrop Street two years later. I asked him how my mother would know where to find us when she came back. He answered me by telling me to pack another box. I didn't ask again. After all, we wouldn't have been moving if he didn't have to spend all his time caring for me. He didn't need me complaining about anything, right? We rented a bungalow off Monroe Street, and he got a job teaching at the local community college. The two bottles of wine it took to soothe his pride each evening cost him that position my sophomore year in high school, and we moved to a two-bedroom apartment over a pie shop. He was never employed again. When I left for the university, his moves took him to smaller apartments in shabbier buildings. He'd been in the one-bedroom place off Midvale Boulevard for the past three years.

By the time I got to that star intersection, I was thinking about how my mother and I had cost Sanford Kincaid everything. I by my presence, she by her absence. I was also thinking about how small my life and my father's were. For all intents and purposes my father's entire world was a four-hundred-square-foot apartment. Mine wasn't much bigger. In six square miles of Madison real estate I was born, raised, and educated from kindergarten through two years of college. I still work at the same place that hired me when I dropped out . . . that library where my bike went missing all those years ago . . . and I rent the bottom floor of a three-flat two blocks away.

The Kincaid corner of the world is pretty damned minuscule. That's what I was thinking about when I saw her.

It was what she wore that caught my attention first. I saw a woman come out of the Hotel Red wearing a black suit and high heels. She was walking up the sidewalk, toward where I sat waiting for the traffic to clear. *She's not from around here,* was my first thought. You rarely see that level of dress-up here in Madison. And you certainly don't see it on a late workday afternoon when temperatures are in the high nineties with enough humidity to make your car windows sweat. I figured she must be from Chicago, up here on business. Traffic was barely moving. It wasn't quite six o'clock, and it seemed as if every automobile, motorcycle, bicyclist, and bus in town was making its way down Regent Street. I watched her walk closer. First it was her hair. It was so like mine. Not exactly the dishwater blond mine is, but close enough. A few blond streaks and highlights perked it up. She wore it short, bobbed to a chin as square and level as mine. My mother used to tell me it looked like God got done with my face, grabbed a straight edge, and ran it under my jaw for a nice, clean finish. Then she'd kiss the top of my head and tell me I was her beautiful doll.

My chin's still as square, but it's been many, many years since anyone's called it beautiful.

The woman got closer. I moved forward one car length, following the little electric roller skate impersonating an automobile in front of me. I could see her better. She took her right hand, combed it through her hair, and flexed her fingers at the top of her head, giving herself a little scalp massage.

Like I do.

She was about parallel with my car when the person behind me honked. I'd been so focused on the woman, I'd missed the opportunity to move ahead. The horn blast caught her attention, too. She turned, and for a moment our eyes locked. She had large blue eyes, spaced wide under a high forehead.

Like mine.

I could tell something registered with her. She wrinkled her brow. The movement was identical to the furrow I get when I think something's not adding up. Her nose dipped at the tip. Like mine. Her lips formed an anxious smile. Only for half a second. More nervous reaction than sincere greeting. Thin lips. Like mine.

The car behind me honked again. The woman on the sidewalk looked over her shoulder, like maybe she expected someone else to be there. I remember thinking she seemed startled. Maybe a little afraid. She looked at me one more time, real quick. Then she turned around and walked back toward the hotel. I inched my car ahead, keeping my eyes on her. I saw her re-enter the hotel. I didn't know what to make of it. I mean, you gotta admit, the whole thing was kind of freaky.

Then I got this queasy sensation in my stomach. Thought maybe I was going to throw up.

Like I said, it was real hot and muggy.

The asshole behind me laid on his horn again, like it was vitally important to world peace that he move forward the one car length that had opened up in front of me. I flipped him the bird and followed the traffic two more blocks until I could turn onto my street.

"What did you do then?" Sally Normandy asked.

"Nothing. Went about my evening. Probably read a little. Maybe caught some TV."

"You didn't think about the woman you saw?"

I glanced at Anderson. He was sitting there, taking it all in. Looking like there was a certain correct answer I was supposed to give, but he wasn't about to hand me any clues.

"No," I said. "I didn't think about her at all."

Sally kept her eyes on mine for a few moments.

"Go on, Tess. What happened next?"

CHAPTER 3

I like to keep my mornings pretty routine. That way I can fool myself into thinking I'm sleeping a little longer while I go on autopilot through all the showering, dressing, and breakfast-eating
rituals. So you can trust me when I say that by the time I woke up
the next morning I wasn't thinking about the woman I'd seen
down on Regent Street. It wasn't like I thought it was all a dream
or anything like that. I mean, she didn't enter my mind at all.
After my morning at-home stuff I locked the front door behind
me, walked the two blocks to the library, and started another,
more beloved routine.

It's always my favorite time of the day. *Opening the store* is
what my father used to call it. I like being the first one in . . .
snug behind a locked door . . . me and all those books . . . flipping on lights . . . dialing up the air conditioner . . . inhaling the
intoxicating perfume of paper, paste, and ink every volume
sends out to entice the reader to come closer. It's a smell I've
loved since I was a girl, when this very library was my sanctuary
from the lonely silence of a motherless home.

I headed back to the cleared-out corner I call my office and
looked at the reminder sheets the night crew left me before they
closed up. There was always something they couldn't figure out
or simply didn't want to do. I never mind that they leave it for

me to take care of. I like that kind of problem solving, especially early in the morning. That Wednesday I saw that Myra and Don, the two part-timers staffing the library's later hours, had left me with a couple of minor things to do before the patrons showed up. One of their notes said the interlibrary loan system hadn't delivered the books we'd expected and a couple of patrons had raised as much of a ruckus as is acceptable on the near-west side. Another message told me the back door was sticking again. Myra was afraid it was a fire code violation. I checked it out. Sure enough, the humidity had swollen the old wooden door. I lifted my leg, braced my foot on the wall next to the jamb, and pulled on the knob as hard as I could. The door popped open, and I nearly fell back on my butt. As I steadied myself I saw a flash of movement outside the door. Like I'd interrupted someone by jerking the back door open. I leaned out but didn't see anybody. I think I even might have called out, but nobody answered. I had to shove my shoulder against the heavy wood to get the door to close again. I double-checked the lock and wrote a sticky note reminder to call the building manager, then set about the familiar dance of preparing the library for opening. By the time I unlocked the front doors at precisely ten a.m., I'd forgotten all about what might have been moving there in the back alley.

The morning eased by with a steady stream of regular patrons. That's the joy of working in a neighborhood branch. The main library downtown draws people from all over the county. All over the state, probably. It's like a destination in itself, designed by a famous architect and decorated like some kind of spaceship from the planet Literati. Folks get dressed up to go there. They make a day of it: browsing the stacks, wowing themselves with the latest high-tech gadgets, listening to lectures from big-shot university scholars. They take it all in, then go have cocktails at whatever overpriced saloon the hipsters have designated *the* place this month.

My shop is better than that. In my place it's people who live nearby making the library a regular part of their day. Paige

Williams came in with her mom that Wednesday. I first met Paige when she was two and she'd toddle in for story hour. She and her family live in a refurbished four-square on West Lawn. It didn't matter if the snow was three feet high or the thermometer climbed into triple digits, Paige and her mom could be counted on for three visits a week.

"Miss Tess, guess what?" Paige wore pink shorts and a T-shirt proclaiming *Girls Rock* in rainbow glitter. "I'm going to school! I start kinney . . . kin . . . kinsle . . ."

"Kindergarten," her mother prompted. "You start kindergarten."

Paige's enormous blue eyes beamed with the news.

"Oh my," I said. "We better find something to get you ready for such a momentous event." Paige followed me to the children's section. Her mother promised she'd be back in an hour. I knew she was headed to the coffee shop at the top of the block. Our head librarian, Brian Erickson, has strict rules about unattended children, but as usual he wasn't in that morning. Besides, Paige was no trouble. Park her in that gingham rocker in the corner with a stack of picture books and you won't ever hear a sound from her. Neighborhood gossip has it Paige's father is never afraid to shriek insults or threats at his wife, anytime, anyplace, it doesn't matter. I figured if an opportunity presented itself for Paige's mom to spend a little quiet time with a cappuccino and the morning paper while her daughter was lost in a world filled with singing puppets, talking puppies, or flying carpets ready to take her to safer lands, well, I was more than pleased to help make that happen. It's not really that hard for people to look out for one another.

A big part of my job is supporting the people who give time to the library. The same two women have been volunteering at our branch for the past twelve years. Agnes is eighty-seven, and Innocent just turned ninety. They've known each other more than six decades, can you believe that? Their husbands, each long dead, moved them into a shared duplex over on Vilas Avenue just after the Korean War. The men had served together in the navy and brought their wives with them when they came to Madison to study on the G.I. bill. Agnes and Charlie raised their three girls on the top floor, while Innocent and Eddie lived childless, happy lives one floor below. Charlie retired from Oscar Mayer. He started in the plant skinning hogs and worked his way up to product management. Agnes liked to joke her husband had been "the big cheese in bologna." Eddie, on the other hand, took his degree in philosophy and hired on with the Postal Service. He didn't get a chance to retire. One January day he was delivering the mail in near white-out conditions. A bicycling commuter, unable to see much in the blizzard, ran into Eddie and knocked him into Mineral Point Road in time for a passing salt truck to grind him into the pavement. Innocent was home baking Eddie's birthday cake when the police came knocking on her door. Eddie would have turned thirty-four had he lived to see the next day. Innocent says after all these years she still can't stand the smell of spice cake with cream cheese frosting. The settlement Innocent got would have let her live anywhere, but she stayed in the only home she and Eddie knew and became a surrogate aunt to Agnes and Charlie's daughters. And though not one drop of shared blood ran between them, Innocent and Agnes were closer than any pair of biological sisters could ever hope to be.

I helped the two old friends get organized for the day. There were books to be re-shelved and mailings to coordinate. It took them longer to get things done than when I first started at the library nine years ago. I guess a lot of aging can happen when you get that close to the finish line. Truth told, I didn't care if they got one thing done. They smelled like lavender sachet, wore hand-carved mother-of-pearl combs in their hair, and whispered in respectful library tones as they shuffled across the tiled floor showing newcomers where to find things. They patted the youngsters with soft, age-spotted hands in a way that made their parents straighten their spines with pride. Brian stayed away from the library when Agnes and Innocent were scheduled. He called them the Reaper Twins.

Rosie Verdon came in around eleven o'clock. She wasn't scheduled to start her shift for another thirty minutes, but Rosie's always early. She's an undergraduate at the university, studying writing, and I swear she's read every book on the *New York Times* best seller list from the past five years. Works half-time to cover her expenses. She's twenty-one years old but handles herself like someone with twice that many years under her belt. She's got that friendly kind of energy everybody is attracted to. Even Brian likes her, and I don't think he likes anyone.

Rosie's got a sister. Violet's two years older than Rosie, with a personality that's polar opposite. Where Rosie's burning that midnight oil in order to graduate and is already planning on going down to Iowa to pick up her MFA, Violet's focus is men. I've overheard her more than a few times when she drops by for a quick visit, clucking her tongue at Rosie and calling her a chump for working so hard.

"Don't waste the pretty, Rosie," she says. "Get yourself down to that business school library. It's as easy to fall in love with a man who's gonna make the big bucks as it is some dreamy-eyed poet."

Violet's a clerk at an art gallery two blocks up from the library. She's never set foot in a college classroom, but she dresses and talks like someone from the royal family. Rosie once told me Violet doesn't give a flying fig about art. She's just interested in the men who have the money to plunk down thousands of dollars for an original painting to hang over their fireplace. I asked her one time, didn't most men who go to the gallery get there because their wives dragged them in? Rosie got that cute little grin of hers going and told me Violet doesn't think of the men as married.

"She thinks of them as between divorces."

Violet came into the library that afternoon to bring Rosie a pair of sandals she'd borrowed. The minute I saw her I flashed on the woman I'd seen the day before. You see, even though you'd be hard-pressed to find two young women more dissimilar than Rosie and Violet Verdon, if they weren't speaking you'd have to do an extralong double-take to tell them apart. It doesn't matter that twenty-six months separate them in age. Those two are mirror images of one another. Same dark hair worn in the same slick pixie cut. Carbon-copy turned-up noses with a constellation of freckles floating over each. Identical cheekbones—high and sharp in the middle of the same heart-shaped face. Each with eyes as green as an Irish morning. They were different women, that's for sure. But on the face of things they were identical.

Violet stayed all of three minutes. Her drop-offs were never much longer than that. It was only when she wanted to borrow something that she hung around the front desk, gossiping and telling Rosie all the things wrong with the way her baby sister was living her life.

"Did you two always look so much alike?" I asked after Violet sang out her good-byes and walked out the door.

Rosie thought for a moment. "I don't think I noticed it until I was in high school. I spent a long time in my gangly stage. The way my parents tell it, Violet was born graceful and stayed that way. I lingered in the all-arms-and-legs phase. Acne declared war on me but never bothered with Violet. A few years ago, my junior or senior year at West, I guess, I started to see it. Then we got more and more alike. Physically anyway. Why?"

I don't know why I didn't tell her about the woman at the star intersection. "Is it weird at all? Having someone look so much like you?"

Again Rosie took her time before answering. "I don't really think about it all that much. Violet's her own person. But I admit it's kind of intriguing when I see her wearing an outfit of mine. It's different from looking in the mirror. I get to see how I look to others, full-on. Not in a reflection." Rosie scrunched up that elfin face of hers. "I guess it is kind of strange, now that you mention it. I wonder how twins feel. Identical ones, I mean."

We were having this conversation behind the front desk. The library is always slow that time of day. I guess most folks would rather spend a hot afternoon down by one of the lakes.

"I've heard people say there's a twin for every person on the planet," I said. "Do you believe that?"

"I don't know. Maybe. Look at me and Violet. We look plenty alike. Of course there are twins who are the spitting image of each other. And when you get right down to it, how many different ways can you arrange two eyes, a nose, and a mouth? Think of it statistically. Sooner or later you're gonna come up with an identical combination. So, yeah, I guess I have no trouble believing there's an exact duplicate running around somewhere." She tossed the dust rag she was using to wipe down the counter into the bin under the desk and smiled at me. "Maybe your doppelganger is strolling along some river in Amsterdam this very moment. Or maybe on some wild African safari. Armed only with a camera, coming face-to-face with the deadliest predators on the planet. Wouldn't that be cool?"

I didn't tell her I thought my look-alike might be a whole lot closer than that.

Around six o'clock, after setting the evening crew up with their to-do list, I left the library. The air was heavy and hot as I walked home. It would be another couple of hours before the humidity broke and folks dared to venture out to their front yards and porches. I turned my own AC up when I stepped inside my apartment. Then I peeled off my sweat-soaked clothes and indulged in a cool shower. I had turned off the faucet and wrapped a towel around my wet hair when I heard something that sounded like a thud coming from my kitchen. I stood stock-still and listened, fully aware of my vulnerability as I stood naked beside that claw-foot tub.

The only sound I heard was my AC humming.

I pulled my robe from the hook on the wall and wrapped it tight around me. I stood behind the closed bathroom door for several seconds, listening. I grabbed a can of hair spray, opened the door, and stepped into the hallway, ready to spray aerosol lacquer into the face of any intruder.

But no one was there.

I checked the rooms. I double-checked the closets. Nothing seemed out of place. I looked under my bed. Then I went to my front door.

It was closed but not latched. Like someone had pulled it shut quietly but had failed to secure it completely. I opened the door and looked outside. The two geranium pots on my porch were undisturbed. The wind chime hanging from a rafter was motionless in the breezeless evening.

I closed the door, threw the dead bolt, and slid the chain lock.

Maybe I didn't close the door tight when I came home. I remember being so hot I wanted nothing more than to start that AC and get into the shower. I must have been careless.

Funny what we can get ourselves to believe, isn't it?

CHAPTER 4

I woke up with another one of those headaches. I never used to get them. I mean, like, ever. Truth is, I'm one of the healthiest people I know. But in the last month or so it's been like a ninja warrior has been taking sword practice inside my skull. Stabbing and lunging. Lunging and stabbing. Sometimes the back of my eyes are his favorite target. Other times it's straight up the center of my skull. That morning my ninja was mounting a lateral assault across the back of my head, slashing his razor-sharp saber in a straight line, about two inches up from where my neck and skull meet. Ear to ear. And just for giggles he punctuated his onslaught with the occasional kick to my left eardrum.

Rosie tells me it's stress. Probably caused by Brian.

I thought about calling in sick. But it was Thursday. That's a busy day for us. Interlibrary loans are reconciled on Thursdays, and a whole lot of folks are chomping at the bit to climb up a few notches on the book reservation list. So I dragged myself to the bathroom and showered and dressed. I felt a little better when I went to the kitchen to make my breakfast and pack a lunch. My favorite knife, the only one I ever bother to keep sharp, wasn't where it was supposed to be. I keep it in its own little box in my silverware drawer. When I went to cut my ham sandwich, the box was there but the knife wasn't. That irritation brought the ninja back off the bench with a vengeance. I swallowed a couple of aspirin, hoped for the best, and headed off to the library. Told myself I'd find the knife when I got back home.

It was a normal day, I guess. Maybe I spent a bit more time back in my office than usual, but like I said, my head was killing me. Everything got done, though; I'm pretty good at soldiering on. Next thing I knew it was already quarter past four. Rosie came in with a printout of the books I was supposed to pick up as part of the loan program. She reminded me Elaine Vogeller had been in twice that week already, asking when exactly the latest Lee Child thriller was going to be available for her.

"She's been tracking the reserve list as if it's the countdown to Christmas," Rosie said. "Elaine knows she's finally made it to number one. If it's not ready when she comes in tomorrow, you can be the one to break it to her. Have you ever heard how high her voice can get when she's peeved? I swear neighborhood dogs start howling."

So I scrambled to finish what I was working on, did a brisk walk home, picked up my car, and drove the few miles to Sequoya Library. I barely made it before Belinda, the librarian in charge of assembling the packages for the exchange, ended her shift at five-thirty. I ran through the listings, made sure Elaine's book was right on top, loaded the two crates into my car, and headed home in time to join all the other commuters. I was creeping along, air conditioner blasting, in the same traffic clog that got me two days before. It's a route so familiar I could have driven it blindfolded. As I was oozing my car down Regent Street, the Hotel Red came into view and I remembered the woman I saw before.

For a moment, I thought I saw her again. Near the same spot. A group of seven or eight people was crossing Regent. I was about four cars back, but I could have sworn I saw that same bobbed hair toward the rear of the pack. I recognized the trendy blond streaks. Her head was turned, as though she was looking at that dreadful statue outside Camp Randall. But I couldn't see her face. Once the group crossed the street, the members dispersed in several directions.

But the woman wearing a black sheath dress, the one with the sharply cut bob, walked straight to the Hotel Red and went inside.

The blaring horn behind me reminded me it was my turn to creep forward. I did, fully intending to head home. All I needed to do was make it two more blocks. Then I could turn, be out of the traffic, and have a clear shot straight to my apartment.

Instead, I turned into the Hotel Red's parking lot.

I didn't have a plan. What was I going to do? Knock on every door in the hotel? And if I did meet her, what would I say? *Excuse me, but isn't it funny how much we look alike?* I know how crazy this all sounds. A Christmas carol popped into my mind despite all that sunshine and humidity. *Do you see what I see?*

It was past six o'clock by the time I parked and went inside. The lobby was pretty full. The bar, too. Happy Hours are all the rage in Madison. I didn't see her.

I thought about getting a drink and grabbing a table with a clear view of the elevator. Maybe she'd gone upstairs to change out of that black dress. If she was from out of town, she'd probably want to come down for dinner. There were plenty of restaurants within walking distance, but she wouldn't want to stroll in this heat wearing panty hose and heels.

I got to thinking about how idiotic this was. What? Was I a stalker now? Besides, it hit me how out of place I must have looked. Hotel Red is for the chic and trendy. I was in my typical go-to-work outfit. Loose denim skirt, sleeveless cotton blouse, Birkenstocks. Hair pulled back in a scrunchie. No makeup beyond Burt's Bees lip balm. Nowhere near the sundresses, strappy sandals, and full-face makeup of every other woman in the place. I'd seen a woman who looked like me. Big deal. I decided to take myself home before I could embarrass myself further.

But first I had to go to the bathroom, so I made my way through the crowd to the restroom off the lobby. It was a two-stall setup, and I was glad to see only one was in use. When I was finished I went to the sink to wash my hands. Looking at myself in the mirror, I gave myself a mental talking-to for giving in to what was obviously a heat-related delusion or an easily explained something else. The toilet flushed in the other stall and then a woman stepped up to join me at the double sink. Our eyes locked in the reflection of the mirror. Both of us looked more than a little startled. Maybe there was even some amazement sprinkled in, I don't know. We stared in silence while warm water ran over my hands. I finally turned off the spigot but made no move for a towel. The other woman didn't move, either. We stared at each other. She was the first to speak.

"Well," she said. "I'll be damned."

CHAPTER 5

"It's like looking in a mirror. I mean, I know we're actually looking in a mirror, but . . ." She let out a long sigh. "This is just plain bizarre."

The bathroom lighting might have been unflattering, but it was bright enough for detailed accuracy. "I saw you walking the other day. Tuesday. I was in my car."

"That was you? I thought I saw someone familiar. I chalked it up to my general disorientation."

"You're the reason I'm here."

She pulled her head back in a pose of guarded curiosity.

"How's that?" she asked.

"I don't know. I saw you on Tuesday. You looked so much like me. Then I saw you again a couple of minutes ago. You were crossing the street. Maybe I wanted to make sure I wasn't hallucinating."

She wiped her hands dry and tossed the paper towel into the trash. "You live in Madison?"

"Yeah. I'm Tess, by the way. Tess Kincaid."

She nodded but kept her eyes on me, like she was sizing me up.

"I'm Mimi," she said. "I flew in from Boston on Monday."

She didn't have a Boston accent. In fact, I didn't hear any accent at all. Her voice sounded an awful lot like mine. Maybe a little deeper. Fuller somehow. "What brings you to town?"

"Job interview," she said. "At the university."

The door opened and two laughing women entered the bathroom. They stared at us for a moment, probably silently counting the number of cosmos they'd imbibed. If it weren't for our different styles of dress, they'd have been certain they were seeing double.

"You in line?" one of them asked me.

"No," I said. "We're finished." I turned to Mimi. She nodded toward the door and suggested we continue our conversation outside the bathroom. The two women gave us one last look. I heard their tipsy laughter resume as Mimi and I walked out into the busy lobby.

"Should we get a drink?" she asked, pointing to the outside patio. "Out there, if it's okay with you. It'll be hot, but at least we'll have some quiet." She must have sensed my hesitation and pressed a little harder. "Come on. How often does a person get to sit across the table from her own face?"

So we pushed our way through the crowded bar and took a seat at a table in the middle of the empty patio. The heat and humidity didn't bother me. In fact, I like those dog days of summer, even though most people can't stand them. The world seems smaller somehow when the air is that heavy and close. More manageable.

Mimi told me she wasn't much of a drinker and wanted nothing more than a glass of water. We waited, but no server came.

"Maybe they figure anyone insane enough to sit outside in this soup doesn't have cash or even room enough on their credit card for a couple of drinks," Mimi said. "But I'm used to it. It gets so humid in Florida during the summer you swear you're gonna have to sprout gills if you hope to keep on breathing."

"I thought you said you were from Boston."

"Only the past five years. I took my PhD from Tufts. Florida's my home. Well, since we moved there when I was about twelve. Coral Gables."

"Near Miami, right?"

"Actually, Coral Gables is like a donut hole of tranquility surrounded by the spicy Latin wildness that is Miami." Mimi looked back into the restaurant. There was no sign of anyone coming out to see what we wanted. "Should we stand and flap our arms?"

I offered to get our drinks. She reached for her wallet, but I waved her off. Mimi was a visitor to my town. Besides, she wanted only a glass of water. The least I could do was get it for her while I picked up my own drink. I headed back into the hotel, elbowed my way up to the bar, and returned a few minutes later with two glasses. She thanked me as I set her ice water in front of her. I sat back down and took a sip of my gin and tonic.

"You're here interviewing for a faculty position?" I asked.

She held up a finger, signaling me to hold on. I realized she'd taken a sip of water and was holding it in her mouth for a second or two before swallowing.

Like I always do.

"My PhD's in history. I research American popular music. Faculty positions are hard to come by these days. I'm applying everywhere and doing the face-to-face wherever I get asked."

"Any luck?"

"Here?" She shrugged. "Who knows? The position I interviewed for is only for one year. Somebody's taking their sabbatical. I met with a lot of people. Even the man whose classes I'll be covering. That must be strange, huh? Sitting across from the person who's replacing you?" Mimi's eyes were teasing. "I mean, how do you convince someone you're genuine enough to step into their shoes?"

It seemed easy. Talking to her, I mean. I've never been the kind of person who likes to make small talk. Particularly with someone I've just met. They always seem to be asking questions. Prying, really. How do you feel about this? When's the first time you whatever? I operate on the assumption that if someone wants me to know something, they'll tell me. Other than that, I figure it's none of my business. But having a conversation with Mimi was different. Thirty minutes after we sat down, I was halfway through my gin and tonic, talking to her as easily as I do Rosie. She didn't pounce on me with questions. We just shared. We learned neither of us was married. We were both only children, and each was more a dog than cat person. Anyone listening to us would never guess we'd met less than an hour before.

"What was your dissertation topic?" I asked.

Mimi rolled her eyes in self-mockery. "I did three hundred forty pages on the healing influence of Barry Manilow. Don't laugh. I put a lot of solid research in there. The man was a god back in the day. I would love to have been living when he was in his prime. Every heart broken in the seventies and eighties was made a little better with a Manilow tune. I'll bet you don't even know who he is."

"Are you kidding?" I asked. "My mother was addicted. I remember her cranking up 'Copacabana' every Saturday morning while we cleaned the house. To this day, whenever I smell furniture polish I think of Lola and Tony. And good old reliable 'Mandy.' You could always count on her to give without taking."

"Ah," Mimi added. "But he sent her away."

"And yet has the nerve to ask her to kiss him and stop him from shaking."

It had been a long time since I laughed that hard.

"What about you?" she asked. "Where'd you go to school?"

I pointed over my shoulder. "Right here. General studies. Got slogged down second semester of my sophomore year and withdrew instead of taking the hit to my GPA. Never finished." I pointed again. This time to the west. "I work down there. The Monroe Street Library."

"You like it?" she asked.

"Depends on what you mean by *it*. I like the library. The patrons are all neighborhood people, so that's great."

"I hear a 'but' in there. And that could mean one of three things. You're underpaid, there's too much bureaucracy, or your boss is a jerk."

"How about all three?"

"You deserve better. I can already tell."

We were quiet for a bit, content to watch the people coming

and going. Things were slowing down. Madison closes up pretty early on a Thursday night. Even in summer. Midwesterners would never let a night of revelry interfere with their up-with-the-sunrise attitude. There was another day of work tomorrow. Around these parts you'll hear middle-aged folks still referring to weekday evenings as "school nights."

"So, back to the elephant in the room," Mimi said to break our repose. "What's your theory on what's going on?"

I looked into a face so much like mine. "I don't know. I've always heard there's a duplicate of ourselves somewhere. Today I had a discussion about how there's only so many permutations you can make with facial features. I've read there's even an app that will help you find yours. Maybe that's what we are. A pair of those look-alikes people talk about."

She drained the last of her water and pushed the glass away. "Still, it's odd that we'd meet, wouldn't you say?"

I thought about that. "I work with this woman. Rosie's her name. She's the analytical type. Rosie would call our meeting a statistical fluke. The whole damned world's nothing but a chaotic, random shuffle and deal according to Rosie. Maybe she's right. I mean, you could as easily have been on a job interview at Columbia this week. Or North Nowhere Community College. I could have missed the traffic jam on Tuesday if I'd left my dad's two minutes earlier and not seen you walking down the street. Sometimes paths cross. It might seem like something more, but it's really a coincidence."

"You seem way too young to be such a Polly Pragmatist. Where's your sense of mystery and magic?" she asked. "How old are you, anyway?"

"Twenty-nine. How about you?"

"When's your birthday?"

"October 11th. Which means I'll be turning thirty soon. I guess I hadn't realized how close it was. Maybe I'm growing into my Polly Pragmatahood."

Without preamble, Mimi pushed herself away from the table and stood. "You said you lived near here?"

THE WRONG SISTER   31

"Two blocks away from that library I told you about." I had the feeling she was dismissing me.

"Let's go to your house. If we stay here we'll end up spending money we don't have drinking more than we should."

"You seem in a hurry. What's up?"

"Maybe you and your friend Rosie are right. Maybe our meeting was the randomness of the universe." She pulled her purse over her shoulder. "But, like you, I have a birthday coming up. And I'm turning thirty. On October 11th. Does that sound like a coincidence?"

CHAPTER 6

Mimi ran her hand along the back of my sofa. "Nice place." She pointed to the black-and-white photographs over the fireplace. "You take these?"

I nodded. "It's been a hobby since high school. I'm not very good. But it's cheaper than buying wall art, I guess."

She walked over to study the trio of pictures. I'd taken them two days after a favorite restaurant burned down. The place had been a Madison landmark, and I wanted to make sure part of it stayed alive.

"Don't sell yourself short," she said. "These are good. All jagged edges and stark destruction. Like what was once so familiar is gone." She turned toward me. "Stuff like that happens all the time, doesn't it? Now you see it, now you don't. People, too. Here one minute, gone the next."

"I don't know about that," I lied. "You want something? Chips? Soda?"

She shook her head and continued her stroll around my apartment, then picked a book up off my sofa and thumbed through a few pages. "You always read stuff this literary?"

"Not always. It's a best seller." I poured myself a glass of ice water. "I need to stay up on what's current so I can make recommendations to library patrons."

She closed the book, tossed it back on the sofa, and looked at me. "You take things very seriously, don't you, Tess? I'll have to remember that."

An awkwardness hung in the air. "What now?" I asked.

Mimi pursed her lips, as though considering our next move. "Let's start with the physicals. Kick off your shoes."

We stood barefoot back to back in my kitchen and laid our hands across the tops of our heads. Exactly the same height.

"I'm a size six," Mimi said. "Straight off the rack. How about you?"

"Same here." We shopped in different stores, though. You could tell she spent good money on clothes. While I envied her polished look, it never made sense for me to make those kinds of purchases.

I pulled out my phone and snapped a photo of Mimi. A close-up of her face. Then she took one of me. We compared them, straining to find differences. With the exception of her hair—highlighted with blond streaks and cut an inch or two shorter than mine—we found none.

"What's your ethnic background, your heritage?" she asked. I remember thinking a history scholar would ask that.

"My paternal side comes from Scotland," I told her. "Not that long ago, actually. My father's grandparents came over and started some kind of printing business in the early 1900s. My father's father was the first in his family to be born in the United States. My dad was born in Massachusetts. Not far from Boston." I recalled Mimi had said she'd taken her PhD from Tufts. I started to wonder how many coincidences were going to pile up. "I don't remember which town."

"Was he by any chance an identical twin?" Mimi asked. "I knew a guy in undergrad. His father was a twin and so was his mother. The twins married each other. I guess one set started dating and then hooked their sibs up on a blind double date. You should see the kids these two couples had. They all look alike."

"Double cousins," I said. "We have some around here. But I don't have anything like that. No uncles, no aunts."

"What about your grandparents? Where are they?"

"They died before I was born. Car crash."

Mimi considered that for a moment. "So you never met them?"

"How could I meet them if they're dead?"

"Sorry. Thinking out loud." She sat down. On my sofa. In my spot. Legs curled up under her. Just the way I like to sit. Anyone looking at her would see she was completely comfortable occupying my space. "So you have no family here in Madison? Beyond your father, I mean."

"How do you know my father's in Madison?"

"He's not? I'm sorry. I assumed. When we were talking about coincidences back at the bar. You said you'd been coming home from visiting your father when you first saw me. Did I get that wrong?"

"No. I guess I forgot I mentioned him."

"So there's no one else? No family?" Her voice dropped into a seductive huff. "No lover?"

"I thought we were following coincidences." I'm sure my tone was sharper than it needed to be.

"You don't like talking about yourself. That's another thing I'll have to remember." She looked at me for a few moments before speaking again. "Back to your father and his Scottish roots. Let's see what we can deduce. You never met your father's family."

"Like I said, that's tough to do since my grandparents died before I was born."

"Don't get testy. We're following leads. Let's say your dad's an identical twin."

"But he's not."

"I said let's say. Your fuse runs short, doesn't it?"

"Okay," I said. "*Let's say* my dad's an identical twin."

"Then let's say he disappoints his family in some way," Mimi continued.

My father has disappointed a lot of people, I thought.

"Or maybe his family disappointed him," she said.

My father's had that experience, too. A lot of people have let him down. My mother and I lead the list.

"It had to be something big." Mimi's gestures picked up as she built her scenario. "Something that led to a big family fall-out. Who knows what it was all about? Religious differences, maybe? You know, back in the day people took that kind of stuff a lot more seriously. Your father a religious man?"

I shook my head. "It never seemed to interest him. At least he never talked to me about it."

"Maybe he fell in love with the wrong girl." Mimi's smile got devious. "Or maybe even the wrong boy."

"Never happened."

"So it was something else. A youthful indiscretion. A run-in with the law. The particulars aren't important right now. What-ever it was, it was big. There was a major family blowout. Yelling, screaming. Threats, warnings, denunciations." Her arms waved as she spun the tale. "I can totally see it. Your fa-ther finally had enough. He made the decision to walk away from the whole bunch. His own twin included. Disowned his entire family, grabbed your mother . . . that is, if he even knew her at the time . . . and struck out on his own. When you were born he told you your grandparents had died. He became a man who promised himself he'd live his life on his own terms."

I thought about my father, alone in his small apartment. I doubted those would be the terms he would have chosen.

"His twin might have been devastated, but life goes on. Un-beknownst to your father, his twin meets a girl, marries, and goes on to become *my* father." Mimi's blue eyes were wild with the explanation she was giving birth to. "And then, three decades later, you and I meet. Not with that universal random-ness crap you suggested earlier but in some karmic script writ-ten by an eternal hand. We become friends, unravel the mystery, heal the wounds, and find a way to reunite our long-estranged family."

"Are you sure your PhD's in history? That much drama

sounds more like hysterical fiction. And you've got enough *let's say* in there to make the whole thing sound like a farce."

"You think so? I read about this exact thing happening, not too long ago. In New York City. A girl is sitting in her first day of graduate school at Columbia. The professor tells the students in his seminar class to introduce themselves. Tell a little bit about their upbringing. Some girl she'd never met tells the story about how she'd been put up for adoption as an infant. Describes the story her mother told her about her birth mother. The whole thing rings a bell with the other girl. Long story short, Girl A starts putting two and two together, sits down with Girl B for a cup of coffee, and a couple of weeks later DNA tests confirm they're sisters. Never laid eyes on one another before they walked into that seminar room. Does that sound like hysterical farce?"

I didn't want to hurt her feelings. I've known some people who need to be right. Always, no matter what the topic. Maybe Mimi was one of those. Still, it felt like a betrayal to my father to sit and listen as she spun stories about a man she'd never met. A man who'd sacrificed his entire life to take care of me.

"Odd things happen," I said. "I'll admit that. But there's a piece of this pie you don't know that eliminates your entire premise. My grandparents left my father a trust fund after they died. That doesn't sound like someone who's been disinherited."

Mimi wasn't one to let facts stop her once she got on a roll. If you want to know the truth, the more I got to know her, she struck me as someone who wouldn't let anything stop her.

"What proof do you have it's a death-related trust fund?" she asked. "Maybe it's money his parents gave him to stay away. Hush money for never again speaking of the dark family secret."

I almost wished Mimi's story could be true, dark skeletons in the closet and all. At least it would mean there was family out there somewhere for my father. But the cold, hard truth was, with the exception of me, Sanford Kincaid was alone in the world. Parents dead. Denied the circle of colleagues that would have come from the long and rewarding career he was robbed of when he had to step away from academia to raise me. Abandoned by his wife. Left alone in a low-rent four-plex to imagine there might be friends waiting to share a cup of coffee at a neighborhood shop.

The urge to protect my father was as near as skin to me. I'm sure my voice was firmer than needed. "It didn't happen that way, Mimi. Let's talk about something else."

She didn't argue with me. But while she may have been gracious enough to move off the topic of my father, the mystery in which we found ourselves was too juicy a bone for her to stop gnawing. "What about our birthday? Explain away that one."

My irritation was growing. Maybe I was tired, maybe I was frustrated. Whatever it was, I wasn't enjoying our conversation anymore. "Millions of people are born every year. There are only three hundred sixty-five days for them to do it. Tens of thousands of babies were born that October eleventh."

"Do they share the same face?"

When I didn't answer, she watched me for a while. The Nancy Drew sense of adventure left her eyes. "Have I said something to offend you?"

I didn't feel like answering her. Maybe because I wasn't quite sure what was irritating me. Instead, I looked at the clock. "It's almost nine. I have an early day tomorrow. You ready for me to drive you back to the hotel?"

"You're pissed about something."

My irritation mushroomed into a full-blown anger. And my headache was back. So I did what I was taught in that anger management class I was forced to take my senior year in high school. It was my punishment for kicking in the front of my locker after Deidre Cummings told me it was better if Thomas Franke took her to the homecoming dance instead of me because at least she'd have something decent to wear. Stupid teenaged thing, I know. Probably the hormones raging. I thought the whole idea was bogus, but I've got to admit, the class taught me skills that help me keep my snarling dog of anger chained up tight.

So rather than going off on Mimi I closed my eyes, took in four deep breaths, and focused on slowing my heartbeat. It was a minute or two before that dog settled back into its cage. I appreciated her staying quiet long enough for me to calm down.

"I'm not like you," I said.

"What do you mean?"

I struggled to find the right words. "I get it. This whole thing intrigues you. But I'm not used to making up stories about my family."

"You're telling me you're not even curious about what's going on here?"

"Let's stop, okay? This isn't what I want to be doing right now."

"Then why did you come looking for me?"

"I don't know. I saw you. It was weird. Then I saw you again." I knew I wasn't answering her question. "I don't know why I went into the hotel."

"Because you wanted to meet me." She was as calm as I was agitated. "Because there's an answer to this riddle, and you're as interested in finding it out as I am. So let's get to it. You don't like talking about your dad and his family. Okay. There's plenty of strings to tug on to solve this mystery. How about your mom? Where is she? Where do her people come from?"

I took my glass of water into the kitchen and emptied it down the sink.

"Uh-oh," Mimi said. "Another nerve hit. Sorry. Do you see her often?"

Forcing myself to stay calm with every step, I returned to where I'd been sitting. I looked across to Mimi. She seemed so relaxed. So interested in what I had to say. It was a story I didn't like telling.

Yet for some reason I did.

"My mother left us. I was twelve years old."

Mimi's voice dropped into the sympathy register. "Oh, Tess. I'm sorry. What a rotten move. Where is she now?"

I shook my head. "I have no idea."

"She doesn't keep in touch?" Mimi sounded incredulous. "With her own daughter?"

Something hot was crawling up from my stomach, burning its way higher and higher in my throat. Once again, my anger dog pulled on its tether. "No. I haven't seen her since she left."

"What happened? She and your dad fight all the time? Was she feeling trapped by the responsibilities of motherhood? Some sort of psychotic break?"

The burning found its way into my mouth, and my snarling dog broke away from its chain and lunged forward. "This isn't a parlor game, Mimi! What business is it of yours, anyway?"

My rage was immediately replaced with spine-crushing shame. Just like it always is.

"I'm sorry. You didn't deserve that. I guess we all have pieces of our family history too tough to discuss. You happened to bump into mine. That doesn't mean I should yell." I apologized again and hoped she knew I was sincere. "Let's chalk it up to me being a private person."

She smiled in what I assumed at the time was forgiveness. "I know how you feel. That gives us something else in common. You grew up mostly with only your dad. It's always been Mom and me. My dad died about six weeks before I was born."

"Was this down in Florida?"

"No. I was born in Colorado. Boulder. Nice town. But kind of lonely, I guess."

I was relieved to have the focus off me and my family. "Was it tough growing up without him?"

Mimi's eyes sparkled through a shine of tears. She bit her lower lip and took several long breaths before she spoke. When she did, her voice was choked. "Don't ever let anyone tell you it's impossible to miss something you never had." The calm sophistication she displayed throughout the evening disappeared. She appeared vulnerable. Fragile, maybe.

"Did your mom ever remarry?"

Mimi shook her head. "It was always her and me. Dad left

her pretty well fixed financially. There were never any worries about money, and she worked only because she loved it so. I'm not quite sure what it was she did, actually. I was a kid. All I knew was that she traveled a lot for business. And I had a wonderful nanny named Lily. But one day Mom came home and announced she'd quit her job. I was thrilled. I wasn't so happy when she announced we were moving, but I got used to it."

"Why'd you move?"

Mimi shrugged. "Who knows? Maybe Mom needed a fresh start. Away from memories of my dad. All I know is she came home one day, pulled me out of school, told me everything was going to be different, and boom! We were off to sunny Florida. After that, she made raising me her full-time job. She'd be there for me every day when I got home from school. She was my Girl Scout leader for years until I begged her to let me quit." Mimi laughed. "She enjoyed that chapter of our lives way more than I did. We traveled. Around the country at first, but as I got older we'd go wherever she thought might be fun. When I went off to college her wanderlust took off with a vengeance. Without me to tie her down she's free to roam the world. I get postcards and Skype messages from places I have to Google so I can find out where the heck my own mother is."

As she told me about some of her mother's adventures, I remember thinking I'd kill for the opportunity to see that kind of spirit in my father. To see who he might have been without having me to tie him down.

"But she always stays in touch." I hated to admit it, but I felt jealous. "You always know where she is."

"When she can. I haven't heard from her in over a week. She doesn't even know I'm here. This job interview came up after she left for Brazil. She's cruising with some rain forest salvation league. Volunteering to gather water and soil samples. At least I think that's what she said she'd be doing. There's no Wi-Fi where she is. No phone service."

"Do you miss her?"

Mimi's face softened. Her smile was wistful. When she spoke, her voice was barely a whisper. "I do. I miss her a lot. For a long time my mother was all I had." She stayed quiet for several moments. "But life goes on and all that rot. Time for moving ahead, going our own ways, Mom and me. And she's not the only one having an adventure right now, is she? I can't wait to tell her all about this. She'll want to meet you, that's for sure."

In that moment I knew I wanted to meet her, too. And another, very different, realization hit me in the same instant. I was tired. Very tired. I didn't know whether it was the time or the circumstances, but I was suddenly weary to the bone.

"It's late," I said. "My bed is calling out to me. Come on. I'll drive you back to the hotel."

Mimi took her time surveying my apartment one more time. From my kitchen to my breakfast nook, across the living room and down the hall toward my lone bathroom and single bedroom.

"You've created a cozy space here, Tess. I like it." She patted the sofa with both hands. "It's been a hell of a day, to say the very least. If you don't mind, I think I'll stay right here."

I was taken aback at her assumption she'd be welcomed. "I don't know if that's a good idea. I'm not exactly set up for houseguests."

"Oh, I'm no bother. I'll camp out here on the sofa. We'll have breakfast together. I'll walk you to work. Then you can point me in the right direction, and I'll get myself back to the hotel."

It's odd, isn't it? Those in-the-moment decisions we make that seem so innocent yet cost us so very much. I guess now I could blame it on my fatigue. But that wouldn't change anything about how things turned out, would it?

"Why not?" I said. "I have lots of new toothbrushes from past visits to my dentist. Let me go get you some blankets."

Mimi took her time in the bathroom as I readied a sleeping spot for her, but she finally emerged, face scrubbed, teeth brushed, and wearing my favorite pajamas.

"All set," I said. "This sofa is actually more comfortable than you'd think." I turned to head down the hall to my bedroom when it dawned on me.

"You know, I don't know your last name." I'm sure I sounded as silly as I felt. "If I wake up tomorrow morning and all my furniture's missing, I'll need a name for the police report."

She snuggled down under the covers. "Didn't I tell you? How rude of me. It's Winslow. Tell the cops to be on the lookout for Mimi Winslow from Coral Gables, Florida."

The floor beneath me seemed to give way. A hum buzzed in my ears, growing to a deafening roar in less than one heartbeat. I held my arms out to my side to steady myself and willed the noxious liquid gathering in the back of my mouth to return to where it came from. I turned around slowly, certain I'd collapse. I walked back over to the sofa and looked down at her.

"Did you say Winslow?" I asked.

"Yes. Tess, are you okay?"

I wasn't sure of much at that moment. But I was most assuredly certain I wasn't okay.

"Winslow," I said. "Winslow is my mother's maiden name."

CHAPTER 7

Mimi wanted to stay up and talk more, and the bombshell I'd dropped erased any fatigue I felt moments before. But a primal urge throbbed inside me. Some ancient instinct to protect myself filled the space between my ears, screaming at me to hurry away. An irrational impulse to grab Mimi by the scruff of her neck and toss her out of my house surged through my muscles.

But that was ridiculous, of course. At least that was what the thinking part of my brain was insisting. Mimi was still the woman she was before I learned her last name. Lying there on my sofa, in my pajamas, she looked like a vulnerable teenager. I needed to be by myself and make sense of what was happening. So I overrode my instincts and told myself to calm down. Get some rest. Everything would make sense in the morning.

I went to my room, locked the door, and flopped on my bed. My arms and legs were heavy, yet weak. Every inhale and exhale demanded purposeful effort, as though deep structures in my brain had forgotten how to go about the basic business of staying alive. A burning fatigue stung right behind my forehead, dancing incongruently with an incendiary burst of energy. It was even money which one would take the lead. My throat was dry as dust. Sleep was out of the question. I suppose that might be natural after all the events of the day. But nothing felt natural anymore. I tried all my tricks to make myself drowsy. I counted backward from two hundred to zero. When I got all the way down to three, two, one, my body was exhausted, but my mind was as alert as a sniper on night patrol in Kandahar.

I didn't have a clue what was happening, but whatever it was, it had jumped way beyond being explained away as one of Rosie's statistical coincidences.

I must have fallen asleep at some point, because I woke to the smell of coffee brewing. It took me a few groggy moments to convince myself I hadn't been invaded by caffeine-loving burglars. Then I remembered I had a houseguest and lifted my head off the pillow, only to be greeted by what felt like the U.S. Olympic boxing team using the back of my eyeballs for speed-bag practice. I forced a halfhearted focus to my bedside clock and kicked myself free of the tangled sheets. It was almost seven-thirty. I had to open the library at ten. And there was always that forty-five minutes of paperwork left by the closing crew that had to get done before the first patron walked through the doors. If I didn't hustle I was going to be late. I slipped my feet into some flip-flops and headed down the hall.

Mimi stood by my kitchen sink, wearing my lightest-weight jeans and my favorite Green Bay Packers T-shirt, freshly showered and ready to greet the day. While I was certain I looked like something someone might put on a poster to warn kids against the evils of talking to strangers, whatever mystery the two of us were involved in didn't seem to have had any impact on her sleep at all.

"Are you wearing my underwear, too?" I stumbled forward to accept the mug of coffee she held my way. "I'm sorry. That sounded mean."

She nodded toward the bathroom. "I left you plenty of hot water. I like the smell of your shampoo, by the way. You want me to fry you some eggs while you shower?"

I took a long sip of coffee, and the pain behind my eyes eased a bit. "No. Thanks anyway. I save big breakfasts for the weekend. Most mornings I make do with toast and a couple of pieces of fruit." I glanced at the bowl on the counter. Four apples, two oranges, and three bananas. Same inventory as the night before. "But you go ahead. Help yourself."

Mimi shook her head. "I've already eaten. Must be the time difference. Maybe all the excitement of our paths crossing. I know we said we'd have breakfast together, but my stomach was growling."

I drank more coffee and made note of another distinction between us two seemingly identical women. Mimi was far perkier than I had ever been that early in the morning.

"I'll have your toast ready when you're dressed," she said as I headed down the hall. "We'll have a nice chat and I'll walk you to work."

Despite my sleep deprivation, I was beginning to feel as if I might be able to handle the day ahead. Mimi sat across from me at my breakfast nook table while I ate my toast, banana, and apple. We didn't talk about whatever cosmic convergence led to our meeting one another. Instead, we shared more about our lives. I learned she dated off and on but hadn't met anyone she considered worthy of a long-term commitment. She talked a bit more about her love of American popular music and her belief that it was more than mere soundtrack.

"It holds a masterful sway over our emotions and memories," she said. "I could play a couple of cuts from Metallica, for instance, and in no time you'd be fired up and ready to throw a punch at me for no apparent reason. Or a song can come on the radio and all of a sudden you're seventeen again and that handsome Sammy Barlow is trying to get you into the backseat of his parents' Buick after show choir practice."

She insisted I relax with a third cup of coffee while she cleaned up the dishes. She asked me what it was like growing up in America's heartland. "Is it the magical world of drive-in movies and summer nights at the ice-cream stand that Bon Jovi and John Mellencamp make it out to be?"

I told her about ice skating in winter, hanging at the lake in the summer, and part-time jobs at fast-food restaurants. She asked me if I was popular in high school.

"Isn't that the goal of every Midwest teenager, after all?" I didn't care for the judgment in her tone. "To have three parties to get to on Saturday night? Wear your boyfriend's letter jacket and beat out your girlfriends to make homecoming court?"

"It wasn't like that for me." There must have been something about the way I said it that told her not to push any further. She smiled, turned her back, and focused on one final wipe to the countertop while I crammed what I needed for the day into my canvas backpack.

"What time's your flight?" I locked my front door behind us and pointed in the direction of the library.

"I fly out a little after two. The hotel has a shuttle. I'll be back in Boston in time for dinner. And I'm sure I'll be spending time with my journal the entire flight back. I want to capture every minute of this whole freaky thing while it's fresh in my mind." We walked a few steps in silence. "I'm going to miss you," she said. "Isn't that strange? I haven't even known you for twenty-four hours. But somehow you seem close to me. Like it's important we know each other. Does that make any sense?"

I told her it did. And that I felt the same way.

I wish I hadn't. I wish I'd told her she meant nothing to me. That our meeting was a mistake. That I wished I could hop on a time machine and go back to the moment I saw her walking out of that hotel. Because if I could, I'd find a way out of that damn traffic jam. Even if it meant crashing into somebody's car or driving up on some stranger's lawn. I'd get myself away . . . far and fast . . . from that star intersection. And I'd never look back.

But that's the thing about any given moment. You can't know what the next one's going to bring. You do the best you can without one stinking clue about what's going to happen five seconds from now . . . hell, even half a second from now. You roll the dice based on what you've got at hand. Your heartbeat hands you off to the next moment, and you hope it all works out. Most times it does.

This time it didn't.

Mimi and I turned north on Garfield, and the library came into view. She said she liked my setup. I remember thinking that was an odd word to use. I asked her what she meant, and she told me it was nice that I could walk to work or restaurants or shops. She said she thought it was a nice way to live.

"Yeah," I told her. "I do have a nice setup."

"Trader Joe's!" Mimi pointed across the street while I unlocked the front door to the library. "Oh, my god! I'm hooked on their Triple Ginger Snaps. Have you ever tried them?"

My breath caught in my throat. I don't know why. I should have been immune to being stunned by our similarities by then.

"No." Why did I lie about something so small? "I don't think I've ever had one." I stepped inside, and Mimi followed me.

I went about my business while Mimi strolled the aisles. It felt good to have her there. Looking back, that was one of the most confounding things about this whole situation. One minute my instincts screamed at me to run away from her, and the next I felt as comforted by her presence as a newborn hearing her mother's lullaby.

Maybe that was part of her plan.

That morning in the library, I glanced at her from time to time, trying to determine what held her interest as she visited the various sections of our small neighborhood outpost. Was she curious about my job? Or was she lingering, delaying the time she'd have to leave our odd confederacy of confusion? She came back to my office and stood in the doorway while I put the finishing touches on last night's reports. I got the feeling she was about to say something when a familiar code knocked on the front glass door. Three long, two short, three long.

"What's that?" she asked.

I closed the program, shut off the computer, and stood. "Not what, who. A regular. He's on his way to work. Comes by twice a week. Drops off the book he's finished and picks up another. In and out."

Mimi feigned a look of exaggerated disappointment and spoke with a deep, authoritarian voice. "What's this, Miss Kincaid? Are we stretching the rules? Playing favorites?" She pointed to the clock on the wall behind my desk. "The library doesn't open for another fifteen minutes."

"Be quiet. It doesn't hurt a thing. Think of it as providing excellent customer service."

Mimi craned her neck to see the man standing in front of the glass door. "Oh my. We're a handsome sort, aren't we?" She turned to me with one eyebrow raised. "What's the story? And if you haven't made a move on him I'm going to need a full explanation why."

"There's no story." I came around the desk and stood in front of her. "John's a very nice man. It's a small kindness I do, that's all." The coded knock came again. "Stay here. I'm not supposed to have anyone in the library off hours."

She pointed toward the door. "And what do you call letting him in?"

"That's different. He's a patron. He belongs here. Now stay put and be quiet. This will take all of three minutes." I didn't wait for an answer before I headed to the front.

"Good morning, John." I opened the door wide enough for him to enter, then locked it behind him. "It's going to be another hot one, isn't it?"

"Makes it a little easier to be stuck in my cube all day." John Rappaport, I'd come to know from almost a full year of brief twice-weekly conversations, worked in the business office of the university's athletic department. He oversaw contracts, particularly those from manufacturers wanting to use any of the scores of trademarked logos tied to the various sports teams. "Won't have to be out in the hot soup all the cool kids are calling air these days." He handed me the book I'd given him the past Monday. "This one was terrific. Maybe in need of a little editing, but still amazing."

"Stephen King knows what he's doing. Not a better storyteller working today. He'll use as many pages as he needs to get the job done." I set the book on the return desk and handed him three I'd selected for his review. John was always in a hurry. It

hadn't taken me long to learn what types of books interested
him. About eight months ago I offered to make suggestions. He
seemed to like the efficiency of that idea, and our early morning
arrangement was born. "Pick one."

"Guaranteed?" He always asked the same playful question.

"Or there's no charge." I always gave the same response.
John headed to his favorite table by the window. I went back to
my office, knowing he'd make his pick in short order.

"Well, he's not ugly, is he?" Mimi was all smiles.

She didn't need to know I agreed.

"So? Is there some secret code of library ethics that says you
can't date a customer? What are you going to do? Break some
confidence that he likes bodice-ripping romance novels?"

I stifled a laugh. "He likes thrillers with a bit of a horror or
supernatural twist."

"Is he married?"

I glanced over my shoulder. John was still at the table, reading the back of one of the books. "I don't know." It must have
seemed odd that after nearly a year of chitchat I didn't know that
about him. But there was something about him that tweaked my
awkwardness quotient and kept my tongue tied about anything
beyond book reviews. "We don't talk about things like that."

"Does he wear a ring?" she asked. "And don't even try to lie
and tell me you've never looked."

This time my laugh was born of embarrassment. Still, it was
nice to tease with someone like this. "No. There's no ring."

"Then ask him out. I can tell by that cute little blush crawling
across your cheeks you think he's as handsome as he most assuredly is."

"I couldn't do that." I wasn't interested in mischief anymore.
"Maybe you could, but I couldn't."

She thought about that for a moment. I hoped she wasn't of-
fended.

"Okay," she said.

"Okay, what?"

"Okay, I'll ask him out. Like I said, my plane doesn't leave until two." She broke out a devilish grin. "And I do have that hotel room right down the street."

My eyes must have grown wider than I realized, because Mimi burst out a laugh. "You *do* like him. I knew it. And I have a hunch he likes you, too."

I felt vulnerable. Curious, but vulnerable. "Why do you say that?"

"A guy who looks like that?" She nodded toward John. "Let me tell you something, Little Miss Library Staffer. Books you can get any number of places. Day or night. But he comes in here twice a week, makes the same jokes, always when you're alone, and reads what you want him to. He's interested. Poor guy's probably as shy as you are." I started to disagree, but she cut me off. "Don't think I don't see behind your fast-talking bravado. You're timid, so what? Lots of people are. Maybe John is, too. But the two of you are going to die lonely unless one of you makes the first move."

A hot flush crept up my neck. I felt a line of sweat form at my hairline. "That's not going to happen."

Mimi took a tissue off my desk and mopped my forehead. Without asking she ran her hands through my hair, shaking her fingers as she went, fighting August's humidity to achieve maximum fullness. Another quick move had her unbutton the top two buttons of my shirt and widen my collar, exposing a significant amount of skin while keeping my décolletage nothing more than a discreet allusion.

"I want you to seize this moment." Her tone left no room for dissent. "Go out there and do whatever you need to do to make his checkout legit. Then ask him again what he thought of the Stephen King. When he starts to tell you he liked it, interrupt him, look him square in the eyes, and say this: 'Actually, I'd love to hear all about it over a glass of wine this evening. What time are you free?'"

I took a step back. "Are you crazy?"

"Maybe. But I know you'd be nuts to miss this opportunity. Do it, Tess."

Self-assurance radiated from eyes so identical to mine. I never allowed myself to think anything would come of my attraction to John. But there were her eyes . . . my eyes . . . filled with the conviction that this would be an easy and logical step.

"Look, Tess. This is how it's going to go, and we both know it. I'm going to get on that plane. We're going to promise to keep in touch. And for a week or two we might even do that. But then our lives are going to go on. I'm going to get hired somewhere. I'll build my career, and if I play my cards right, a life with a good man, a couple of kids, a dog, and a few crazy friends is out there waiting for me. You're going to stay here and be an underappreciated library staffer who walks to work and takes care of her alcoholic father unless you do something different. The odds of our paths crossing again are like ten million to one. But we have this moment. Our paths *did* cross. Do this, Tess. Do this for you. Do this for us. Mark this odd little shimmer in the celestial sea that brought us to one another by doing something completely out of character."

"What if he says no?"

"Then he's either married or a fool. Either way you wouldn't want him."

She made it sound so easy. But a part of me whispered that maybe she was right. Maybe it was me making it difficult.

"One of us is right, Tess. I'm betting I'm the one. I'd stake my money on the possibility you're ninety seconds away from a first date with a good-looking man." She nodded toward the front of the library. "Now get out there and see which one of us wins the wager." She spun me around and gave me a gentle nudge out my office door.

"It's going to be the Koontz," John called out as I neared the counter. "It was the tease about Elvis that got me. Is he really in the story?"

I held a finger to my lips. "Library oath. We never give away a plot twist. Especially once we know a reader is interested."

"Well"—he handed me the book—"you've never steered me wrong before. I'm sure you don't intend to start now."

I processed his loan and handed the book back to him with a nervous little tremor in my hands. My breathing became more rapid as my heart raced. "You really liked the Stephen King?"

"I did, especially the way he . . ."

I interrupted him and jumped off that cliff. "Actually, I'd love to hear all about it over a glass of wine this evening. What time are you free?" The words came out faster than I intended. And I forgot the part where I was supposed to look him in the eyes.

John's head snapped back as if I'd slapped him. He looked toward the door. Then he looked back to the table where he'd been sitting. He looked down at the counter. My legs melted in humiliation's heat, and I leaned against the same counter for support. A scorching wave of embarrassment rose from my stomach and climbed toward my chest.

And then he looked up and smiled.

"I could meet you here at six. Does that work? We could grab a table at Barriques."

CHAPTER 8

Truth told, my good-bye to Mimi could have been more gracious, but I was dancing with some unfamiliar emotions after I made the date with John. I wish I could remember what she said exactly or recall something about the tone of her voice. That might have given me a clue as to how this whole thing was about to go down. I keep thinking there must have been something I missed. But all I could think about then was that John was coming back at six. We were going to walk down the block, sip wine, and talk about our days. I know to some folks a first date with a guy they'd had a crush on for almost a year might be just another Friday, but stuff like this doesn't happen to me. Like ever. I remember Mimi gloating when I went back to my office. You know, that told-you-so kind of attitude people can get when . . . well, they just told you so. She did take a harsh look at what I was wearing and made me promise to scoot home on my lunch break. She even told me what outfit to wear. It was a mix-and-match of things she must have pulled from her memory of stuff she'd seen at my place. That could only mean she'd been shuffling through my things. I see that now, but at the time it didn't register. I was swimming in unchartered waters and grateful for the advice.

Before she left, Mimi said something again about me meeting her mother. But to tell you the truth, I don't recall much beyond that. She waved and walked out the door. Said she could see the hotel from the sidewalk. I had a fleeting thought about how she told me the odds were against our ever seeing one another again. I guess I believed her.

I'd give anything to have been right.

But on that day nothing mattered except my date with John. The morning crawled by with a steady stream of regular patrons. Innocent and Agnes arrived to start their volunteer hours, so I got some things together for them and tried to focus as they each raved about their current favorite mystery series on PBS. Rosie came in around eleven. Early as usual. I asked her if she minded if I took a little extra time at lunch. She said okay. Rosie's okay with everything.

I trotted home and took a long shower. Mimi was right. My shampoo does smell great. I took the time to lather-rinse-repeat and shave my legs extra close. I turned the air conditioner up full blast. When it's this humid it's tough to hold off a sweat and I wanted to look as fresh as I could for as long as I could. I took my time blow-drying my hair. I even put a few curls in it. I liked the final result. I thought about adding a few highlights next time I went for a haircut.

I stood in front of my closet for a long time, trying to find the perfect thing to wear. I wanted to look good, but I didn't want to come off like I was desperate to make an impression. In the end I put on the exact outfit Mimi suggested. A gauzy cotton skirt. Pale blue with small white dots. Bias cut and falling to my ankles. I teamed it with a sleeveless white cotton T-shirt. Mimi suggested I wear a navy blue sports bra underneath.

"Sure, it'll show," she said when I balked. "But it won't look like you're pushing the goods. It'll just make him realize you're wearing a bra. Let him have some fun thinking about what's inside."

I gave it a try and, son of a gun, it looked great. Mimi thought my turquoise corn blossom necklace would spice up the outfit. I even wore the flat white sandals she recommended, and I smoothed moisturizer over my face, arms, and hands. A brush of mascara and some pale lipstick was my only makeup. When I looked in the mirror, I liked what I saw. I drove my car back to work. There was no way I was going to walk and let August deflate what I'd spent ninety minutes putting together.

Rosie gave a whistle when I got back to the library. Agnes and Innocent had left for the day. Brian, our seldom seen head librarian, called and said we shouldn't expect him. Said he was meeting with board members about fund-raising. That may or may not have been true. Brian and the truth have more of a nodding acquaintance than what you might call a real working relationship. I'd know soon enough, of course. If Brian really was meeting about fund-raising, he'd call me into his office the next day with a list of things he expected me to do to produce the money he promised the committee. I call Brian "the bread man." He thinks it's because he brings in a lot of dough, but really it's because in the great sandwich of fund-raising, he's the two yeasty bookends. He's there for the promises and he's there to take the credit. But when it comes to the meat of creating, developing, and pulling off the programs to actually bring in the money? Well, that falls to me, Rosie, and all the volunteers I can corral.

The afternoon passed more quickly than the morning. Rosie had called out the ten-minutes-to-close warning when John walked in. His lunch hour must have been as busy as mine. He'd worn cargo pants, golf shirt, and sneakers when he came by that morning. But he picked me up wearing jeans, a soft white cotton shirt, and brown leather sandals. He walked straight up to me. He smelled terrific, and his cheeks had that just-shaved look.

"You look great," he said. "Are you ready?"

I turned to Rosie, who waved me off. "Go. I've so got this."

I shot her a look of thanks, picked up my purse, and walked through the door John held open for me.

Barriques was crowded. It always is. It's located in the heart of the Monroe Street action, so in the morning there's a steady stream of retailers, neighborhood commuters, university types, and police from the nearby station coming in for their favorite to-go beverage. After that come the grad students. They plug in their laptops and stake claim to any available square inch of table space, nursing one cup of three-dollar coffee while they use the establishment's electricity and Wi-Fi for hours. Between eleven-thirty and two, the place jumps with local employees on lunch breaks. Then it's the students and their computers again. Quitting time brings the Happy Hour crowd, drawn by Barriques' wine list and half-priced Mediterranean appetizers. When John and I walked in a few minutes before six, it seemed that every table was taken, and several people were standing with a wineglass in one hand and a plate of hummus and pita in the other.

John led me to a table in the far corner. He removed the RE-SERVED sign, folded it, and stuck it in his pocket. "Bartender's a buddy of mine. I swung by around three and staked my claim. He said he couldn't enforce it but wouldn't remove it, either. Never underestimate Wisconsin folks, Tess. They like rules. This place could be shoulder to shoulder and no one would dare sit at a reserved table."

"People like rules, huh? Tell that to any policeman and watch 'em laugh."

John smiled. I'd always thought his eyes were blue, but sitting this close I could see they were gray, with greenish specks throwing off light.

"Yeah," he said. "But those sorts of people don't hang out at a near-west wine bar. Speaking of which, my bud the bartender says he's got just the thing if I'm looking to impress a date. Shall we give it a go?"

I nodded, and John got up to fetch our drinks. I turned his phrase in my mind. Was he out to impress *me?* I looked around the crowded room. Nobody glanced my way. They were all busy with their own conversations. Laughter came from some of the tables. Two women, each holding a glass of white wine, strolled toward me. They were looking this way and that, scouting for open seats. One of them, a tall blonde in a thigh-skimming sundress, looked right at me. She and her friend walked closer. I steeled myself.

"Nice necklace," she said. "Did you get it in Arizona?"

She was smiling, waiting for my answer.

"No. Down the street." I got a little braver. "Katy's. You should check it out. She's got some great stuff."

The tall blonde nodded. "Thanks. I will." Then she turned and walked away.

John came back to the table with an icy bottle of wine and two glasses.

"Don't feel pressure," he said as he poured. "We'll drink what we want and you can take what's left home." He handed me my glass and raised his. "To Stephen King. And to the lovely librarian who calls him the best in the business."

I focused on his hair and held on to my glass. Anything to keep from blushing. It was brown. Light, like maybe he was blond as a kid and it darkened over the years. He wore it loose but neat. Not touching his collar and trimmed around his ears, but long enough to let the natural wave show off.

"Is it time for me to tell you everything I liked about the book?" he asked. "Or can we talk about other things?"

Was he making fun of the way I'd asked him out? "We can talk about anything you'd like."

"Good. Let's start with what you think about the wine."

I hadn't taken a sip yet, so I did.

"Tell me the first thought that pops into your mind," he said.

I shoved my nervousness aside and complied. "Flowers. I smell flowers. And if I ever tasted a rose, I imagine this is what it would taste like."

Those green specks in his gray eyes started to shimmer. "Good on you! That's as apt a description of this Riesling as I've ever heard. Tell me more."

I took another sip. This time I let it linger on my tongue. "Sweet, but not in an icky way. Like a snowflake dusted with one single crystal of sugar."

John leaned back. "There's a poet inside you. *A snowflake dusted with sugar*. I'm going to steal that, if you don't mind."

"And where will you abscond with it?"

He dipped his chin. A sheepish look came over him. "On my blog. I write about wine. Does that make me sound like the most pretentious asshole in the world?"

I was surprised. "So it's contract negotiator by day and wine connoisseur by night? I would never have guessed. I'm impressed you have time to knock off two novels a week."

"Oh, there's more, I'm afraid. I'm also a law student."

I had no idea. But then again, how could I? "Here?" I was instantly embarrassed by the stupidity of my question. "Of course it's here. What am I saying? How do you manage?"

John took a sip of his wine. I liked the way he held the glass—low on the stem, as if he didn't want the warmth of his hand to take the chill off the contents.

"Well," he said. "First off, it helps having a great boss. And I do. He knows my goals and he supports me. As long as I keep up with my work, he doesn't care when I do it. I work full time during the summer and half-time when classes start. My third and thankfully final year begins the end of this month."

"Don't most folks at your stage clerk for some judge?"

"Hmm, I see you're familiar with the tedium that is law school." I was glad he didn't ask how I knew what I did. I wasn't ready to talk about my father's failed career at the very school he was attending. "A lot of people use this summer to clerk. But I want a career in sports management. Wisconsin's Athletic Department is one of the biggest in the nation. I can't imagine one that's better run. Like I said, I have a great boss. He's got me working on all manner of contracts. I interact with the legal department constantly. I sit in on upper management meetings. For the kind of career I want, I'm right where I need to be."

"What about studying? And when do you find time for pleasure reading?"

"You know what they say about law school. First year they scare you to death. Second year they work you to death. Third year they bore you to death. I'm happy the hard work's behind me. This year should be a cake walk."

"That's a glib response." I was impressed with all he was able to manage in a day. "Really, tell me how you do it all."

He was quiet for a few moments. Like he wanted to consider his answer before responding. "I think if you're doing what you love, it's easier. And I love the law. It brings structure to all the chaos we humans seem to naturally carry in our wake. And I love sports. So studying ways to combine the two doesn't seem taxing to me. I also love wine. Writing about it takes no effort at all. And as for the pleasure reading, well, there's a couple of reasons I do that."

His eyes held mine. I typically would have been uncomfortable with someone paying me that much attention. But this time I wasn't. This time I liked it.

"First and foremost, while I love researching the law, it can be pretty dry. I've seen way too many law students lose their love of reading. It's been beaten out of them with all that mind-stunting fine-print precedent. I made a promise to myself when I started law school. I'd keep a novel going at all times. To remind myself how much richer I am when I read fiction. I never want to lose that."

"And the other reason?"

He reached his right hand out and traced my pinky finger. "I know this cute librarian. She feeds me the most delicious books. And now I get to talk to her about them."

I fought the temptation to pull my hand away. To tell him I'm not a real librarian. I'm a college dropout who slogs her way through mundane grunt work. It wasn't that I was purposefully hiding who I was. I didn't want to disappoint him. And I liked the warmth of his hand and the tingling excitement that danced along with it.

So we sat that way for a while. Saying nothing. Letting our hands get to know each other.

"What about you?" he eventually asked. "You're learning my secrets and penchants. Tell me some of yours."

I suppose I could have started with something we shared and told him my father once loved the law. But then I'd have to answer his questions about what became of all that. I didn't want John to know about my mother's abandonment and my father's subsequent overwhelm with caring for me as a young girl. I didn't want one man on the verge of beginning his own legal career to know I'd been responsible for the destruction of another's.

"I'm pretty much what you see," I said instead. "I've lived in Madison my entire life. Always loved books. But I'm not a librarian. Just a lowly staffer. I dropped out of college many credits short of a degree. I'm lucky to have a job I love so much, I guess."

I was surprised at how fast I blabbed my lack of credentials to him. Maybe I wanted to give him an easy out. Maybe I wanted to feel the sting of his rejection early on, before I came to care for him.

"Ever been married?" He didn't even flinch at my academic failure.

I shook my head. "Not even close. I dated some in high school and college. But nothing I ever felt all forever about. How about you?"

"There was someone once. But that was a while ago." He was quiet again for several heartbeats. "You know, my grandfather once gave me some wonderful advice. Johnny, he said, the first thing to figure out is where you're going. Then figure out who you're taking with you. I guess I had the cart before the horse with that relationship. Since then I've been so busy trying to figure out where I'm going I haven't had the time or the inclination to get around to seeing who I might want to ask to join me." He leaned back and spread his arms, an open book ready for inspection. "So here I am, thirty-two years old and getting ready to start my third year of law school. Better a little late than a little never, isn't that what they say?"

"What did you do before?"

"Taught high school. Six years. Math. All levels. From algebra to calculus."

"Here in Madison?"

He shook his head. "Green Bay. That's where I grew up. I taught in the same school I graduated from. Let me tell you, that's a trip. Being able to walk into the teachers' lounge with people who used to send you to the principal's office? Wild."

"I always wondered what goes on in there."

"I don't mean to burst the mystique, but it's a break room. Smells like stale coffee and a community refrigerator nobody wants to clean. There's no wizard behind the curtain."

He was easy to be with. I liked his humor and his candor. He seemed like a guy who didn't have a secret in the world.

"Why'd you quit?"

Again, he took his time answering. I liked that about him, too. He impressed me as a man who knew words were important. He wanted to choose them carefully.

"Public education used to mean something." He shook his head in disgust. "But that's gone. I loved my students. I tried to make as much of a contribution as I could. But I could see the direction things were headed. I didn't want to be the last dumb sailor to jump from a ship that's so obviously sinking. I hope that doesn't sound cold."

I knew exactly what he was talking about. In a lot of ways libraries were taking on ever more of the basic educational functions for young students while the public schools were overwhelmed trying to address the social and welfare needs of the kids enrolled there.

"Sounds like you're following your grandfather's advice."

"We keep talking about me." His smile was relaxed. His eyes were warm. "Tell me what you read, how's that? That should be an easy question for a librarian."

"I'm not a librarian."

He leaned in and put his right hand over mine. "Easy there, girl. No need to be defensive. Nobody at this table's here to hurt you."

Was I that obvious, or was he that sensitive?

"Okay, so you read a lot, I imagine. Part of the job." John returned to the conversation without skipping a beat. "But what's your passion? What does your hand reach for first when you have a free afternoon?"

I knew my answer. I didn't know if it would be as interesting as all his answers were.

"Tell me, Tess."

I took a deep breath. "Time," I said. "I like to read about time."

A curious look came over his face. "You mean like clocks or watches?"

"No, but that's a good example of what I find so intriguing. Time is something, right? I mean, you can see the impact of it all around. Trees grow, people age. But you can't see time. You can't touch it. All we can do is register the effects of time, not time itself. It's not an animal, vegetable, or mineral. It's not an emotion or a thought. And when we try to capture it, we're not even lassoing the actual thing."

"I don't think I'm following."

I paused. "Take those clocks or watches you asked me about. They're nothing more than a man-made attempt to bring measurement to something that truly can't be measured. The click of a watch, if it's running properly, is constant. Time isn't."

"The whole relativity notion. Like an hour in a dentist's chair feels like an eternity." He reached for my hand again, this time holding it. "Yet the past hour feels like ten minutes."

I glanced at my watch and was stunned it was already after seven o'clock. A reflex urged me to leave. To go home, eat my dinner, watch my television shows, and get to bed early in anticipation of a busy Saturday at the library.

But I felt fine where I was. I inhaled deeply and exhaled the impulse away.

I'd give anything to be able to have stayed there. To suspend time in that precise moment. With John holding my hand and smiling.

"That's exactly what I mean." I thanked him as he poured us each another glass. "I like reading about that kind of stuff."

He lowered his voice to an imposing basso. "The steady forward march of time."

I took a sip of wine and shook my head. "Time doesn't march forward. It rushes backward."

John stopped midsip. He set his glass on the table. "That doesn't make sense." He used his hands to indicate my entire being. "Look at you. A fully grown, beautiful woman."

I wasn't even ashamed of my blush this time.

"You weren't always like this," he continued. "You started as a baby. Time marched on and look what happened."

Time marched on and I became an abandoned girl. I pushed the thought away and focused instead on the wine and the man in front of me.

"You became the lovely creature you are today," he finished.

"And time will continue and I will become an old woman, stooped and hobbled. But you see, you're making my point."

He grimaced. "Maybe it's the wine. Maybe I'm too stupid. Either way, I'm not following."

"It's quite simple, really. Time didn't start with the big bang theory and move forward to this moment. Time doesn't go from the past into the future. It comes from the future, rushes headlong at us and gets funneled through a microscopic point called the present, and whooshes its way into the past."

John still looked confused.

"Let me use the example you just gave. I started out as a baby, right?"

"Sure," he said.

"Then I became a girl, then I became a woman, and someday I'll become a crone. Things move from a state of potential to a state of actual. Like a seed is a potential tree or an egg is a potential chicken. Follow?"

"So far so good. I'm right there with you."

I took another sip of wine and felt the buzz. "This is Friday. This particular date in August, right?"

He nodded.

"This day only has the potential to become yesterday. This

day, this particular day, cannot become tomorrow. This day can move only from today to yesterday to the day before yesterday to last week to last year. Then it can only become a few years ago, last decade, last century . . . on and on. Today can go only into the past. Today can never go into the future. Time comes to us from the future and rushes toward the past, impacting us in bizarre ways along its journey."

John leaned back in his chair. The crowd around us was thinning as Happy Hour groups headed home. The noise level dropped. Everything seemed more comfortable.

"I get it," he finally said. "You're right." He leaned forward, resting his chin on his hand as he stared at me. "You're a fascinating woman, Tess Kincaid. I don't believe I've encountered the likes of you before. Tell me more, you captivating piece of humanity. Leave me spellbound with more of your thoughts."

I'm ashamed to say I giggled at his playfulness. Maybe it was the wine. I liked this man. I liked being the focus of his attention. I wanted him to think I was captivating and I wanted to leave him spellbound.

"I met my doppelganger yesterday."

"Your what?"

I pulled my phone out of my purse and screened up the photos Mimi and I had taken of each other the previous night. I showed him the first one.

"Who's that?" I asked.

"I'm not drunk, if that's what you're testing." He looked away from the phone and gave me the once-over. "I like the way you're wearing your hair tonight better."

I thanked him and scrolled to the next photo.

"Who's that?"

"That's you again. With your hair tucked behind your ears. I still prefer this evening's coiffure."

I flipped back to the first photo. "That, indeed, is me." I brought up the second photo. "And that is Mimi Winslow."

John took the phone from my hand. He used his finger to flick back and forth between the two shots. "And you never met her before?"

I drained the final sip from my glass. "Laid eyes on her for the first time Tuesday afternoon while stuck in traffic in front of the Hotel Red. Ran into her face-to-face . . . and let me tell you *that* was something . . . yesterday."

John handed me back my phone. He looked away as though trying to process something but not having anything stored in his brain against which to measure it. He pushed his chair away from the table.

"Stay right there," he said as he stood. "This conversation is going to require more wine."

CHAPTER 9

I probably should have felt sluggish at work the next day. It had been a whole lot of years since I drank that much. But the memory of my evening with John kept me sailing from one project to the next.

It had been almost nine o'clock when we left Barriques. I told John how busy my Saturday was going to be, and he told me about two important projects waiting for him in the morning. We said we needed to call it a night three times before we finally pushed away from the table and headed to the door. He offered to call me a cab, but I wanted to walk home. My car would be all right in the library parking lot, and the dusky evening was still light enough. Kids were playing on their front lawns while fireflies flickered and their parents watched from wide porches. It was only a few blocks. He didn't press to learn where my apartment was. I liked that. Instead, he pulled me close and kissed my cheek. I liked that, too.

"I'm that way." He pointed across the street. "I had a great time. I want to do this again. Soon."

I told him that sounded fine to me and started to walk away.

"Hey, Tess."

I turned around. John reached into his pocket and handed me the RESERVED sign he'd used to save our table. "For a bookmark." The green flecks in his eyes glistened. "Maybe in a volume about time."

I slipped the sign into my purse, waved, and left. Sleeping came easily that night.

Brian Erickson stomped in sometime around noon the next day, chomping on a donut and complaining about the window display.

"What good is it to pimp a summer reading list when it's less than two weeks to Labor Day?" Brian brushed crumbs off his short-sleeved plaid shirt. He'd gained about fifteen pounds since his son was born six months ago. "Change it to Back-to-School. You need to be all over this stuff, Tess. Our front windows are our first impression. Board members drive down this street every day."

"By all means, let's worry about the board members and not the actual patrons," Rosie whispered to me.

"There's an entire closet full of decorations," I suggested as he walked past the front desk where Rosie and I were checking out a line of people. "If you'd like to get started, I'd be happy to join you after I finish this month's catalogue supplement. Oh, scratch that. I've got book orders for Young Adult and Science Fiction due by close of business today. Anytime I'm not at the circulation desk I'll spend finishing those. Looks like you're on your own."

Brian stopped in his tracks. He glared at me, then Rosie, then the line of patrons. Then back at me. I couldn't believe I'd said that out loud. But what I really couldn't believe was what I did next.

I smiled at him. I didn't look away. I didn't bow my head. I didn't come up with some sort of snappy patter to let him think I was joking. I simply smiled until he walked back to his office. Rosie elbowed me and gave me a wink.

"Atta girl," she said.

Still, when I locked the door behind me at six-thirty, I stopped to admire my new Back-to-School window display. Then I drove to my father's house. I didn't stop at the grocery store. It wasn't that kind of night.

"You're late." My father slipped into the front seat and snapped his seat belt on. "I know this is difficult for you, but it's important."

I inhaled deeply. I always do that when I first see my father. The smell of his breath helps me gauge how much he'd been drinking. I figured he'd had only two or three drinks in him. Dad usually made an effort on that particular day.

"It's seven minutes 'til seven, Dad." I backed out of his driveway and headed down to University Avenue. "It's not like we've got people waiting for us."

"Sooner we get started, the sooner we get finished." He turned the fan on my air conditioner higher. "I've got a lot to do this evening. I'm sure you do, too."

The only thing on his agenda after this outing was whiskey, a couple of crossword puzzles, and reality TV. He'd be passed out in his recliner by nine o'clock. Same as every other night. But it was important to him that I believe he still had a full life. So I apologized for my tardiness and drove on.

We got to the parking lot at the trailhead five minutes later. The sun was still more than an hour from setting, so I wasn't surprised to see at least a dozen cars there. Three lakeside trails in the heart of the city were jewels too lovely to ignore on a hot August evening. Especially on a Saturday. From this spot, one short trail headed west, the least popular of the trio. Another headed east, winding through old-growth trees and following the lake for over a mile, culminating at the Student Union Building, where hundreds of people would be drinking beer, eating brats, and listening to music on an enormous stone lakeside terrace. My dad and I started off on the trail in the middle, a half-mile stretch through the woods ending at a peninsula called Picnic Point.

It was my mother's birthday, and we'd come to mark the occasion.

I can't remember when my dad first came up with the idea. These annual treks seemed like they'd been a part of my life ever since she left us. That first year I'd resisted. I didn't want to be reminded I wasn't important enough to my mother to make her want to stick around. But my father insisted. Just because she's not here doesn't mean you don't have a mother, he'd say. Then he'd tell me how I needed to understand I was part of a bigger system than him and me alone.

Her birthday was the one time of year it was okay to talk about her. I didn't have the heart to tell him I didn't want to. What was I supposed to say? That I missed her? That I wished she'd come home? That I had forgotten the very last words she ever said to me were yelled so loud I thought my eardrums would burst?

I'm done with all this! she'd screamed. *I don't want you!*

These outings were for my father. I guess I always knew that. Even during my angry childhood years I could see it in his face. He missed her so much. He needed to remember the tender times. Back when it was good. I somehow understood, even during my rebellious teens, that I owed him this much. He'd paid such a high price for my mother's desertion. I could give him this one indulgence.

We walked the straight path in silence. We nodded to the strangers we passed, acknowledging their presence in that friendly but distant way Midwesterners do. The land on either side began to narrow, giving glimpses through the trees of Lake Mendota to our right and left. We passed a small clearing where stones were laid in a rough circle, a place where people gathered around the campfire. I knew it to be especially popular with groups of women celebrating their fiftieth birthdays.

My mother would have marked her fiftieth birthday six years ago. I wondered how she had marked that milestone. Was there a circle of friends to welcome her into their coven of crones? Would the laughing celebrants dancing around her know she had a husband and daughter missing her in Wisconsin?

I hated those outings.

We passed families throwing Frisbees, tossing beanbags, and eating basket dinners that gave the point its name. A memory flashed through my mind. My mother and I having our own private picnic in our backyard on Lathrop Street. Had our little family . . . my father, mother, and me . . . ever come here for a picnic?

My father laid an awkward arm across my shoulder when we arrived at the tip of the peninsula. He withdrew it several tense seconds later and suggested we sit. In the early years we'd find an old log or dry patch of grass, but the university had made improvements to the point over the past decade. Now there were fine stone perches on which to sit, contemplate the beauty of the lake and the city's skyline, and think great thoughts.

"This is your mother's fifty-sixth birthday." His ritual always started with him announcing her age. "That makes me fifty-eight." Again, sticking to his script. We were both quiet for a while. I had nothing at all to say. Maybe he had too much. He turned to me with sad eyes. "How'd that happen, Tessie? How'd I get to be this old with nothing to show for it?"

I wondered what he thought I was. Then I remembered. I was the reason he had nothing more to show for his life than a liquor-addled liver.

"Tempus fugit, Dad." A couple in a neon-yellow kayak paddled by. I focused on them and waited for the next part of my father's tradition.

"What would you say to her, I wonder," he said. "What would you want her to know about what's happened to you in the past year?"

This was the part that creeped me out the most. The part where he wanted me to talk to a woman who was God-knows-where as if she were sitting right next to me. Who knows why it was so important to him? Maybe he read some psychology book that said tossed-aside children grieve less if they're allowed to imagine a conversation with the woman who birthed them. I wanted to scream, Maybe that works in theory, but from where I'm sitting the only thing I'd want to say to her is

"Bite me." The only thing I'd want her to know is that her running away to chase whatever it was cost my father everything. Oh, and by the way, I'm not doing so hot, either. I mean, if my own mother couldn't love me, who the hell else is supposed to?

"I don't know, Dad." I played along. It would be over in a few minutes. "Maybe I'd tell her about my day. Maybe I'd tell her I drank an entire bottle of wine last night."

He shot me a warning look laced with disappointment. "Don't be dramatic, Tess."

The kayakers were a small yellow dot. I concentrated on the sound of the waves lapping against the stone bulkhead.

"I remember the first birthday I spent with your mother." At last we were coming to the end of this pageant. "She was twenty-two." His voice got that faraway sound it always gets when he thinks of her. "She walked into a diner next to the law library. I was with Artie Geiser. We'd just finished a four-hour study session and needed coffee. Your mother came in with two of her friends. They were all laughing and so full of light." He turned to me at the same point in the story he always did ever since I turned sixteen and he figured I was old enough to understand. "Of course, I found out later they were stoned out of their minds and desperately in need of something to satisfy their munchies. Your mother called out to the entire restaurant that it was her birthday. She wanted to know who was going to buy her a hot fudge sundae." He smiled and lingered in the memory. I knew it wouldn't be long before we could head back to the car. "I told Artie to beat it. Said I had to buy my future wife her birthday sundae. I waved her over, handed her a menu, and told her to have at it." He chuckled, like he always does, then said what he always says. "I bought her a hot fudge sundae, all right. After I bought her a pork chop dinner with extra gravy and buttermilk biscuits. We were engaged by Christmas and married on Valentine's Day."

A seagull circled high above us. It was as good a place to rest my attention as any.

"She wasn't always bad, Tessie." At last. The final scene of this morbid play. "I want you to remember that. There was a time she was worthy of all the love we gave her."

I waited about a minute before I stood. His ritual was over. I grabbed his hand and pulled him up. "Let's go, Dad. Like you said, we've both got busy evenings."

We didn't say a word to one another as we hiked back to the car. Not on the ride to his apartment, either. I pulled into his driveway and shifted the car into neutral.

"Don't forget to eat dinner," I said as he opened the door. "There's plenty in your freezer."

His nod was slow. Like he was hearing me but thinking about something else. I watched him walk away. There was a deliberateness in his pace, and his stoop would better fit a man thirty years older. I waited until I saw a light go on in his unit, then backed out and headed home. I decided a hot shower and an early bedtime were exactly what I needed to bring an acceptable end to the evening.

But that didn't happen.

When I pulled into my driveway, I saw I had a visitor. Standing on my porch, leaning against the railing. Waving as I pulled up. The neighbors wouldn't have been alarmed to see her there.

Mimi Winslow, after all, looked right at home.

CHAPTER 10

"Already?" I opened the front door, and Mimi followed me in. "You were in Boston for one day and you're back?"

She curled up on my sofa like a cat pouncing on a favored spot. She tucked her feet underneath her hips and relaxed. "I should have called. But then I realized I didn't have your number. How'd we let that happen?"

I thought about her departure the morning before. I'd been so focused on my upcoming date with John, I hadn't taken the time to give her a proper send-off. "So you flew back? Just to get my phone number?"

Mimi laughed like someone with a secret that gave her a leg up on everyone. I wondered if that kind of confidence came from having a mother around to help you believe the fantasy that everything would turn out fine. "No, silly. I'm back for another round of interviews."

"At the university? So soon?"

Mimi shrugged in that why-shouldn't-good-things-happen-to-me kind of way. "Maybe I wowed 'em. Maybe they're desperate. Who knows? And who cares? I got on that plane yesterday afternoon hoping to get a call back from any place I mailed an application. Didn't matter where. I need a job. By the time I was walking out of Logan my cell phone rang. It was the department secretary here. She wanted to know how soon I could get back to Madison for another day of meet and greets. I told her my time was her time. She asked, 'How's Monday work?' I told her it works great. She told me I'll be meeting with two faculty members I've not met before and again with the guy whose position I'll be taking while he's on sabbatical. And to top it off"—she paused for dramatic effect—"I've been invited to join the department dean and her husband for dinner. The dean of the History Department from the University of By-God Wisconsin and her husband have invited me to dinner. How's that sound?"

I set my purse on the kitchen counter. "Sounds like you got the job. Your interviews are on Monday? This is Saturday. Why'd they want you back two days early?"

Her face lost its enthusiastic smile. "Is this bad that I'm here?" She stood and looked toward the door. "I'm sorry, Tess. I guess I got too excited. I spent the entire plane ride back to Boston thinking about us. I mean, this whole thing blows me away. I drew columns and diagrams in my journal, trying to make sense of everything. I found myself wishing we had more time to explore whatever this is that's going on. When the secretary asked if I had a preference for flight times, I asked her if it would be okay if I came right back. Sorry, Tess. Sometimes I'm too impulsive for my own good. I should have asked you first if it was okay. I got so amped up about the possibility of spending more time with you. And like I said, we hadn't exchanged numbers. So I couldn't call you, could I? The secretary said it made no difference to her when I came, as long as I was at the department, ready to interview, Monday morning at nine. But I'm intruding, right?" She shook her head. "Mom's always telling me not to get ahead of myself. That I have to make sure the rest of the world's prepared before Hurricane Mimi gets ready to blow. Don't worry. I'll get out of your hair." She winked and gave me that glittering smile she uses so effectively. "I know my way back to the hotel. But, hey, maybe we could grab brunch or something this weekend."

A couple of days earlier I was as curious as she was to figure out what the universe had in store by letting the paths of two look-alikes cross. But truth be told, I hadn't given Mimi and our situation much thought since she left, other than using our eerie encounter as first date amusement with John. I know it sounds odd, but between my date and the whole mother's birthday thing with my dad, I kind of shoved Mimi to the back of my mind. Then there she was, energized and excited to continue solving our mystery. And seeing her again, what can I say? Maybe I realized I still wanted to see where this whole thing would lead.

"No," I said. "Don't even think of going back to that hotel. You'll stay here."

"Really?" she asked. "I don't want you to feel pressured to take me in like some stray puppy who turned up on your porch."

"But isn't that what you did?" I teased. "Show up on my porch?"

She smiled that secret-keeping smile again. "I guess so."

I pointed to the stove. "You want some tea?"

Mimi crossed the room and sat at my breakfast nook table. "I'd love some. Then I want to hear all about your date with the handsome book borrower. Tell me every detail."

It was an hour before our conversation made its way back to the mystery of the carbon-copy women. It had been fun sharing my date with her. She sighed like a twelve year old when I told her about John saving the table for us with his RESERVED sign and later handing it to me to use as a place marker.

"Oh, my god," she said. "A true romantic. And he listened! He actually held in his memory for longer than it takes to order a beer that you read books about time. How cool is that?"

I blushed and told her I thought it was pretty damned cool. She told me to go on. Thinking back on it now, Mimi seemed especially curious when I mentioned I'd told John about how I'd met my look-alike and all the coincidences linking the two of us.

"Did he say anything about me?" she asked.

"He doesn't know you. What could he say?"

Mimi waved her question away. "Good point." She wanted to know when I planned to see him again. I told her I didn't know.

"You haven't called him, have you?"

I hadn't. She said that was a good tactical move. That I should go about my life and not give him any cause to think I was sitting around waiting for him to crook his finger so I could come running.

"And it wouldn't hurt to not be available next time he asks you out," Mimi said. "Men like the chase. Honor his inner Neanderthal. Make him work before he drags you back to his cave."

"Our date ended less than twenty-four hours ago," I said. "John said he wanted to get together soon, and I told him I felt the same."

"You think that was wise? Maybe it would be good for him to wonder if you have any interest in him at all."

Her advice irritated me. "Listen, Mimi, I like this guy. I haven't had a date in way longer than I care to admit. I don't see any harm in letting him know I'm interested in him. Besides, aren't you the one who all but pushed me into his arms?"

Mimi wiggled in place—a little chair dance of pride. "I did, didn't I? See how well this is turning out? Remember that next time I suggest you do something."

I took my last sip of tea and asked if she would like another cup. There weren't any more details about my date with John to discuss, and we both knew there was another topic she was itching to give some attention. She passed on the tea.

"Tell me about the columns and diagrams," I said. "The ones you outlined on the flight back to Boston. Have you come up with any working ideas for what's going on here?"

"Have you ever heard the expression, 'If you hear hoofbeats, think horses'? It's one of the first things my research design professor taught me."

I hadn't, but it seemed like something even a college dropout such as myself could decipher. "Things are probably what they seem? Is that it? Don't go looking for exotic justifications when a straightforward explanation is bound to be correct more times than not?"

"Exactly. See, Tess? You've got the mind of a scientist. You really ought to think about going back to school."

Mimi's opinions on what I ought to be doing stoked my irritation. Especially given they were so in tune with what my own inner voice had been yammering at me for years. But that nag always got drowned out by the self-damning screams of my more vocal interior critic.

"Tell me what you came up with, Mimi."

She took a long deep breath, as if she was preparing for a big announcement. "I think we were ignoring the horses when we first met. You tried to push all this stuff away as nothing more than a coincidence. I, on the other hand, couldn't wait to springboard into some wild adventure. I blame my mother for that. She's always up for the next exotic escapade. I think I come by it honestly. I got myself convinced that this was going to be a twisted mystery. Remember that dramatic story I spun out about hush money and family secrets?"

"How could I forget?" I asked. "I still have whiplash from all the let's-say things you threw my way."

"See? We were hearing hoofbeats and thinking butterflies. At least I was. But I've had two plane rides to calm down. I think what's going on is nothing more than precisely what it looks like. I think the hoofbeats we're hearing really are horses."

"Meaning?" I had a good idea where she was headed, but I didn't want to be the one to say it. I didn't even want to be the one to hear it.

"There's a word for what we are," she said. "One that describes two people who are mirror images of one another, share the same birthday, and whose mothers have the same last name." Mimi swallowed hard, as though the word required the strength of Hercules to spit out.

"Twins," she said. "Identical twins."

A humming buzzed deep in my inner ear. I remember shaking my head. At first it was slow, like I couldn't believe what she was saying could possibly hold any merit. But the words *identical twins* hung there in the air, and when Mimi didn't take them back, chalk this off as some sort of misguided joke, or offer any alternate options, my head shaking picked up speed. Faster and faster. I thought if I could only wave my head hard enough and fast enough it would erase the dreaded words from the very ether into which they'd been spoken.

Mimi stood and brought the pad and pen I keep on my kitchen counter over to the table. She wrote something on it. I couldn't see what. I was too busy shivering.

"My mother's last name is Winslow." She held her hand over the pad. "Your mother's maiden name is Winslow. Tell me your mother's first name."

My head shaking stopped. So did my shivering. I stared into Mimi's eyes. What I saw there compelled me to answer even though I had no desire to take one more step down this twisting road. The consequences of verifying Mimi's assumptions were too overwhelming. Still, her eyes urged me to speak. It wasn't a dare I saw in the blue of her irises. It wasn't even a command. What I saw was an assurance that I could do it. I could say the words I had to in order to resolve this.

"Audra," I whispered. "My mother's name is Audra Winslow Kincaid."

Mimi slid the pad across to me.

My eyes flared as I read what she'd written. I thought of that time in chemistry class my sophomore year at West High. Kevin Richter was at the lab station next to mine. He was too busy flirting with Cindy Norstlin to pay attention to the steps our teacher had listed on the blackboard. He picked up the wrong bottle and mixed something into his beaker of ammonia, and a wicked cloud of light blue gas streamed straight toward my face. I remembered the yelp I let out and Mr. Tencil grabbing me by the shoulders. He pulled me to the corner and held me under a special shower that flooded water directly into my eyes.

My eyes felt that same acidic burn as I read Mimi's note.

Happy Birthday to Audra Winslow.
My dear mother turns 56 today.

I read the note again. Then I read it a third time. I remember thinking how Mimi's handwriting was so similar to mine. It didn't surprise me. In that moment I thought there was nothing in the world that would surprise, shock, or stun me ever again.

I was wrong, of course.

"Now what?" I asked.

Mimi got up and returned to the kitchen. She pulled a bag out from behind my purse. "I brought this," she said. "From Boston. We're going to need absolute proof."

She set the bag in front of me. My hands didn't shake when I pulled out two boxes. Like I said, I was beyond all that.

"They're DNA kits," Mimi explained. "A simple swipe of our cheeks, drop them into a mailbox, and we'll have our genetic proof. One way or another."

One way or another, I thought. Mimi will have her answer as to who this doppelganger is, and I'll have my proof as to why my mother left me.

"We both know how this is going to turn out," I said. *My mother left me to raise another child. My twin. The better me. The one she really could love.*

"We need proof," Mimi insisted.

But didn't we already have it? We'd been buried by the hoofbeats. We'd found our horses. What more would this little piece of commercial science bring us?

I fumbled with the package, pulled out the instructions, and read them aloud.

CHAPTER 11

As you might imagine, I didn't get much sleep that night. Mimi wanted to stay up and run through all kinds of scenarios. Now that we'd actually spoken the words *identical twins,* she was energized and eager to take on this new mission of discovery. She always presented herself that way. Never tired. Never disappointed. Forever interested in what was coming next. As if life for her was one enormous and intriguing riddle and she couldn't keep herself from proving to the world there was no way it was going to outsmart her.

But I wasn't energized. Or curious. I was angry. I needed time alone to settle down. So I lied and told her I was dead tired. Even though if you had to make a mile-long list of everything I was feeling that night, the word *tired* wouldn't show up once. I tossed some sheets and blankets onto the sofa and told her to make herself comfortable.

"You're sure it's okay?" she asked. "My staying here?"

She must have picked up on my anger. I guess I'm not very good at hiding it. Sometimes it seems as close as my next breath. Coming without me ever having to call it. I remember talking to my dad when I was in high school, after that anger management class I was forced to take. I'd been doing okay, but out of nowhere my anger monster had gotten off its leash and I kicked a trash can to pieces in the third floor girls' bathroom at West High. I can't even remember what got me going that day, but I do remember being so hot I needed to get away and hurt something. Maybe I tried to use the skills they taught me, maybe I didn't. But if I had to describe it now, it was as if I had become the very embodiment of rage. Kicking that garbage can seemed safe enough . . . until I realized I couldn't stop. I wailed on that thing. Crushing it with a rain of heavy stomps. Sweating and panting like I'd run six blocks. A couple of girls walked in. I guess I scared them. They alerted the first teacher they saw, and the next thing I knew I was in the guidance counsellor's office. He's handing me pamphlets on that same anger management class and warning me I'd better get my act together because he didn't have time to deal with my shit. That's when I asked my dad if he would take me to a doctor.

But he said all I needed to handle my emotions was to think about what would be waiting for me at home any time he learned I'd acted in a way that brought shame to him. Then he slapped me hard across the face to show me what he meant, and added two more for memory enhancement. He said he knew how to handle my teenage turmoil and someday I'd thank him that I hadn't started the whole therapy merry-go-round.

So here I am, way past being a teenager and still struggling to keep that monster on its chain.

But on that night I did okay. I took a few deep breaths, was able to dial my anger back to irritation, and forced myself to make up the sofa for Mimi while she used the bathroom. When she came out to say good night, I could tell she wanted a hug. Like she expected me to be all sisterly toward her all of a sudden.

I couldn't do it. So I changed topics and sidestepped the whole thing.

"You ever worry about choking?" I pointed to her neck. "Your necklace. Is it safe to sleep with it?"

Her hand went to her throat to touch the small gold rectangle hanging from a chain. "I never take this off. My mom gave it to me." She paused. "I wonder if I should start saying *our* mom. What do you think?"

"What does it say?" I leaned in to look as she held it out as far as the chain allowed.

"It's my name. *Mimi*. Pretty simple, but I love it. It was my first piece of real jewelry."

My mother never gave me a gold necklace. Of course, I was only twelve when she left. That's a little young for boxes from Tiffany. A memory did come to me, though. My mother and I sitting at the dining room table. Tracing our hands on construction paper. She traced her hand first, using a bright blue crayon. Then she put my tiny hand inside the outline of hers. I must have been four or five. She traced around my fingers. I recalled the sound of her voice.

I'll always want your hand in mine, Tess. Always.

I shoved the echo of my mother's lie back into the cellar of my memory, said good night to Mimi, and went to bed.

I guess most people might have spent the night tossing and turning with all kinds of questions about why. But that's not what happened with me. I already knew the why. My mother had, for whatever reason, gotten tired of being my mother. As much as I try to forget her last words, they're always right there. Riding shotgun with my beastly anger. I hear her with crystal-clear high fidelity. My memory rings with the shrill of her frustrated shriek. *I'm done with this! I don't want you!*

I didn't wonder about *why* that sleep-starved night. My mind instead tortured me with questions about *how*. Had Mimi and I been separated at birth? Did my mother not know she'd given birth to twin daughters? Did she find out later, perhaps at the same time she had grown sick of me? Did she run away to join her newly found girl in some sort of dream-come-true maternal mulligan?

Did my father know? And what about Mimi's story about her own father? She said he died before she was born. Was that a tale her mother . . . our mother . . . spun for her?

Or if Mimi and I had been brought home together, what could have happened that might force young parents to separate their twins? I thought about the grandparents I'd never met. Like Mimi's father, they'd died before I was born. Were these pre-birth deaths a coincidence? Or were they a convenient way to explain why family members who should have populated a child's life were nowhere to be found?

My brain became a sticky spiderweb littered with unanswered questions. Somewhere in the deep darkness of predawn, right before my body gave in to exhaustion and slipped into a short and dreamless sleep, I made the decision to speak to my father. But I'd wait until the DNA tests came back. Maybe a part of me was still holding on to the fantasy that there might be some sort of explanation other than being Mimi's twin. But if the tests came back saying what she seemed so sure they would, I'd have no other choice but to confront him. The test would prove that my father and mother were partners in a complex cover-up tampering with the lives of both their daughters. As difficult as it would be, I'd wait.

I left my apartment early the next morning. I wasn't doing myself any good churning scenarios in my brain, and I certainly didn't feel like going for another ride on Mimi's magical mystery rickshaw. I wasn't scheduled to work that Sunday but I knew the library's routine would give me the focus I needed to steer clear of unanswerable riddles. I tiptoed into the kitchen and collected an apple and two bananas from the counter. I didn't see Mimi beneath the mound of sheets and blankets on the sofa, but I hoped sleep had somehow found her. For all the chaos that stormed into my life from the moment I first saw her, I did feel a kind of tenderness toward her. As I locked the door behind me, I remember wondering if that was how sisters felt.

The air was comfortable as I walked toward the library. I waved to moms drinking their morning coffee on porches, enjoying the fresh air before the oppression of summer drove them inside to their air-conditioned sanctuaries. They'd be back out again after sunset, sipping lemon beers or chilled white wine and watching their children chase fireflies in the finally bearable humidity. Soon enough the earth would tilt, and autumn would bring crisp, delightful days. But for now, time outdoors were morning and evening bookends to the stifling heat of late August.

I busied myself with paperwork left over from the closing crew. Brian had written me a short to-do list, accompanied by a note saying I shouldn't expect him in again 'til Wednesday. He said he was off visiting a library similar to ours in order to get "expansion ideas." He didn't mention where the library was. Since Brian Erickson is the kind of man who loves to bore you with tedious details, I assumed there was no library visit at all. Our jerk-off head librarian was extending his weekend. Probably going up north, where lakes and pine trees promised visitors a break from the heat of deep summer. I'm not a betting person, but if I were, I'd lay money that he wasn't taking his wife or baby son with him. Brian's the kind of guy who always thinks of himself first, last, and only.

After I finished with the overnight chore list, I responded to an e-mail from a second-grade teacher from Randall School. What she was doing working while there were still ten days of summer vacation left was anybody's guess, but she had sent me a list of possible dates and wanted to know if she could schedule a September or October class field trip to the library. I was unfamiliar with her name, and since I knew all the teachers in our area, I figured she must be new. That would explain why she was planning field trips instead of soaking up sun at Bernie's Beach. I was cross-checking her dates with the library's master calendar when I heard a familiar rapping on the glass of the library's front door. Three long, two short, three long.

I hadn't expected him. John had picked up his last book on Friday. He'd typically drop it off Monday afternoon. I looked down at my outfit. Denim capris and plaid sleeveless shirt. Not the worst I could have pulled out of my closet, but not the cutest, either. I ran my fingers through my hair, fluffing as I went. I took a quick pump from the dispenser on my desk, smeared a drop of the lotion across my lips, and headed to the front door.

"You're early," I said as I let him in. "We don't open for another hour and a half." I noticed his hands were empty. "You haven't finished the Koontz?"

John Rappaport smiled and brushed a damp strand of hair away from my eyes. "Haven't even started it. I'm glad you're here. I don't know what got into me this morning, but I was up at the crack of dawn. I figured I'd take a chance you were suffering from the same affliction. What d'ya say we go grab some breakfast?"

I pointed over my shoulder. "I've got some fruit on my desk. I'll split it with you."

John leaned in and kissed my cheek. "Hope that's okay. You just looked so pretty standing there, offering to share."

My hand went to where his lips had just been. I figured it would sound stupid to tell him it was more than okay to kiss me, especially all casual like that, so I just stood there like an idiot.

"Go on," he said. "Get your purse. Let's take a couple of pancakes off Mickey's hands before it gets too hot to think about food. I'll have you back in plenty of time to unlock the doors and start another day stamping out ignorance on Madison's fashionable west side."

Brian's to-do list leapt to mind. So did the new teacher's field trip, the teen group reading list, and the organization I'd need to do before Innocent and Agnes showed up for their volunteer hours. I opened my mouth, about to tell him all the reasons this wasn't a good time. Then I realized I wasn't even supposed to be at the library that morning.

"Give me two seconds," I said. "And Mickey's Dairy Bar is the right place. I'm starving."

*   *   *

When the waitress asked me if I was finished, half my breakfast was still on my plate. That wasn't unusual. Mickey's pancakes are the size of pizza platters. Besides, I'd been so busy bringing John up to date I hadn't given my food the attention it deserved. I asked her to take it away but told her I'd be interested in one more cup of coffee.

"Wow," John said as the waitress topped off both our cups. "I can see there's never going to be a dull moment with you around. That's quite a story. Way more drama than I'm used to." He blew a cooling breath over his fresh coffee. "How do you make sense of all this?"

I shook my head. "Beats me. Mimi was sleeping when I left. She doesn't have anything to do until her Monday morning interview. Which means her mind's going to be working overtime churning up theories. I plan to sit tight and see how this thing plays out. I mean, she's the one who's so gung ho on this twin thing. It's safer for me to simply be an observer."

"It's a logical leap, you gotta give her that."

"Maybe." I somehow felt calmer with John knowing what was going on. I especially liked how easily he accepted what I told him. This *was* a lot of drama, yet he didn't seem to be judging me for it. "My head can't get around the logistics of it. How do you pull off something like separating twins?"

"Hospital snafu?" he offered. "That might explain the separated at birth part. The way I see it, the other part's the tough one."

"You mean how my mother managed to raise Mimi in Colorado . . . remember, that's where they lived before her mother moved them to Florida for what she called a *fresh start*. Do you mean how'd she do that while she was still here in Madison, stuck with me?"

John's face clouded over. "You were a kid when your mom left. And if the adult I'm sitting with is any indication of the child you were, I'll bet you were terrific. No one was stuck with you, Tess. Besides, just because Mimi's shouting *Twins!* from every rooftop doesn't make her right."

I didn't respond. The last thing I wanted was to come across as some whining girl bathing in self-pity, but I could see the truth even if John couldn't. My mother left me without so much as a backward glance and spent the next seventeen years happily raising someone else. If Mimi's weird theories were good for anything, they were good for making that point abundantly clear. My mother didn't even have the old "out of sight, out of mind" prattle to fall back on. She would have seen the face of the child she left behind every time she looked at Mimi. And not once, not in all those years of adventures with Mimi, did it seem to bother her. Any kid that easily forgotten had to be some real special kind of rotten.

"I once met a John Rappaport when I was out in Los Angeles visiting my uncle," John said. "He even had the same middle name as me. It's Aaron, by the way, in case you're interested in jotting that little tidbit down in the notebook you've started about me."

I rolled my eyes, but I was glad to learn his middle name. "Yeah, but did he have your birthday? Did he look exactly like you?"

I knew what he was doing, and I appreciated his effort. As far as I was concerned though, any ship carrying the slightest notion that my mother and Mimi's mother coincidently shared the same name and birthdate had long since sailed.

"He was old enough to be my grandfather and spoke with a heavy Yiddish accent." John took his last bite of pancake and another sip of coffee. "Let's step back a minute. Other than Mimi looking like you, what is it we know? For sure, I mean."

Hadn't he been listening? There was the anger again.

"Hear me out," John continued. "Other than your physical similarities, has Mimi offered any proof of what she's saying? Have you seen a photograph of her mother? Or what about her own birthday? Has she shown you a driver's license? Anything at all that could confirm these similarities you two allegedly share."

"What are you saying?"

John's gray eyes were serious. "What if she's playing with you? I mean, what do we really know about this woman? Your paths cross in a hotel, the two of you see facial similarities. What if she's someone who sat at the mean girl lunch table and wants to have a little fun at your expense? Play with your mind and stave off boredom while she's waiting for her job interview."

"You don't think that sounds a bit paranoid? It's not like I have anything she might want. What would be her motivation?"

"Maybe she doesn't need one. Could be she's interested in nothing more than a few days' diversion and a fun story to tell at the next monthly meeting of the Bitch on Wheels Society. Or it could be something more sinister. Identity theft. That's big business. What better person's life to steal than someone you could pass for in a photo lineup?"

I wasn't buying it. My grandparents' trust fund belongs to my father. It's not like I was sitting on a pile of dough. And, to be perfectly honest, my credit score isn't what it could be. It didn't make any sense. Then again, nothing about this whole escapade did. I needed a break from all these theories and suppositions. Suddenly a day at work sounded terrific.

I looked at my watch. "I gotta go. The library opens in twenty minutes and I still have a few things to finish up before it does." I got the attention of our waitress. John handed her his credit card when she brought the check by.

"My invitation, my treat," he said. "Besides, Mimi could be out there right now screwing up your good name, so your card might be declined anyway."

John and I talked about our day's agenda on the walk back. He said he had back-to-back meetings 'til noon. Apparently Sunday is just another workday for the athletic department. He had volleyball with his rec league in the evening. He asked if I'd come watch their team play one day soon. I told him I'd be glad to.

He followed me into the library, helped me turn on all the lights, then said he had to go. I was leaning against the checkout desk, liking how he was standing so close to me.

"I wish it was December," he said.

"Come on. The heat's not that bad. Soon enough there'll be snow and frosty wind. Don't wish the summer away."

"It's not that." He pointed toward the ceiling. "If it was Christmas there might be some mistletoe hanging from that beam. Then I'd have an excuse to kiss you."

A very pleasant warmth that had nothing to do with August surged through me. "Do you need an excuse?"

He inched closer. "Oh, no, Ms. Kincaid. All I need is permission."

I inhaled. He smelled like fresh shampoo and soap. Those green specks in his eyes danced in a way more suited for evening than midmorning. "Permission granted."

And that's when John Rappaport kissed me. Long and slow. I tasted a mixture of coffee and maple syrup on his lips. He pulled me into him, snug against his chest with strong arms. His chin brushed mine, rough and male. I felt the muscles in my back and shoulders relax as I leaned into his embrace.

I heard the front door open.

"Oh!" Rosie mumbled an apology as she approached. "I didn't expect to see . . . I didn't know . . . What the hell, Tess, it's Sunday."

John released me and let his eyes smile into mine before he turned toward Rosie, his arm extended in greeting. "I see you in here all the time, but we've never officially met. John Rappaport. I work over at Camp Randall. I'm in here a couple times a week." He nodded his head in my direction. "And unless I'm totally misreading the signals, you may be seeing a lot more of me."

Rosie's grin was wide as she shook his hand and introduced herself. John looked back at me and asked if it would be all right if he called me soon. I scribbled my number on a scrap of paper, handed it to him, and told him to have a great day.

"Thanks for breakfast," he called out as he walked to the

door. "Oh, and Tess?" He turned back around for one last smile before leaving. "This is all going to turn out fine. Nobody's gonna hurt one hair on your pretty head. They'd have to get through me." I can still see the way his eyes sparkled. "And that's never going to happen."

CHAPTER 12

Detective Andy Anderson patted the table in front of him. "At last! I thought we were going to spend all night listening to stories of romance and mystery." He turned his crew cut head toward his companion. "I heard a lot of animosity toward the deceased. Some folks might call that a beginning of a motive. Did you hear it? Or were you as caught up in this tall tale as Miss Kincaid here?"

Sally Normandy held up a hand, like she was reminding him to take it easy. She was, after all, the one who told me to start at the beginning. She didn't want me to leave out any details. So if Detective Double A was upset with me, I didn't much care. I was giving them what they asked for. Besides, Sally seemed like a person I'd be much more interested in pleasing than Detective Turn-Sideways-And-He-Disappears Anderson. Unfortunately, he ignored Sally's gesture and kept talking.

"Miss Kincaid, let's get back to that necklace." Anderson flipped a few pages back in that yellow legal pad he'd been taking notes on all the while I talked. "When was the first time you saw it?"

I wasn't sure what he was looking for. "What necklace?"

Anderson made a disgusted face. I thought he'd probably not be as irritable if he'd allow himself a slice or two of pepperoni and sausage pizza every so often.

He turned again to Sally. "Is this how she's gonna play it? Pull the I-don't-know-what-you're-getting-at routine every time we trip her up?"

Trip me up? Is that what was happening here? Did they want all my details in order to build a case against *me*? Were they seeing me as someone who would be even remotely capable of murder?

I looked into Sally's blue eyes. They seemed as concerned and supportive as when she first walked into the room. Had I misread her intentions? What if the two of them were playing some sort of good cop–bad cop role like on those TV crime shows?

"Do I need to call an attorney?" I asked.

Neither of them answered. I suddenly felt very cold, as if the air in that little interrogation room had dropped fifteen degrees in the time it took me to ask my question.

Sally reached into the deep plastic tray she'd set on the chair beside her when she first walked in the room. It looked like the kind our mailman, Darryl, carries when he has an especially large delivery to bring to the library. She pulled out a small manila envelope. Today's date was marked on the outside, along with a long row of digits and letters I could only imagine to be the case number.

This is what it's come to, I thought. The Madison Police Department has assigned a case number to my life. An even more sobering realization hit me. *I'll bet that big letter H stands for homicide.*

Sally opened the envelope and shook it. A clear Ziploc plastic bag fell onto the table in front of me. A gold necklace was inside. The chain was twisted and chinked. From where I sat, it looked like there was mud caked into the links.

I stared at it. Anger surged up inside me, slamming into my chest. Trying to force an opening. Eager to spit words of accusation and damnation to anyone within shouting distance. I squeezed my fingernails into my palms.

"Do you know where we found this?" Anderson asked.

Words wouldn't come. I sat there, paralyzed, mute, staring at the delicate gold necklace with the solid little rectangle dangling from it.

Sally inched the plastic bag toward me. "Take a good look, Tess. Turn it over, look long and close. Don't take it out of the bag, but look hard. Tell us if it looks familiar."

Of course it was familiar. I knew exactly what it was. Still, I did as she asked. I picked up the bag and examined the necklace. This close, I could see something green tangled in the chain along with the mud. Grass maybe? Moss? Like the necklace had been someplace other than around the neck of a newly minted PhD from Tufts. The one who specialized in the history of Barry Manilow. I ran my finger over the inscription on the gold fob.

Mimi.

"You know this necklace, Tess?" Sally Normandy's voice was kind.

I nodded.

"You've seen it before?" she continued.

I nodded again.

"Can you tell us where?" she asked.

My mouth was as dry as an oven. My tongue felt heavy and large against my teeth. It was a struggle to get the words out. "She had it," I said. "Her mother gave it to her."

"That's what she told you, huh?" This time Anderson asked the question. And his voice wasn't anywhere near as kind as Sally's. "Out of her very own mouth. You heard her tell you her mother gave her this necklace."

I nodded.

"You have any reason to touch this necklace?" Anderson continued. "Maybe during one of your all-night gab fests? Or maybe when she might have been showing it off?"

I tried to think. Had I touched it? Was this another time they were trying to trip me up? Maybe catch me in a lie?

"I don't know," I finally said. "Maybe. I know I saw it. She said it was a gift from her mother. She never took it off." A filmy slip of memory drifted into my field of awareness.

Detective Anderson seemed disinterested in my new recollection. Sally Normandy's face revealed nothing.

Andy Anderson leaned back and crossed his wiry arms across his chest. "What are we to make of the fact that this necklace was found with the body?"

Body.

The *body*. I forced myself to swallow hard in order to start my next breath. The body. I tried to picture where it was right now. In the morgue? In a refrigerated drawer? What happens to bodies once they're discovered? Once they're no longer a person, but a vessel for clues in a murder investigation.

I started to shake.

Sally looked toward the one-way mirror and asked for a blanket. Less than a minute later the door opened and a set of hands offered a folded piece of heavy red fabric. I saw only the hands. I didn't see the arms they were attached to. I didn't see the *body*. Maybe it was down in the morgue, too. Maybe this whole place was filled with bodies that didn't belong anywhere else. Like a warehouse for thrown-away humans whose only value is whatever service their bodies can perform. Ask these questions. Record these notes. Fetch some water. Bring a blanket.

Give us enough clues to hang a killer.

What becomes of the bodies after the services are performed? Do they rest in some sort of suspended animation until needed again?

I laughed at the absurdity of my thought. A short guffaw huffed unbidden from my chest, and the next thing I knew I was laughing so hard my shoulders were heaving. Tears ran down my face. I couldn't catch my breath.

I couldn't catch myself.

Sally stood and stepped behind me. She laid her hands on my shoulders and pressed down. "Stay with me, Tess. I know this is hard." Her tone was so soothing. Like a whispered promise that normal was out there and I'd find it again someday.

That was a lie, of course. Nothing would ever be the same again. But in that moment her voice was so seductive. I focused on her words and let them pull me back from my hysteria.

"You're safe here, Tess." I could smell Sally's perfume. It smelled like fresh rain. "We want to hear more."

She offered me my glass of water when I was calmer. I couldn't hold it in my quivering hands, so she held it for me, pressing the rim against my lips. She cooed encouragement as I took a few sips.

"Thank you," I said.

"You're welcome." There was something reassuring in her simple response. Like watching my meltdown was no great whizbang for her. Like she'd seen it a thousand times before and now it was time to get back to business.

"So John left for work after taking you out to breakfast last Sunday morning," she said. "Then what happened?" The glare she tossed toward Andy Anderson was more warning than here-we-go. "And remember, tell us slowly. Details are important."

Don't leave out anything that might trip me up. Isn't that what you mean?

CHAPTER 13

The rest of that Sunday went pretty much like any other. Rosie wanted to know all about me and John. She may be mature beyond her years, but she is, after all, twenty-one years old. And a twenty-one-year-old doesn't walk in on two people kissing without wanting to know the entire backstory leading up to that moment. I enjoyed sharing what had happened between me and John over the past couple of days. That's not like me. Normally I keep things private. My dad always told me that our lives were of no interest to other people and it was always important to realize that whatever was going on in our own world was best kept locked up in our own heads. He told me over and over: *Still lips make for a happy mind. Nobody needs to know our private business.* But telling Rosie how I got the courage to ask John out, and how our time at the wine bar flew by, well, it was like I got to re-experience the whole thing. It made it nicer because it was shared.

Rosie about melted when I told her about the RESERVED sign.

"You have to hold on to it forever," she insisted. "Try to imagine showing it to your grandkids and telling them the story about how Grandpa stopped you before you could walk away, handed it to you, and asked you to keep it."

Agnes and Innocent came in for their three-hour volunteer stint.

"It's the weekend, Tess." Agnes pulled out a chair to make it easier for Innocent to settle her ninety-year-old bones at the table laden with envelopes for the two of them to stuff. "Why isn't a good-looking girl like you out there on this fine day? Put on a sundress. Let the boys get a good look at you."

"Tess doesn't need to do that." Rosie plopped herself down beside them. She wasted no time bringing them up to speed on what she saw that morning. Agnes raised an eyebrow toward me. I felt for sure I was in for some sort of lecture on proper library decorum. Instead, Agnes's eyes lit with a memory that wiped two decades of wrinkles off her beautiful face, and she told us about the first day she met her Charlie.

"He'd gotten this old Studebaker. His very first car." Her eyes glistened with a chuckle she couldn't contain. "The thing cost him all of twenty-three dollars, and I swear it was held together with baling wire and rope. My daddy and I were driving down a dirt road having just picked fifteen bushels of sweet corn for Mama to put up. It was a day as hot as today's going to be, and I was wearing my brother's hand-me-down overalls, covered in sweat and corn silk. Well, there was Charlie, pulled over and kicking his car like he thought he could knock some sense into it. Daddy stopped, of course. He was like that, always a helping hand to anybody in need. But nothing could save that Studebaker. Daddy offered him a lift into town. I don't know what got into me, but when Charlie, as strange to me as Old Carver's goat, crawled in the back of Daddy's flatbed, well, I got myself out of that cab and hopped up there with him. Daddy asked him to come by for supper as we dropped him off in front of the boarding house where he was renting a room. Charlie looked at me and asked what I thought of that. I told him that sounded fine to me. Mama was making a ham, and we sure had enough corn to go around." She patted an age-pocked hand over her gray hair. "I spent nearly two hours getting myself presentable that afternoon. Made my brother shuck all that corn himself while I took a swim down in the creek to get the big dirt off, then came back to the house for a long soak in the tub. Anyway,

I looked as pretty as I could muster. When Charlie stepped up onto our porch I was right there to answer the door, and that was all she wrote." She laughed out loud. "You know, he was a loyal Studebaker man the rest of his life."

I asked Innocent how she met Eddie. She smiled in that sweet and soft way she has and waved her hand. "In a place very much like this," she said. "I met him in a library. Eddie loved books. I loved Eddie. Not much to tell beyond that."

Rosie said that day in the library felt more like Valentine's Day than the waning strain of summer.

I stayed at work despite it being my day off. I sent Rosie home a few hours early. I closed up at six and for some reason turned left instead of right when I locked the front door. As I walked along Monroe Street, the late afternoon was scorching, but I didn't mind. I strolled past the shops. They stay open later on Sundays in the summer to take advantage of all the walk-by traffic. I popped into some stores to say hello to owners I knew. I ran into Carl Crittens while I waited to cross the street. Carl and I both graduated from West High. He went on to pharmacy school and worked with his dad. He'd take over when Mr. Crittens decided it was time to retire, and that would make four generations of Crittens running the drugstore on the corner.

"We gonna get our quarterback this year?" Like most of Dane County, Carl was an avid University of Wisconsin fan. "We got the offensive line. We got the D. We're one good arm away from a national championship."

The light changed and I wished him a good evening before we crossed in different directions. I walked on, past bungalows with front lawns fading to yellow straw in the relentless heat. I passed the Edgewood Complex, its cluster of buildings set in an urban oak forest behind a tall iron fence. There, a person could study from kindergarten straight through to their master's degree without ever leaving the campus. I wondered if there was another educational system like it in the country. Maybe it was only Madison that could support an operation like that. It was a place where anyone lucky enough to find themselves there pretty much planned on staying right where they were until they rested for all eternity in the cemetery on top of the hill.

Except for my mother, of course. Nothing could stop her from leaving this lovely town. Not even a husband or daughter.

I dodged cars pulling into the Laurel Tavern parking lot. Sunday meant chicken dinner, and the Laurel had one of the best. When I crossed the sidewalk in front of Michael's Frozen Custard, I was surprised how far I'd walked. I don't know where my mind had been, but a glance at my watch told me it was nearly seven o'clock. My legs were tired. My shirt was sweat-marked. I decided to buy a cone and relax by Lake Wingra, in the park directly behind the custard stand.

I got a double scoop of chocolate custard. I'd have a long walk home, and since lunch was nothing more than the pieces of fruit I'd intended for breakfast, I figured the caloric indulgence could be justified. The lowering sun was working a number on my cone as I walked across the park's grassy expanse toward the lake. I had to lick fast to keep up, but I made it to a table at the lake's edge with no chocolate rivers running down my arm.

There were at least a dozen families picnicking. Charcoal grills heavy with steaks, brats, and burgers scented the air. Kids in bathing suits ran with the unhindered joy of a summer evening. The boathouse was doing a brisk business. Teenagers hung around the snack bar while people took rental kayaks and canoes out onto the water. Entire families of ducks and geese swam across the lake, oblivious to the paddleboarders gliding alongside them.

It was a lovely end to a lovely day. I enjoyed my spot at the table, alone with my cone, observing the happy comings and goings of Madisonians at play.

"Fancy meeting you here." Her voice came from behind me. "Looks like we had the same idea." She hopped up onto the table and sat next to me. "Mind if I join you? I was taking a walk." Like she was confident that as soon as I got over being startled I'd be glad she was there. "I got bored in your apartment. No offense. I figured I'd go out exploring. And look at this—our paths cross again. Do you think this is like what you read about? You know, with twins? How they have their own special bond and private language? Maybe some internal twin radar pulled me right to where I'd find you. Wouldn't that be something?"

"Yes, I guess it would."

"You hungry?" she asked.

I told her I'd had an ice-cream cone. I pointed to the boathouse. "You could grab a burger or brat over there."

She shook her head. "I'm good. Where were you today?"

"I dropped by the library this morning. Good thing I did. Brian was MIA. I'm sure he planned to stick Rosie with everything."

"Brian's an ass," Mimi said.

I smiled and thought she might be onto something about internal twin radar.

"You left awfully early. I was hoping we could have breakfast together."

"I couldn't sleep."

She nodded her understanding. "Last night was pretty heavy. I hope I didn't freak you out. Springing that DNA kit on you."

"I'm fine."

We sat there in silence for a long time. I focused my attention on a class taking place about twenty feet in front of me. Six middle-school girls were learning logrolling from two college-aged women. I was impressed. The girls not only looked to be picking it up easily but also seemed to be taking great joy in flopping into the water when they couldn't get it right.

"That's pretty cool," Mimi said. "I don't think I could stand up on a wet and rolling log. How about you?"

I didn't say anything.

"I wonder what it would have been like," she said.

My attention stayed on one young girl, dressed in denim cut-offs, sports bra, and a tie-dyed T-shirt while the rest of the girls were in bathing suits. Her wet hair was held tight in a ponytail.

She didn't seem to be part of the group. The rest of the girls giggled and hugged one another, offering encouragement. This girl kept her attention riveted on the instructors, watching every move and copying their technique.

"If we had been raised together, I mean." Mimi leaned back and closed her eyes against the sun. "I wonder how our lives would have been different."

The little girl I was watching was alone on her log. Her feet moved in tentative steps, rolling the log forward, then stopping. She held her arms out wide for balance and reversed her motion, sending the log spinning in the opposite direction.

"One thing's for sure, I never would have let you drop out of college. I mean, you're wicked smart. Anyone can tell that. No, sir. There's no way I would have let you quit if I'd been around."

The girl stepped up her pace. She seemed to be gaining confidence and didn't use her arms as much for balance. She rolled the log forward and back. Back and then forward. Picking up speed. An instructor stood on the dock, hands on her hips. She must have asked the girl something, because I saw her nod and inch away from the center of her log to the far end, making room for the instructor to join her.

"And I don't think you'd be as tied in to your father if I'd been around, either. One thing's for sure. Either *my* father's our father, and you wouldn't be dealing with a washed-up alcoholic, or *your* father's our father and the two of us would have ganged up on him years ago and demanded he stop his foolishness and be the kind of parent we both deserve."

The instructor started off slowly, rolling the log forward. The preteen girl kept up with her, grinning as she focused on her feet. The instructor signaled for the two of them to stop, then shifted to a backward roll. Again the girl kept up. The other girls were watching her now.

"How about you?" Mimi asked. "How do you think things would be different if we'd been raised together, as we should have been?"

The instructor picked up her pace, spinning the log backward with increased velocity. The girl struggled. She wasn't grinning anymore. Her arms waved wildly as she struggled to keep her balance.

And then the instructor shifted direction. Fast and without warning. The girl fell backward into the lake. The other girls laughed and draped themselves over one another.

"Stop it." I know my tone was sharp. "Isn't it enough I agreed to the DNA test? Let's wait and see what it says before we get any deeper into this identical twin thing."

"But can't you see I've got to be right? I mean, what else could it be?"

I watched the instructor hoist the girl she'd thrown off the log onto the dock, then climb up next to her and lay a condescending hand on the girl's wet head. She was probably offering some meaningless words of consolation, but I could see the girl's red-faced humiliation.

"I don't know, Mimi," I said, turning toward her. "I want to wait. And lay off my dad. You don't know one solitary thing about him or what he's been through. He wasn't perfect, but he was there for me. Always. In a way my mother never was. If you're right, and we *are* twins, while you and our mother were off having adventures and growing close, all the while never having to worry about money or jobs, my father was sacrificing everything he'd worked for to keep me safe. The fact is, neither of us has a flying clue what's happening here. Until we do, lay off my dad. Can you do that?"

For once Mimi's nothing-can-hurt-me bravado fell away.

It didn't take long for it to return.

"Fine. You don't want to talk about your dad, that's understandable. Let's talk about your mom."

"No, Mimi. Let's talk about *your* mom. Let's see some proof."

"What more proof do you need? Same name, same birthday?"

I shook my head. "So you say, Mimi. All I have is your story that your mother and mine share those. Give me something else."

"Like what? You want a birth certificate or something?"

John's words came back to me. "How about a photo? Let's start there. You and your mom are so close, I'm sure you have dozens of pictures. Show me one. My father's got lots of pictures from my mother's time with us. Her face is burned into my memory. Granted, I haven't seen her in seventeen years, but I'm sure I'd recognize her."

Mimi seemed shaken by my anger. Most people are when I'm sloppy enough to let it get the better of me. "Of course I have pictures. My apartment in Boston is filled with them. I have photo albums, too. I should have brought some. It didn't occur to me. I guess I was so excited to get back here to see my sister it completely skipped my mind."

I looked at Mimi, seeing her from a new perspective. "You came scurrying back to Madison, two whole days early for your interview, with the expressed intent of solving this mystery. It occurred to you to bring a DNA kit but not one photograph?" I got off the picnic table and stood in front of her. "How about your phone? As close as you and your mother are, I'm sure it's loaded with selfies of the two of you. Maybe in front of the Eiffel Tower or the Grand Canyon? Hell, show me a picture of the two of you getting mani-pedis together, I don't care."

"I don't have my phone on me." She looked over her shoulder, to the far end of the park. Like she was looking for someone to swoop in and rescue her.

"Then let's go back to my apartment. The walk will do us both good. You can show me the photos then."

Mimi's jaw quivered. She looked back over the park again. Scanning from east to west. "I don't have it, okay? When I woke up this morning and you were gone, I wanted to call you to make sure you were all right. I didn't have your contact info, but I was going to look up the library's number. That's when I realized I didn't have my phone with me at all. In my excitement I must have left it back in Boston. I was going to tell you about it. Ask you if it would be okay if I gave the department secretary your number in case they needed to reach me." Her eyes were wide, filled with a pleading sense of urgency. "Tess, I left my phone back in Boston. It's stupid, I know. My mom's always saying I get so excited I overlook important things."

"Why didn't you come to the library, then? You know the way. If you were so worried about the History secretary having a number to contact you, why not come and tell me?"

Healthy color drained from Mimi's face. Red blotches began to appear on her ashen skin as she sat there saying nothing.

"I didn't know where you were," she finally said. "It was supposed to be your day off. Why would I go looking for you at the library?"

My back stiffened. My hands formed fists. I had to consciously keep them dangling at my sides. My heart pounded, and I felt a headache coming on. Mimi had an answer for everything. It was all so pat, so neatly wrapped in logic.

"I'm leaving now." It was difficult to force my voice to stay level and calm. "I'm walking home. Alone. I'm going to check my apartment from top to bottom. If anything has been removed or disturbed I'm calling the police. Do you understand me?"

She sat there, wide-eyed and silent.

"And if I have to call the police, my second call will be to the History Department. I don't know what you're up to. But whatever it is, it's over. It's done." I pointed to the playground equipment at the far end of the park, probably two hundred yards away. "When I get over there I'm going to turn around and look back to this bench. I'd better see you sitting here. If you're not, I'm calling the police. There's no way I want you getting to my apartment before I do. When you see me turn around, you can leave. I don't care where you go or what you do, so long as it doesn't involve me. I don't ever want to see you again."

"But . . ."

I interrupted her. "I will put any belongings you may have left at my place out on the curb. Pick them up and be gone. I don't want to hear you knock. I don't want you to come by the library. If you do either of those things I will call the police. Do you understand me?"

Tears ran down her cheeks.

"Tess, please, don't . . ."

I interrupted her again. "Stay away, Mimi. I mean it. I'm done with you."

I turned and walked away, each step pumping raw energy into my rage. I walked straight across a field where four people were throwing Frisbees. Mothers guiding their toddlers down the playground slide stopped and watched me as I stormed past. When I got to the far end of the park, I turned and looked back.

Mimi was still there, sitting on the picnic table looking out at the lake.

I turned and crossed into Michael's parking lot.

"Miss Tess! Miss Tess!" I turned toward the child's voice calling my name. It was Paige Williams, the library patron so excited about starting kindergarten. She stood squirming on an outdoor table while her mother wiped remnants of custard off her face. I went over to them.

"Been to the lake?" Paige's mother asked. "We were there earlier. I promised this one if she managed to stay dry I'd treat her to a cone before we headed home. You see the logrollers?"

I tugged on Paige's pigtail and told her mother I had. "You heading home now?"

Paige scrambled down off the table and took my hand.

"We are," Paige's mom said. "Need a lift?"

I glanced back at the park.

"That would be great." I picked the little girl up and parked her on my hip. "Really great."

CHAPTER 14

I checked my apartment; nothing seemed to be missing. Then I checked again, and locked my doors and windows. I got on my computer and reviewed my bank accounts. I had $3,715.49 in savings and $299.87 in checking. The balances were right where I expected them to be, and there had been no activity beyond my own in either account. I changed the passwords anyway.

I have two credit cards in addition to my debit card, and I logged into those accounts, too. My one credit card had a $415.02 balance and showed no purchases since that toaster oven I bought myself last February. My other credit card had a zero balance. That's the one I keep for emergencies. To be safe I called their customer service numbers and reported each card missing. Both credit companies assured me that my new cards, with new account numbers, would arrive within three days. I asked them what would happen if someone tried to use the old accounts.

"That can't happen," they each told me. "It's all electronic. Those accounts are already dead."

Then I went online and password protected my cell phone. I sent an e-mail to my landlord saying I had reason to believe my personal security may have been compromised, asking that she be on the lookout for anyone trying to change anything on my lease.

Then I did the same for my utilities and my cable account. I even changed my passwords for Netflix and Hulu.

John had brought up the idea of identity theft. If that was Mimi's angle, she'd have to find a new target. I was proud of myself for taking charge of things. I·felt safe.

For a while anyway.

I went to bed, put my head on the pillow, and the next thing I knew it was Monday morning. I hadn't slept that well in days.

I didn't have any special programming that particular day, nor did I have a shift to cover. But I decided to swing in on yet another day off. I told myself it was to make sure everything was running smoothly. Truth was, I felt like I needed a big dose of normal, and the library offered me that. I got there a little before eleven. Rosie was managing things well. She was behind the desk while Clifford, a high school kid working off community service hours he picked up when he got busted for tagging a police cruiser, shelved books and answered Internet questions for patrons using our community computers. Cordon was there, too. Cordon Balaclay is a retired librarian who subs when local branches are caught short-handed. I wasn't surprised to see him there. Brian was supposed to be working. I remembered his note about checking out other libraries. He must have called Cordon in to cover his shift.

I waved to Rosie and thanked Cordon for coming in on what I was certain was short notice.

"Always happy to help," he said. "I was glad to get your call. Millie's got a birthday coming up, and I want to get her something special. The extra money comes in handy."

Millie is Cordon's Cavalier King Charles Spaniel. She's a sweet dog, and Cordon, a lifelong bachelor, spoils her beyond distraction.

"Well, I'm glad you're here." I went behind the counter to see if Rosie needed any help. She assured me she didn't and asked if I'd heard from John.

I checked my watch. "You mean in the entire twenty-five hours since I last saw him? No, Rosie, I haven't heard from him."

"Well, keep me posted." She gave me a wink. "The way my

life's going, I have to get all my romance through you. But if you don't stop coming in here on your days off, you'll never have anything to tell me."

I promised I would keep her in the loop regarding my love life, swore I was stopping by for only a second, and told her to call if she needed anything. "Keep an eye on Cordon, would you? I think the isolation of retirement might be getting to him. He's under the impression I called him in. Brian must have done it. Probably figured he could stretch his weekend and I wouldn't be here to notice."

"Brian's an idiot," Rosie said.

I got to my father's place around twelve-thirty. I don't know why I bother to knock. Maybe it's out of courtesy. Maybe I want to give him a heads-up that I'm there. Who knows? But it's always the same thing. I knock a couple of times, he ignores me, and I wind up letting myself in with my key. I keep hoping one day he'll get up off that damned chair and answer the door for his daughter.

But that Monday wasn't the day.

His apartment was dark. All the curtains were closed. The only light came from the television. The History Channel was rerunning a piece on secret Nazi training compounds.

"There she is." I heard him before I saw him. He came around the corner from his bedroom. "How's my girl this fine evening?"

He wore baggy, plaid sleep pants and a torn cotton T-shirt. A three-day stubble glazed his cheeks, and his hair looked as if he hadn't showered since our annual hike out to Picnic Point. The entire place stank of whiskey, coffee, and rotting food.

"Dad, it's twelve-thirty in the afternoon."

He swiped a hand over his face. "It is? Well, where's the time go? I get so wrapped up in things, Tessie. You know how I can be." He stepped toward me, laid a heavy hand on my shoulder for about two heartbeats, then pulled it away with a self-satisfied grunt for performing a textbook fatherly greeting.

"Do you know what day it is?" I asked.

He patted his hands over his chest, like an absentminded professor looking for a day planner in the pocket of a suit jacket. Then he stood still and struggled to hold himself steady as he tried to focus.

"It's not your birthday, is it? For God's sake, Tess. You've got to remind your old man about things like this. Happy birthday. What shall we do to mark this fine occasion?"

I watched him shuffle his way to his recliner. He fumbled with the remote and finally got the television set turned off.

"It's not my birthday, Dad. I meant the day of the week. Do you know what today is?"

He stared at me, and I held his gaze. Sometimes, if I look hard enough, I can see the man my father used to be. I can make out the contours of his once-strong chin hidden there behind the loose and ashen skin. Those shoulders that once inspired people to lean on them . . . every once in a while, when he's standing a certain way, I can see them, too. And if he's wearing the right clothes, which happens rarely, but if he does get himself cleaned up, now and then I catch the power of his broad chest.

In those moments I can see why my mother fell in love with him.

That day wasn't one of those times.

"You want a multiple choice, Dad? Or do you want to take a stab at it? Odds are one in seven you'll get it right."

"Don't sass me, Tess. I put up with a lot, but I'll not tolerate disrespect. Not after everything I've done for you. Besides, when you're retired every day is Saturday."

Retired, I thought. *Is that the lie you tell yourself?*

"I've got groceries in the car. You feel like helping me lug them in?"

"Why don't you let me rest my old bones? I'm sure you've only got a bag or two. Can you do that for me?"

"Sure, Dad." I made two trips to the car and brought in enough food and supplies to last him four days. I started emptying the bags and putting things away while he kept his focus on some announcer with a dramatic voice listing off the sins of Josef Mengele.

"I got you those berry yogurt bars you like." I put them in the freezer. "There's six of them. They'll make a nice dessert for you after your dinners this week." I left the canned goods and cereal boxes on the counter. I figured putting them away might give him something to do other than drink and chase Nazis.

I looked around the house. Maybe I should have pulled out a trash bag and started shoveling the place out, but it seemed like such a useless effort. I'd be back there in a few days and the place would be re-littered with dirty dishes, plastic wrappings, and stacks of newspapers. Instead, I shoved a load of unfolded laundry to the side of his couch and sat down.

"It's Monday afternoon, Dad. The sun is shining. The humidity is finally tolerable. You got plans?"

He lifted the remote and pointed toward the television. "I'll see what cable has in store. I've had a busy week. I think I'll take it easy for a couple of days."

I'd lay good money the only trips he'd made out of the house in the past three days were to walk to the end of his porch to get the newspaper.

Thank God for liquor delivery, huh, Dad?

He focused on the remote, moving his fingers over the buttons as if he were exploring an exotic relic from some far-flung civilization and his life depended on figuring out how it worked. More than likely he was counting the seconds until I'd leave and he'd be relieved of having to make idle chat with his only daughter.

His only daughter. An image of Mimi sitting on that picnic table in the park flashed through my mind.

"How long were you and Mom married before I was born?"

He kept his focus on the remote.

"You and Mom ever think about having more kids?" I asked.

His fingers froze.

"I mean, did you want more? Did she?"

He turned toward me. His face stern. "Where's this coming from, Tess?"

I was violating the rule. Our one day to talk about my mother had come and gone.

"I don't know," I said. "My birthday's coming up. Gets you thinking, I guess. Reminiscing. Wondering. Did you and Mom always intend for me to be an only child?"

He waved me away and set his attention on the Gestapo killing machine being described in resplendent baritone.

"Did you?"

"Subject never came up, I suppose."

I nodded. "Maybe it was a tough pregnancy. I know some women swear off having another child if they have a particularly rough time with the first. Was it that way with Mom? Was I a difficult pregnancy?"

"That was a long time ago, Tess. What good does it do to talk about this now?"

"How about the delivery? Were you there? Were you in the room?"

"I don't want to talk about this." He sounded far older than his fifty-eight years.

"Did you catch me when I came out? Maybe cut my umbilical cord?"

He shook his head. Again and again. It never occurred to me that I might have been inflicting real pain on him with my questions.

"Maybe times were different then. I mean, it was thirty years ago. A dad out in the waiting room might not know a thing about what was happening in delivery, right? His wife could be in there giving birth to twins or triplets and he wouldn't have a clue."

His hands opened and closed into fists. There had been plenty of times I would have been frightened to see them. But that day wasn't one of them.

"Were you there, Dad? Were you in the room when I was born?"

"We had an agreement, Tess. We wouldn't talk about her. She's gone. We move on. You agreed to that. It's important to honor promises."

I looked at him . . . hard . . . but try as I might I couldn't capture so much as a shadow of the tall man who inspired both awe and fear that he'd been when my mother was here. All I could see now was an old man, shriveled and small. Deserted by his wife. Beaten by the world. He didn't need more cruelty from his daughter. I got up and went to his kitchen. One clean glass was left in his cabinet. I put two ice cubes in it and poured three fingers of whiskey over them, then carried the glass to my father.

"Here you go, Dad. Put the groceries away when you can. Try to have a nice day."

The sounds of Luftwaffe strafing accompanied me out the door.

CHAPTER 15

I spent Monday night doing chores around my apartment. I don't know how to describe it, but doing laundry, paying bills, making sure everything in my refrigerator is still within its use-by date . . . those things connect me to my body. I feel somehow more real when I do them, if that makes any sense.

My phone did that little jingle when I have a text coming in. My first instinct was not to look. I figured it could be Mimi. I mean, she told me she didn't have her phone, but that girl's resourceful. Maybe she'd be apologizing. Or explaining. Maybe she'd ignore our whole scene and ask me if I wanted company for a *Breaking Bad* binge. But I was in no mood to hear from her, no matter what her motivation. I may have cooled down enough to be past my threat to contact the police, but I still didn't want to hear her. I didn't want anything from her at all, at least not until I was sure what her end game was.

But the part of me wanting it to be John checking in to see what I was doing made me look. I'm happy to say I got the payoff I was hoping for. His text was simple.

Why aren't we together? Aren't couples supposed to be doing stuff in the evening?

He called us a couple. I know it probably makes me sound like a twelve-year-old girl swooning over some mop-headed acne-pocked singer in a boy band, but his text made me smile. A real, cheek-busting, eye-crinkling, red-blushing smile.

I went to the kitchen and made myself a cup of tea. I didn't want to look too eager to return his text. I remembered what Mimi told me about men loving a good chase. I ran over my response options, and finally settled on one I hoped would set just the right tone.

Sorry we can't hang out. Armando's here. He's teaching me the tango.

Those little bubbles started churning on my phone right away. You know the ones I mean? The ones that show you the other person is composing his text right then and there?

Tell him if he steps on your toes he'll have to answer to me. And if he tries anything other than dancing he'll answer to my whole damned posse.

I think I may have laughed out loud. Right there in my kitchen. I remember looking up from my phone to make sure no one was watching. I was alone, of course; it was sort of a knee-jerk reaction to how fun I thought his flirtation was. Maybe a part of me was hoping someone *would* have been there so I could share it. I texted him back. This time I was braver.

How about I promise to teach you every smooth move I learn from my handsome Latin lover?

Again, I didn't have to wait to see those bubbles flashing.

That sounds like a plan. I'm playing hooky tomorrow. How about you do the same? I'll pick you up around eleven. We can go for a walk before I take you out for lunch. It's about time I get your address, by the way.

I leaned back into my chair and sipped my tea. I liked John's style. We'd already had a date where we each drank a bit too much. He followed that up with a breakfast. This time he was opting for a midday get-together. Was he trying to see me in all different lights? I texted him my address, said good night, and told him I was looking forward to tomorrow. I saw the bubbles in action for one last time.

I'll be knocking on your door at eleven. Please answer. Good night.

I called Rosie, told her that based on her advice I'd like to take the next day off, and sealed the deal by telling her Brian wouldn't be in until Wednesday. She said she'd be glad to cover for me, told me to have a great day, and reminded me of my promise to tell her everything about my time with John.

For the second night in a row I had no trouble sleeping.

Sure enough, John was standing on my stoop when he said he would be. I'd been awake since seven. I'd had my usual breakfast of coffee and fruit, then set about getting ready. He'd told me we'd go for a walk and then out to lunch. After trying on a couple different outfits I settled on a pair of pink plaid shorts, turquoise tank top, and hiking sandals. I drew my hair up into a high ponytail. At the wine bar, he had mentioned how much he liked my hair when I wore it down around my shoulders, but today was going to be another warm one. If we walked any distance at all, I'd need the hair off my neck.

"You look like you should be on a magazine cover." That was the first thing he said when I opened the door.

"I might be flattered if I knew what magazine you had in mind," I said. "For all I know you may be talking about *Zombie Today*." I stepped aside so he could come in.

He gave my apartment the once-over. Of course I'd taken an hour that morning to make sure the place was in show-off shape. I even snipped a few hydrangea and day lilies from Toni Streckert's garden next door. She was always offering me cuttings, and the pink and green color combo looked great on my breakfast nook table. Even in that cheap water pitcher I bought for fifty cents when the library hosted a community-wide garage sale.

"Your place is nice," he said. "It looks like you. Comfortable and lovely."

I fought the urge to respond with a self-deprecating jab. Instead I thanked him and asked if he wanted a glass of iced tea.

"No! Let's get out of here. I'm cooped up in an office or study room way too many hours every day. And you spend too much time in that library. Today we play. Let's get while the getting's good. Stretch our legs. Move our bodies. Celebrate the fact we don't owe anybody one moment of our time for the next"—he looked at his watch—"twenty-one hours."

"Sounds perfect. Which way are we headed?" I slipped my phone into the pocket of my shorts and grabbed my keys.

"How would you feel about an urban hike? I was hoping we could walk downtown. State Street up to the square. Then maybe Graze for lunch. How's that sound?"

The students had recently returned to the university after summer break. State Street would be filled with anxious undergrads trying to look cool sitting at outdoor cafés. There'd be street musicians and sidewalk artists. And since this was Madison, there'd likely be some sort of protest or demonstration on at least one street corner.

"Sounds terrific." I pointed to the door and locked my place up behind us.

"You don't carry a purse?" he asked.

I patted my pocket. "Phone, a little cash, and ChapStick. Can't think of anything else I need."

John stood still and looked at me, long enough for me to notice but not so long that I felt uncomfortable. "I like a woman who travels light. You, Tess Kincaid. I like you."

I don't know if I have the words to tell you how I felt hearing that. Not that any of that matters now. But then it did. I started walking in the direction of downtown. I was eager to begin our stolen day together. I guess I didn't realize how fast I was moving.

"Whoa! Slow down there, partner." John beckoned me back to him. "Like I said, we got twenty-one hours. Let's enjoy every minute."

And I did. For a time, at least. We talked about a lot of stuff as we walked through the neighborhood toward the bike path. I asked him about his experiences growing up.

"Well," he said. "You already know I'm from Green Bay. Town's big enough for a kid to always find ways to get in trouble. Small enough that everybody knows it two minutes later. And let me tell you, nobody wasted a second telling my parents what I'd been up to, either."

"I imagine the Packers played a role."

An exaggerated look of surprise crossed his face. "A role? You imagine? Tess, where I come from, Vince Lombardi is a saint. I mean a real one. Without even thinking I could rattle off the names of at least thirty people I know who truly believe a prayer sent up to Saint Vince at just the right moment is the sole reason we made the playoffs last year. My best friend in high school, David Goronsky . . . everybody called him Butchie . . . his parents' house was less than a block from Lambeau. We'd watch every game in Butchie's basement. When the Pack scored, the whole house would shake from the roar of the crowd. Like a fighter jet was getting ready to land in the backyard."

"And what would happen when Green Bay lost?"

We walked several yards before he stopped. His brow furrowed and he put his hands on his hips. After a few seconds, he shook his head. "I'm sure it's happened. But for the life of me, I can't recall one loss. Guess that's the kind of trauma a dedicated cheesehead doesn't let linger in his memory banks."

We laughed. When he slipped his arm around my waist and pulled me back into the walk, it seemed like the most natural thing. Like of course we'd walk along holding each other. He'd pull me closer when a bike passed. We'd break apart when we had to negotiate our way around a slow-moving group of mommies pushing strollers. But once we were clear, his arm would go back around my waist, his thumb hooked inside my belt loop.

John told me about his dad, a machinist at a local paper mill. "His name is Arthur. Arch to everybody in Green Bay. He says he's going to retire next year. I'll believe that when I see it. Wait 'til you meet him. He'll be seventy years old on his next birthday, but he looks twenty years younger. Still splits a cord of wood every spring so my mother can keep a fire going all winter long."

My spine stiffened at John's casual reference to my meeting his father. I don't think he noticed. He went on walking and talking. By the time we got to the mall at the foot of State Street I'd learned his mother's name was Leona. She worked part-time in the cafeteria at the same high school John and his brothers attended. The same school where John once taught math.

"She was disappointed when I quit," he said. "Used to say our working together made her the envy of all the ladies in her circle. None of them got to see their adult sons every day. She understood, though. She'd been at the school long enough to see the decline."

"Are they hoping you'll go back to Green Bay after law school?"

The look on his face as he thought about his answer made me wonder if he missed his hometown as much as his parents obviously missed him. "Green Bay's a great sports town," he said. "But it's not a big sports town. If I want a career in sports law, I need a bigger market. My parents support my dreams. My brothers', too. Green Bay's their place to grow old, not ours."

John told me about his three older brothers. Allen, the oldest, was an IT specialist in Minneapolis. He was married to Janice, whom no one in the family particularly liked, but they all tolerated out of love for Allen. "My brother would make a great dad," he said. "But Janice is devoted to what she calls her retail career. She's been a three-day-a-week cashier at Target since she was in high school. She says kids and careers don't mix."

Donald was the second son born to Arch and Leona Rappaport. "He works the iron boats on the Great Lakes. Lives in Duluth. Spends weeks at a time on the water. Then comes home to Richard and their three cocker spaniels. Then there's Mike. He's two years older than me. Military man." John's smile was more warning than joy. "Great guy. But don't get him started on politics or you're in for a lecture. Mike's married to Amy. Everybody loves Amy. And we're all thrilled that come December Amy and Mike will present my mom and dad with their first grandchild. My folks are buying out every toy store in a thirty-mile radius. Mike and Amy are stationed in New Jersey at the moment. Mom will go spend a few weeks with them after the baby's born."

State Street served up its usual carnival as we walked east toward the capitol. Skateboarders and bikers rolled down the pedestrian mall. It was a weekday lunch hour and the sidewalks were filled with the kind of people that make Madison unique. Here, a person sped by on a unicycle. There, a woman trotted next to an oversized Great Dane with a head the exact height as its owner. A group of women, obviously faculty members, ambled down the street in front of us, giving us full access to their conversation weighing the merits of online learning versus traditional lecture-style instruction. Anyone walking in groups had to talk loud to be heard over the din of bus traffic and music. Those walking alone kept their eyes straight ahead, earbuds filling their skulls with a soundtrack of their own choosing. I wondered what they were listening to. What could possibly be more entertaining than State Street on a warm summer day?

And as we walked John held my hand. We didn't say much. Every now and then we'd stop by a store window and check out the displays. But I thought we both enjoyed just being with each other and watching the show. I know I did.

Once we got to the square, things shifted to a more professional scene. Men and women in suits too formal for such lovely weather scurried about the walks surrounding the capitol building. John and I walked counterclockwise around the majestic building and made our way to Graze. The hostess told us there'd be an hour wait for an outside table. John asked me if I'd be all right eating inside. To tell you the truth, I preferred it. The sun was high, and the outdoor patio seemed more like a place to grill your lunch rather than eat it. We were shown to a great table, where we could see the entire capitol building framed by two-story windows.

"I'm not drinking," he told me when the hostess asked us what she could bring us from the bar. "But I've heard they make a great Bloody Mary if you're so inclined."

The walk back to my place would be too long for me to consider anything alcoholic. I asked for an ice water, and John ordered the same.

"I've never eaten here," I said as I looked over the menu. "What's good?"

"This is only my second time here." John strained to see the specials marked on the chalkboard by the entrance. "I had the burger. It was great. I think you can't go wrong with anything, actually."

A hamburger sounded good to me. I ordered mine with cheese and bacon. John asked for the salmon pasta special. "And we'll have the cookies and milk for dessert," he said. Our waitress promised it wouldn't be long and left us with a small relish plate to nibble on while we waited.

"This is fun," John said. "But I've been blabbing on about me and my family. Tell me all about you. What's happening with your look-alike? Mimi, right?"

I nodded. "I don't think I'll be seeing her again. I did what you suggested."

"Oh? What was that?"

"I took to heart what you said, that all I had was her word for things. I asked her for a picture of her mother."

John drank his water but kept his eyes on me. "That must have been tough. Did it look like your mom?"

"That's just it. She couldn't come up with one photo. When I asked her to show me a picture on her phone, she stammered out some story about how she left her cell back in Boston. Said it was because she was so scatterbrained with everything going on, but that's hard for me to believe. I mean, who forgets their phone when they're traveling? Especially to a job interview. I told her to leave me alone. Then I went home and made sure she hadn't robbed me of anything."

"Why is this the first I'm hearing about this? So she's not staying with you anymore?" His tone was insistent. "When did this happen?"

"Saturday."

He put the radish he was about to eat back down on the table. "You're telling me you haven't seen Mimi in two days? Where is she? Why didn't you tell me?"

"How about because it's no big deal?" I felt my defenses lock back into place. "I met her. It was weird. It got weirder. I asked her to back off, and I don't care where she is. End of story."

He hesitated, then nodded. Finally he smiled, and the furrows in his brow disappeared. "You're right. I'm sorry if I sounded like an intrusive parent." He reached across the table and laid his hand on mine. "You inspire the protective side of me, I guess."

The waitress came with our food, and I pulled my hand free to make room on the table. John and I commented on how great each other's plate looked. We took our first few bites and could only talk about how wonderful it all tasted. I was starting to relax again. Then he steered the conversation back to the personal.

"We've talked about your mom." His voice was soft. "I'm sorry she hurt you like that. Tell me about your dad. What's he like?"

My steel vault of self-defense slammed closed the way it always does whenever people ask about my father. "He keeps to himself mostly."

"Never remarried?" John stole a French fry off my plate.

I shook my head. "Never dated after my mom left. I guess raising a daughter all by himself was enough to handle."

"What's he do for a living? Is he a lover of books like you?"

The room felt hotter. As if the sun coming through the tall windows were turning the whole restaurant into a greenhouse. I took a long sip of icy water and came up with the simplest lie that allowed me to dodge the real answer to his question. The same lie my father tells himself.

"He's kind of retired. Has been for years."

"Oh?" John seemed surprised. "How old is he? I mean, you're only twenty-nine. Did he retire early, or was he older when you were born?"

"My dad's fifty-eight. I guess you can say he's lucky to be able to have this time of freedom while he's still relatively young."

John seemed to buy it. "That's cool. What did he retire from?"

My heart was racing. Any true answer I gave would only bring more questions. And I never liked answering questions about my father and the reasons for his failed career. He'd given me so much. The very least I could do was protect his privacy. Not to mention my own. I didn't particularly like explaining what a burden I'd been to him through the years.

"He was a professor." I wiped my mouth and set my napkin down. I wasn't hungry anymore. "Here at the university."

"And he's retired? Already?" John's curiosity was piqued. "How's that work?"

"An opportunity came up." I wondered if I could tell pieces of the truth without revealing too much. "My grandparents died and left him a trust."

He pulled another fry off my plate and smiled as he ate it. "So I'm dating an heiress, am I? It must have been some trust to let him retire so early. What did he teach?"

I sounded cold. I'm pretty sure I didn't mean to, but I wanted to stop talking about my dad. "Listen, why don't you list all your questions about my father, his career, his funding . . . write them all down. I'll take it to him and see if he wants me to tell a perfect stranger all the details of his life."

That stopped John in his tracks. He stared at me for a few seconds, then apologized. Said he didn't mean to pry. He looked past me. Then he set his fork down and excused himself. "Maybe when I come back I'll be more polite company. I'm really sorry, Tess. I didn't mean to push any buttons."

I never know what to do when I'm alone at a restaurant table. I spent a few moments moving the food around on my plate. Then I turned my attention to the comings and goings of people out on the square. A small group of middle-aged people walked by. They carried signs lamenting what they saw as the latest heavy-handed act by the governor. I could tell from the way their mouths moved they were singing. But even though they were close enough for me to read their banners, the heavy glass separating us kept me from hearing the words. When they passed from view I watched a trio of preteen girls waiting at the bus stop. I remember being intrigued with how physical they each were. Not unlike the girls I saw rolling logs down at the lake. They struck poses and twirled. They rearranged one another's hair. When their bus arrived they hopped in place, eagerly waiting their turn to board.

When the bus pulled away I realized John had been gone longer than a person might expect for someone using the bathroom. I looked toward the direction he went and didn't see him. An embarrassing thought came over me. What if I'd been ditched? Had my abrupt reaction to his questions about my dad been enough to scare him off? I looked the other way, toward the door.

That's when I saw her.

She was leaving the restaurant. I knew that back. I knew that hair. I knew the way she walked.

Mimi Winslow was exiting Graze. I saw her walking fast . . . like I do . . . down the steps. She turned left on the square and disappeared into the crowd.

I jumped when I felt a hand on my shoulder.

"Whoa," John said as he sat back down. "I didn't mean to startle you."

I watched him as he picked up his fork and twirled another bite of pasta onto it. He smiled as he chewed. My mind raced with dozens of thoughts, none of them soothing.

"Is something wrong, Tess?" John took a drink of water. "Are you feeling okay? You look a little pale."

I reached into my pocket, pulled out a twenty-dollar bill, and laid it on the table. "I have to go."

John reached across the table, but I stood before he could touch me.

"What's going on? Tess, I told you I'm sorry. No more talk about your father, I promise. Please stay."

I shook my head. "I've got to go."

I left the restaurant without looking back. I headed home.

This time I was oblivious to the magic of State Street.

CHAPTER 16

John texted me a few times that day. I ignored every one of them. I needed time.

Time, I thought. My favorite subject.

My mind was twisting with all kinds of thoughts I wasn't able to make sense of. I'd been having a pleasant lunch with John. Then he asked about my father.

An innocent-enough line of conversation. Didn't I ask him an ungodly amount of questions about his family? He had no way of knowing how touchy I was about certain topics.

And he had asked about Mimi. He seemed surprised I was no longer in contact with her.

He even seemed a little put out that he was just learning I'd asked Mimi to leave me alone. He brushed it all away by saying he was being protective of me.

Then he excused himself from the table. He'd been gone so long.

And she was there. He came back to the table right as she was leaving.

I didn't know what was happening, but I was sick of coincidences. And I was glad I had those two earlier nights of good sleep under my belt, because when the alarm went off Wednesday morning I was dragging.

*   *   *

Even though it would have been expected, I didn't hear John's coded knock before I opened the library. That was a good thing. He hadn't texted me since the evening before. That was a good thing, too. But when Brian Erickson rolled into the library around noon, I knew my streak of good things had come to an end.

"What the hell, Tess?" He stomped past me, snapped his fingers, and pointed toward his office. I guess I should have been grateful he waited until he closed his door to unload his big bag of hot and crazy on me. "I put up with a lot of shit around this place. I don't need an extra helping of it from you."

"I'm going to need more details." I was too tired to play the role of obedient staffer. "Is there something specific you want to blame me for, or is this your run-of-the-mill finger pointing?"

Brian put his hands on his flabby hips and stared at me. "What in the world has gotten into you? Are you planning some sort of coup? Do I need to remind you I'm the one who lets you practically run this place?"

Practically? Was doing all the work so he could take long weekends, five-hour lunches, nonexistent meetings, and credit for everything that's done right around here what he considered *practically* running the place?

He continued his rant. "I have busted my ass for you. In the name of job enrichment I give you any number of opportunities to stretch yourself. I give you responsibility far beyond your training and experience. And this is how you repay me?"

Job enrichment? Is that what the cool kids were calling dumping all his work on other people these days?

I'd worked with him long enough to know he needed direct questions. When he got on a tear like this it was like his entire being was starved for the sound of his own voice. He'd never get around to his point. Despite my fatigue and irritation, I slipped right into my standard tactics for managing my boss.

"What are you angry about right this moment, Brian?"

"The phone call, of course." As usual, when given tight parameters, Brian could respond.

"What phone call are you talking about?"

He growled mean but unintelligible syllables. He huffed and turned himself around in circles. I was losing him.

"Who told you about the phone call?" Maybe I could zero in on whatever the heck it was he was talking about with specific questions.

"Mildred Dorchester, of course." Brian named the head of our Board of Directors. "She called me right after she hung up with you. And thank God she did. Can you imagine if she'd taken your accusations at their merit and contacted other board members? I have a wife, Tess. I have a child."

While I was pleased to hear Brian acknowledge his family, even if only for his own self-service, I didn't see how they were my responsibility. But that seemed secondary at the moment.

"Brian, I didn't call Mildred. Perhaps you're confused."

He growled his nonsense sounds and spun again.

"Brian, did you hear me? I said I didn't call Mildred. I haven't spoken to her since the volunteer appreciation luncheon in July."

Mildred Dorchester is the kind of person you want heading up your board. She's smart, well connected in the community, and not afraid to work hard despite having more money than the Pope himself. Among other holdings, Mildred owns at least forty rental properties around town, including the building in which my father lives. She's been on the board as long as I've been at the library and was elected chairman two years ago. I've always appreciated her no-nonsense style, and she's been vocal about her support of all I do for the library.

"Well then, who the hell was it, Tess?" Brian demanded in that condescending way of his. "Who called her, using *your* name, complaining that I don't show up for work as much as . . . let me see . . . how did Mildred say you put it?" His words dripped with sarcasm. "Oh, that's right. You said I didn't show up for work as much as someone paid as well as I am would be expected to.

You left her with the impression that all I'm interested in is sucking up to the board and that I leave all the real work to the staff." He leveled an angry stare at me. "As if I could ever trust a bunch of lowly educated incompetents to run an enterprise as complex as this one."

How the hell would he know how complex this enterprise was? Rosie and I did all the heavy lifting. I shoved those thoughts aside. People like Brian have a tendency to walk away clean from any mess they create. There'd be plenty of time to smooth his feathers and resettle into our routine. There seemed to be a bigger fish that needed frying.

"Brian, when did Mildred say I called you?"

"What the hell difference does it make? When isn't important. I'm more interested in why. What the hell were you trying to accomplish? Do you want a raise? Is that it? Are you looking for more recognition? What the flying hell were you thinking?"

I glanced out the window. No one in the library seemed to react to his anger. Maybe Brian's office was more soundproof than I knew. Rosie was still behind the counter, talking to Agnes and Innocent.

I remember thinking I should be out there getting the ladies started with the day's project. I shouldn't have been stuck in here dealing with his crap. But I stood there, doing my very best not to haul off and punch him in his pudgy gut. Then I realized what was going on.

"Look, Brian. I already told you I didn't call Mildred. There's a lot of stuff happening in my life right now. Stuff you don't know about. Stuff that I'm pretty sure will explain the phone call. So I'm going to ask you again, when did Mildred say I called?"

"I don't care what's going on in your life, Tess. I make it a strict policy not to entangle myself with the personal goings-on of my staff. I pride myself on setting good boundaries with my subordinates. Ask yourself. Have I ever interfered with your private life?"

It took more energy than I thought I had to keep from

screaming. I could feel my pulse pounding behind my eyes. Brian didn't get to wrap up his total disregard for the impact his laziness had on everybody who worked there in some sort of smug, shiny gift paper of noninterference. It wasn't fair, and I would have loved nothing better than to tell him so.

But my father taught me long ago to always know my place. And, like most areas of my life, this was a place where I had no power.

So I looked down at my shoes. Sometimes that helps when I get as angry as I was then. I look down and imagine my feet stuck like glue to the floor. Nothing can make me move, so I might as well take a look around and get a good picture of where I am. That's what I did while Brian continued his tantrum. I imagined myself planted in that library floor, and I looked around to see what I could see. The walls were green. Brian's desk had an overflowing in-basket and a completely empty out-basket. The fern on his windowsill needed water. It might sound crazy, but it's usually enough to break the moment, calm me down, and remind me where I am and what I have to do.

I took a deep breath and tried again. "If you can answer my questions, Brian, I'm sure we can provide Mildred with an explanation. One that will help her understand that I was not the person complaining about your work ethic."

He was quiet for a moment. I figured he was considering what might happen if I let Mildred know it wasn't me, his most trusted assistant, who had called her. Maybe he thought she might be convinced to overlook the complaint entirely. Especially if he could convince me to throw in a few compliments about what a grand job he was doing here at the library. He pulled his phone out of his pocket and scrolled down the screen.

"I got the call from her yesterday afternoon at 1:46. She said she'd just hung up from you. If I hadn't been out of town on important library business I'd have spoken to you sooner about this."

I ignored his lie about where he'd been and reconstructed my Monday.

"I had lunch at Graze yesterday." I almost added *with a friend,* but I didn't want to open up that line of questioning. "I walked there. I would have been walking home when Mildred said I called. Downtown, through my neighborhood, back to my house." A thought came to me. "Hold on a minute."

I didn't give him time to respond. I left his office, crossed the hall into mine, and got my phone from my purse. I scrolled up the list of recent calls while I went back to his office.

"Look." I held the screen up for him to read. "Last call I made was Monday evening, 8:38. And it wasn't to Mildred Dorchester."

"Who was it to, then?"

So much for his policy of noninvolvement with his subordinates.

"Not that it matters," I said, "but I called my landlady to set up an appointment to have my locks changed."

Brian spun around again. He tended to do that when he didn't know what to do next.

"You could have used any phone. This proves nothing."

I looked down at my shoes again. I visualized roots growing out of the soles of my sandals, securing me to the brown and red tiled floor. I took another long, deep breath. I kept thinking I shouldn't have to prove anything. I was not a liar. If I said I didn't call Mildred, Brian could take that straight to the bank.

But like I said, I always know my place.

"I met somebody," I told him once I calmed myself enough to speak. "Last week. A woman. She looks an awful lot like me. She sounds like me, too. Look, I don't know how to explain it, but a lot of crazy things have been happening since she showed up."

"You mean like identity theft?" Brian's disbelief was evident in his tone. "Who would want to steal your identity?"

I was breathing faster than was good for me. My hands closed into fists. My heart pounded out a crazy rhythm. I mentally started chanting along with my pulse. *Calm down. Calm down. Calm down.*

"I don't know her reasons." I could hear the tremble in my voice.

"And you're suggesting she called Mildred? This person you just met? Why would she do something like that?"

"I don't know."

His eyes narrowed. "How would she even know to call Mildred Dorchester? What would give her the notion to complain about me?"

Calm down. Breathe. Calm down. Breathe. Calm down.

"I've spoken with her." Shame flooded my body like liquid fire. "I liked her at first. We had kind of a goofy mystery thing going, you know? Like, who are you? Why do we look so much alike?"

I didn't add the rest of what I was thinking. *Why do we have the same birthday? Why do our mothers have the same name? Oh, did I mention we took a DNA test?*

"And you complained about me?" Brian's hands were back on his hips. "You meet some stranger off the street and the first thing you do is start gossiping about me? And I'm to believe she takes it upon herself to call Mildred pretending to be you? Why? What's in it for her, Tess?"

There was a knock on Brian's door. Rosie poked her head in. "You guys want to keep it down? We can't hear the words, but the whole library can sense the tension." She turned concerned eyes toward me. "Everything all right?"

Brian took a deep breath. His volume was lower. He spoke to Rosie, but his eyes were on me.

"Thanks, Rosie. We're good. Tess here was telling me a story about meeting new friends. I guess I got a little excited for her."

Rosie nodded and closed the door. When Brian spoke again I could tell he was struggling to keep his voice in the civil range.

"You're going to call Mildred. You're going to tell her all about your new friend and whatever prank she's pulling. You're going to impress upon her how much you appreciate the hard work I give this library and that you can't imagine why your friend said anything different. Then you're going to contact your new little gossip mate and tell her whatever it is you need to to make sure this doesn't happen again. Do you understand me?"

I nodded.

"Because if it happens again, I'll have no choice but to fire you. Do you understand that? I'll not keep a staffer who gossips to strangers about library concerns."

We stood there in tension for at least a full silent minute.

"I've got to head down to Janesville," Brian said. "There's a meeting you've already made me late for. Can I count on you to take care of things on this end?"

He turned toward the door before I had the chance to assure him I could.

"You've got a good setup here, Tess. I know how much this place means to you. But I want you to be careful. There's no other job that would allow someone with your lack of credentials to enjoy the kind of flexibility and responsibility I've allowed you to have. Do as I've instructed, or else everything you love can disappear."

CHAPTER 17

I used the phone in my office to dial Mildred Dorchester. I identified myself and launched right into why I was calling. I recapped what Brian had told me and let her know it wasn't me who'd made the call.

"I don't understand, dear." The concern in her voice was obvious.

"It was someone else, Mildred. Someone pretending to be me."

"Why would anyone do that?"

It was the same question Brian asked. I still didn't have a decent answer. I didn't have a clue as to Mimi's motivations. Brian was right. Why would anyone want to steal *my* identity?

"I don't know. But there's this girl. We met by chance, and we got to talking because we look so much like one another. Have you ever met anyone who looks like you?"

"I don't see what this has to do with the phone call, dear."

I hesitated. Telling Mildred about Mimi suddenly seemed shameful. I don't know how to explain it. Maybe I realized for the first time how ridiculous my explanation sounded to Brian, which meant it would sound equally absurd to Mildred. I couldn't tell her the entire story. How could I ever expect a board member to understand that I may have stumbled upon the answer to where my runaway mother has been all these years?

I couldn't tell Mildred any of that. She'd probably wonder which number to dial first. Should she call Brian and tell him to fire me as quickly as possible, before my insanity had a chance to reach library patrons? Or should she take the more direct route and call the nuthouse to tell them where they could pick me up? Forget about passing go and the lousy two hundred dollars. Grab a straitjacket and head on over to Tess's house. Bag yourself a certified looney bird.

I couldn't risk either, so I chose my words carefully.

"I think this girl . . . the one I recently met . . . I think she thought it might be funny to call you and pretend to be me. I'm sorry, Mildred. But that's all I can come up with. I'm sorry she included you in her little practical joke. I'll make sure she doesn't call again."

"But she introduced herself as you, Tess. She seemed to know so much about the library's activities. I even asked about your father, and she assured me he was doing well."

That should have been Mildred's first clue. I mean, in all the years she'd been my father's landlord, when had she ever had the opportunity to hear anyone describe him as well?

"And she had some not-so-nice things to say about Brian," Mildred added.

"I understand that. Brian gave me the gist of your conversation."

"How would someone whom you've recently met know so much?" Mildred paused. Her tone shifted. "Tess, did Brian tell you to call me with this foolish story? Are you being forced to make up this explanation in order to recant the concerns you voiced yesterday? You can tell me, dear. If you're being coerced in any way, I don't want you to be afraid. My twenty-year-old grandson likes to tell me he has my back. It's an odd turn of phrase, but I understand his meaning. I have your back, Tess. If Brian's forcing you to tell this story, let me know now."

I liked this woman very much. If I'd been lucky enough to have a grandmother like Mildred, I'd have her back, too.

"It's not like that at all," I said. "I know it sounds crazy, but this woman is always geared up. Full of energy. Always looking for the next bit of excitement. Maybe you know the type. I feel bad about it now, but I guess I did talk a little too much to her about some gripes I have about things around here." I flashed on Brian's warning. "Maybe I was in a grumbling kind of mood and made things bigger than they are. I think she decided to play a prank on me and give you a call."

"Are you saying you're happy with the way Brian runs things?"

Mildred's a sharp one. She'd smell a dodge a mile away. There'd be no use for sugarcoating anything. "I'm saying I love my job. I love the people who use this library. Brian's very good about letting me do things around here that are outside my basic job description." I recalled his wording. "He provides a lot of job enrichment for my position."

Mildred was quiet on her end of the phone. When she did speak, I heard the skepticism in her voice. "Um-hm. I think I know what's going on here. Is Brian there, dear? Put him on, please."

Panic jumped into my chest like a five-hundred pound gorilla leaping into a clearing and announced its presence by pounding on my rib cage. "Mildred, please. Don't take the ramblings of this girl as proof of anything . . . indication of anything. It's nothing. Everything's fine here. Really."

"Relax, dear. I'll take care of this. Let me speak to Brian."

For once I was glad he was off chasing whatever it was that occupied him all those hours he wasn't here in the library.

"He's not here," I said. "He left for a meeting down in Janesville." My throat was so tight I could barely speak. "I'll leave him a message. Have him call you." I swallowed hard. "Please believe me, Mildred. It wasn't me who called. It was some stupid, foolish joke done by someone I wish I'd never met. Someone I doubly wish I hadn't taken the time to vent my frustrations to." I realized I was making matters worse. I wanted to end the call, but I needed her not to follow up with Brian. I couldn't afford to be without a job.

"Please believe me," I said. "I wasn't the one who called."

"I understand, dear. You're saying it was someone you met. She looks like you. Sounds like you. She wanted to play a prank and posed as you." Mildred didn't sound like she believed me one bit. "Perhaps you can clarify one thing for me."

"Of course." I hoped I could. The problem was, I wasn't that clear on things myself.

"I've been on the library board for years. You know that."

"Yes. Yes, of course I do. And I've benefited from your years of service. The entire community has."

"I conduct a lot of business for and with the library. I like to keep myself fully available to the staff."

Where was she going with this? "You've been there for me, Mildred. I've always appreciated that."

"I have the contact information for the library stored in the phone my grandson got for me. I typically don't care for all this new technology, but I'll admit it makes it so much easier when I need to call someone."

"They don't call 'em smartphones for nothin'." I grimaced as that triviality left my mouth. I couldn't think of anything else to say.

"That's why I picked up the phone yesterday afternoon, dear. I was here with my bridge club, holding a winning hand. My partner and I were set to eviscerate that smug Pansy Goldmueller and her sycophant nephew whom she lugs around like a little purse dog. There are precious few things that could pull me away from a moment like that."

I told her I understood, even though I didn't.

"But when I saw it was the library calling, I stepped away from dealing Pansy and her pimply little puppy the final blow and took your call."

In that moment Mildred's meanderings became crystal clear.

"She called you from here," I whispered.

"Yes, dear. I want you to know I wasn't surprised to hear your . . . or should I say whomever it was who called? I wasn't surprised at all at the list of concerns regarding Brian. I've been harboring more than a few of them myself. Carry on with your day, Tess. And don't worry about a thing. Do have Brian call me immediately upon his return, will you? He and I have a great many things to discuss."

I promised I would and hung up. Then I sat down before I fell down.

Mimi had been there. She had posed as me. In my library.

It took me a few minutes before I could be sure my legs would hold me. I stood and shuffled to the door, holding on to any object I passed to steady myself. I called out to Rosie and wasted no time warming up to the subject when she walked into my office.

"Rosie, I called you yesterday and asked you to cover for me, right?"

"Don't worry about it. I was happy to do it for you. But you still owe me the deets on your date with Mr. Cutie." She looked back over her shoulder to make sure no patrons were at the front desk. "And I want to know everything Brian was shrieking about, too. You okay?"

"How'd it go yesterday? Everything run smooth without me?"

"It's a neighborhood library branch, Tess. Not the control room of a nuclear reactor. Like I told you when you came in. There's no need to worry. You didn't have to check in. A day off is a day off."

I leaned against my desk. The room seemed suddenly smaller.

"When I came in? You told me when I came in?"

She blinked in bewilderment. "Yeah. When you dashed in here. Don't you remember? Early afternoon yesterday. I told you to get back to your date. We didn't require any babysitting."

"And did I?"

"Did you what?"

"Did I leave and get back to my date?"

"Of course. Right after you used the phone."

CHAPTER 18

Detective Andy Anderson tossed his pen to the table and leaned back so far, his chair balanced on two legs.

"Sally, do you remember last week when you were reading me the riot act about not getting that Drennan report to you on time?"

Anderson had been so hell-bent on my finishing my account of what led us here, I had no idea why he stopped me from going on with my story. But when he did, Sally Normandy looked up from her own extensive note taking.

Who's Drennan? I thought. *Is that some kind of cop code? Did I say something that . . . what had Detective Anderson said before? Yeah. That's it. He said he was going to trip me up. Was he sending Sally a signal? Did I say something that was going to get me into even more trouble?*

Was that even possible?

Sally's brow wrinkled, as if she didn't understand where Anderson was going any more than I did.

"I remember," she said.

I liked the way she talked to him. Matter-of-fact and straightforward. Like she was his true equal.

"You told me you grew weary of waiting for me to understand that you can't do your work until I do mine," Anderson said. "Remember that?"

"I do," Sally said. "But I don't see how that pertains to what's in front of us right now."

Anderson settled his chair onto all fours. "I like that phrase you used. You said you grew weary. I thought at the time it was a classy way of you telling me to get off my ass and take care of things."

"And?" Sally asked.

Anderson leaned forward and stared right at me. "I grow weary of this, Miss Kincaid. I've been here since seven-thirty this morning." We all looked at that caged clock on the wall. It was nearly 9:15 at night.

"I've already missed dinner," Anderson continued. "Thanks to you I missed story time with my little boy, too. As you can imagine in this line of work, snuggling up with my five-year-old and reading the latest adventures of Thomas the Train is the highlight of my day. So what do you say we cut all the bullshit you're selling and get to the point? Stop talking about bad bosses and little library anecdotes and tell me what I need to know about that body the kid found down at the marsh."

"I don't know anything about that." The back of my mouth filled with some sort of metallic-tasting liquid that was hard to swallow. Fortunately, Sally spoke before I had to say anything.

"Ease up, Andy. Every detail Tess shares with us is vital. I know you want to jump from A to Z, but you're going to have to trust me. We need to hear the entire alphabet. One letter at a time."

Because you need to trip me up?

Sally shifted her attention to me. She rested her hand on my arm and focused those soft blue eyes on mine.

"Go on. You were saying you discovered that Mimi had portrayed herself as you twice. First to Rosie and then on the phone with Mildred."

In spite of sitting in the police station long past quitting time with an angry detective right across from me, Sally's kindness helped me relax a little.

"I think maybe there might have been an earlier time, too," I said.

"Oh?" She settled back in her chair, picked up her pen, and got ready to start writing again. "Tell me about that."

"I told you about Cordon Balaclay."

Sally didn't have to refer to her notes. "The substitute librarian. You were surprised to see him when you went to the library on your day off. You took his presence as proof that Brian never intended to come in that day."

"That's right. Remember, I asked Rosie to keep an eye on him? That I thought his memory might be getting shaky because Cordon said he was happy to get my call asking him to sub."

Sally nodded. "I remember. Cordon's dog, Millie, was having a birthday. He was eager to earn the extra money to celebrate."

Man, what I wouldn't give to have a memory like hers. Scratch that. There are some things I'm trying real hard to forget.

"I think now it could have been Mimi who called Cordon. Maybe that was her very first attempt to see if she could pull off impersonating me."

Sally considered that for a moment. "You're suggesting she might have started with something small, like a brief but welcomed call to Cordon Balaclay. A trial balloon to see if someone would buy her as you."

"That's my guess, yes."

"Interesting. Let's pick up again, Tess. You'd just spoken to Mildred and Rosie. Then what happened? And remember, specifics are important. It's the details that are helping us to understand all the circumstances that led us here. Okay?"

I took a deep breath and focused my attention on how my hands rested in my lap. They taught us that in those anger management classes. Bring your attention to your hands. Focus until you could feel the blood pulsing in your fingertips. It took a while, sitting there with Anderson scowling at me, but I was able to get myself to a point where I could get back to trying to explain this whole mess.

"I needed to stop Mimi. There had to be a reason she was posing as me. But I didn't know where she was. I didn't have her number. Besides, she'd left her cell phone in Boston. At least that's what she told me. But she'd pretended to be me, and I needed to know why. She'd already convinced Cordon she was me over the phone. Maybe after I saw her leave Graze she headed to the library to see if she could pass as me in person. She probably figured I'd be in the restaurant for at least an hour or so. She'd be free to run another experiment. When Rosie assumed she was me, and Mildred sure thought she was me, maybe that gave her the boost she needed to continue posing. For what reason I didn't know, but it makes sense, doesn't it? Do you think that's what happened?"

Sally said nothing. I got the sense she was more interested in hearing my version of events.

"Maybe that's not important now," I continued. "But whatever was going on, I had to talk to Mimi. She was causing me a lot of trouble, and I wanted to know what she was going to do next. I mean, if you could have seen how angry Brian was. He meant it. He'd fire me if Mimi pulled another stunt."

"So what did you do?" Sally asked.

"I first called Hotel Red. Mimi hadn't registered there after I kicked her out of my place. So I left the library and headed to campus. It was a long shot, but it was the only thing I could think of. She had a follow-up interview with the folks in the History Department the Monday before. I thought maybe I could concoct a story about needing to get hold of her and they'd tell me where she was staying. She might have gone out and gotten herself a new phone. You know, so the people in History would have a way to reach her about the job. Maybe they could give me her number. I was desperate."

"Did you ever think of posing as Mimi?" Sally asked. "Maybe get even for what she did with that phone call to Mildred? You could have made sure she never got offered that faculty position. That would have booted her out of your world for good, right?"

Thinking back, that might have been a logical solution, but truth is it never occurred to me. I wondered what Sally thought about my overlooking such an obvious option.

"It turns out I didn't need to do any finagling with anyone. I told you . . . Mimi had this odd way of showing up, and that's exactly what she did. I got to the foot of Bascom Hill around one-thirty or so. I remember thinking I'd made such good time because the lunch hour traffic was over. People were in their buildings. Back at work. I started the climb up, heading toward History. I hadn't gone fifty yards before I heard that familiar voice call out to me."

"Tess!" She was walking down the hill as I was walking up. Even though I'd read her the riot act the last time I saw her, she greeted me with a smile. I mean, I'd threatened to call the police on her if I ever saw her again, and there she was, bouncing her way down toward me like a kitten who'd found someone fun to play with. "I got the job! You're looking at the University of Wisconsin History Department's latest faculty hire. It's only a temporary gig, but I plan on knocking their socks off." She was saying all this as she walked toward me. "Give me six months and they'll be dying to keep me on."

I picked up my pace to close the gap between us. Classes hadn't started yet, but the first day wasn't far off. Bascom Hill was filled with underclassmen who'd probably arrived early to settle into their dorms or apartments. It was a warm day, and hundreds of students were out playing Frisbee or tanning or reading under the shade of those giant oaks and maples. As soon as I got close enough, I grabbed Mimi by the arm and pulled her away from the sidewalk into a small alley between two buildings.

"Ouch," she complained. "You're squeezing a little hard, there, Tess."

I didn't care. My growing rage was looking for a target. I swear it was only the presence of all those sun-worshipping undergrads that kept me from punching her right in that face that looked so much like mine.

"What the hell, Mimi," I snarled at her. "Where do you get off calling Mildred Dorchester? And don't bother lying about it. Brian's ready to fire me after that stunt."

"Did you hear what I said, Tess?" Mimi squirmed free of my

grasp. "I got the job. A job I'm going to love. A job that's going to start me off on a real career. Aren't you happy for me? Don't you want that for yourself? Who cares about that little corner library? We're sisters. Let me inspire you." Her eyes twinkled, as if she had a secret she couldn't wait to share. "I've been thinking, and I'm pretty sure I've come up with a plan that will free you from Brian's abusive clutches."

I didn't know how to respond. I couldn't come up with the words. What little security I had in the world was about to go up in smoke because of her, and there she was, happily concocting her next scheme. It took everything I had to keep from strangling her. When I finally did get around to talking, I remember speaking very slowly, like I was talking to a willful child who didn't seem to want to understand anything.

"Mimi, you cannot—and I mean *cannot*—pretend to be me. Got that? Not on the phone, not in the library, not anywhere. And not with anyone. Anyone! Do you hear me?"

Mimi rolled her eyes. "Of course I hear you. You're standing two inches away."

I stepped back.

"I don't suppose it would do any good to tell you I was trying to help," she said. "I mean, think of all those things you told me about Brian. How he works you like some kind of indentured servant while he sits idly by reaping the rewards. Doesn't that stick in your craw? Don't you ever get tired of people making you feel small?"

I was sick to death of it, actually, but I didn't want her to know it.

"And you thought ratting him out to a board member would help?"

"Did I think the terrible management skills of their head librarian would be something the board should know? Yes. They can't fix an issue they're unaware of. I also thought it was about time they knew who really was running things down there. Maybe get you a little credit along the way." She looked me square in the eye. "I only did what you should have done for yourself a long time ago. Can't you see? I had to. Professional women stand up for themselves, Tess. They use their resources. They escalate when problems aren't resolved and take the issues to higher authorities. If I would have called Mildred as anyone other than you, what I told her wouldn't have carried the weight it needed. The concerns could have been explained away as idle gossip. Mildred needed to hear it firsthand from you. Now she can take action. Thanks to that phone call, she's free to go to the board and address Brian's incompetence. The library will be a better place because of what I did. You should be thanking me, not yelling at me and issuing threats."

What can I say? She made sense. The look on her face, the stubborn plea in her voice. I believed she thought she was trying to help me out by doing the very thing I should have had the courage to do myself. I know it sounds nuts now. But on that sunny hill, in that particular moment, I believed her. I wasn't as angry as I'd been when I headed to Bascom Hill. Still, there was something I needed to know.

"Do you know John?" I asked.

Mimi looked confused. "John who?"

"John Rappaport. The guy from the library."

Mimi's bewilderment evaporated. A sly smile appeared in its place. "You mean your boyfriend? Of course I know who he is. Didn't I tell you exactly what to wear for your first date? I'm already thinking that's going to be one of my roles in this relationship. I'm going to be the sister who gives life advice you should always take." Her eyes widened. "How much do you want to bet it turns out I'm the older twin? The big sister who shows you the ropes. You must promise, of course, to always do exactly as I say."

The anger was there again. It wasn't snarling yet, but it sure wanted me to know it was back.

"Don't do that, Mimi."

"Do what?"

"Don't go building stories about our being twins and how this whole sister thing is going to play out. We don't know anything yet."

"Do you need me to make a flowchart for you, Tess? Maybe come up with a PowerPoint presentation? We know a hell of a lot. There's only one answer here. You're my twin sister. We're going to confront our mother as soon as she gets back. If you want, we can go to your . . . our . . . father right now and settle this thing, but . . ."

"You're not going anywhere near him!" My interruption was probably louder than it needed to be. "Until we know for sure what's going on, you're not saying a word to anyone. Especially my father! So back off!"

Mimi's entire posture eased. It was like she understood for the first time that I wasn't raised in the same fairy-tale you're-wonderful-just-because-you-breathe type of world she inhabited growing up. She lifted her hand and stroked my arm.

"Of course, Tess. We'll wait until you think the time's right to approach your dad. And I'm sorry the call to Mildred made you mad. I'll not do it again."

I realize now, as I'm saying this, she never did answer my question about knowing John. Like a lot of times, as I'm now realizing about Mimi, she sidestepped. She diverted. She maneuvered and led me where she wanted me to go. But on that day she sounded so sincere. I remember feeling softer toward her. I mean, isn't that what sisters do?

"So you got the job, huh?"

Her smile was bright. "They offered it to me not fifteen minutes ago. The bad news is I've got lectures to prepare, like, right now. There'll be no rest for me. But the pay is decent and I'll be able to spend some time writing articles from my dissertation. If I can get a couple into decent journals this year, I'll be in great shape for a tenured slot."

She was always so sure of herself. Always aware of her next step. Confident she was the mistress of her fate. Convinced nothing but success waited for her.

I'd give anything to be able to feel that way. Even for two minutes.

"Well, there's no way I'm going back to the library today," I said. "I'll let Mildred have her chat with him first. What do you say you come back to my place and we celebrate your good fortune over a glass of iced tea?"

"Sounds perfect." She pointed toward the garage on Park Street. "You got your car or are we walking? I better get to know the campus, huh?"

Her enthusiasm was as contagious as a February flu bug. "I drove. Tell you what, I'll give you an overview of the layout and maybe, if you promise to behave, I'll take you on an extended tour later this evening. Once it cools down enough for a long walk."

We headed down Bascom Hill. I named each of the buildings as we passed. We got to my car and I drove home, telling her what I knew about the university's history along the way. At the corner of University and Park, we stopped to let a stream of about fifty teenagers cross the street.

"That's one thing you'll have to get used to," I said. "Traffic on the isthmus is a bear when students are back. Plan double the time you think you'll need whenever you need to cross it."

Mimi was craning her neck to take it all in. "The buildings are so huge." She pointed to a brick-and-steel behemoth across the street. "What's that?"

"That's the new biogenetics building. Wisconsin's famous for advances in that area. It's about quadruple the size of the old one. Lots of federal grant money gets shoveled there. The old place was about three blocks south of here. My mother used to work there. In the old building, I mean."

While the memory gave me pain, the information brought another round of Mimi's seemingly endless enthusiasm. "That's right! You said our mom worked with some researcher or something?"

I didn't feel the need to correct her reference to *my* mother as *our* mother. "Now they'd call her an administrative assistant, I guess. Executive assistant maybe. I don't know her exact title. She worked for Phillip Jasper. He was a new faculty member back then." I pointed back toward the new biogenetics building. "But now it's his work that built that giant place. He's kind of a big cheese from what I read in the paper. But back then he was just my mom's boss."

"Did you know him?"

A strange buzz entered my skull. It started at the base, traveled up over the top of my brain, and planted a jabbing pain smack dab between my eyeballs.

"My mother would take me to work with her sometimes. It's likely I met him once or twice. My memory's not so keen on those details. My mother thought the world of him, I remember that much."

The gaggle of students thinned out enough for me to inch my car onto University. "Let's get out of this sun," I said. "I've suddenly got a headache."

"And its name is Mimi, right?" Her tone was so playful.

"No," I said. "The pain you give me is about two feet lower."

It was almost two-thirty by the time I pulled into my driveway. Mimi got out and walked toward the door like she owned the place. I shielded my eyes against the sun, hoping for a little relief from what was now an iron vise gripping my skull. Out of habit, I checked the mailbox and pulled out two catalogues, my electric bill, and a business envelope bearing the return address of the laboratory where Mimi and I had sent our DNA swabs a few days earlier. I held it up to show her.

"I thought it took, like, ten days," I said as I unlocked the front door.

Mimi hurried in. She stood in my living room as I tossed my purse, keys, and the other mail onto a chair.

"Open it! Open it!" she said. "This is shaping up to be the biggest day of my life so far. First the job, now proof positive that I have a twin sister."

I expected a stack of laboratory printouts with accompanying explanations. Instead, I pulled out a one-page letter. I gave it a quick scan before I looked toward Mimi. She must have seen the confusion on my face.

"Read it, Tess. Read it out loud."

My tongue felt so thick I could barely form the words.

> *Dear Ms. Kincaid:*
>
> *We regret we are unable to proceed with the full genetic comparison of the two samples you submitted. Our screening analysis of the swabs reflect an error in collection. The two swabs are identical. Please refer to the instructions provided in the test kit. There you will find helpful guidance for assuring the two samples are kept separate, thereby avoiding any duplicate submissions in the future.*
>
> *We look forward to receiving your fresh samples. As a courtesy, we will waive all fees associated with this initial analysis. However, should the same collection error occur again, we will be assessing you the full cost of all testing.*
>
> *Yours respectfully,*
> *Anderson Hepple, Ph.D.*
> *Webster-Englehart Laboratories*

"What the heck does that mean?" Mimi asked. "We didn't mix up multiple samples. I did one and you did one. We filled two tubes, we sent two tubes. Did you mark the box saying you suspected we were twins? Could that be why the samples were identical? What's going on?"

I didn't have a clue. But that iron vise torquing against my skull tightened another three notches.

CHAPTER 19

"I don't understand," Mimi said. "The specimens should have looked like duplicates, right? Doesn't that verify our theory? Doesn't that prove we're identical twins?"

Of course, it didn't. No matter how much she wanted to believe it, all the lab's letter proved was that we'd made a mistake somewhere along the way when we gathered our DNA.

"I watched this documentary series once," I told her. "It was all about the human genome and the latest research into the possibility of building human organs so people wouldn't have to wait years on some transplant list. It talked about twins being good organ donors for one another. But there's no such thing as an identical match according to the scientists interviewed in the film. I remember they said identical twins have the same DNA when the egg initially splits. But apparently the DNA changes based on what happens in the uterus while the fetuses are developing. I don't know exactly, but it's like maybe if one twin gets squirted with more of a certain hormone than the other while they're floating around in the mother's womb. Or maybe one twin catches a virus the mother has, but the other one doesn't. Stuff like that causes little changes in the DNA. They'd be identical twins, all right, but they wouldn't have duplicate DNA."

"Then I don't get it. What's that letter about?"

I tried to remember step by step what Mimi and I had done when she insisted on sending in the DNA test she brought with her from Boston. So much had gone on in the past few days. It was hard for me to recall specifics.

"I don't know," I said. "But obviously we screwed up. Or maybe something was wrong with the test. Did you buy it at Logan Airport? I wouldn't imagine travelers have much call for DNA analysis. Maybe the test kit was outdated."

She considered my question. "It seemed pretty straightforward. Swab cheek, stick in tube, mail envelope off. How could we have messed that up? It must have been the kit. Let's go get another one right now. We'll double-check the expiration date together. Then I'll watch you and you watch me, and we'll make sure we send in two different samples."

I was about to tell her I wasn't sure I wanted to go through another week of waiting for test results when my phone rang. I hadn't called Rosie to let her know I'd not be coming back, and I worried something might have gone wrong down at the library. But when I saw the caller ID on the screen, I was surprised to see it was my father calling. I wasn't due to make another grocery delivery for a couple of days. I signaled Mimi to be quiet while I took the call.

"Hi, Dad. What do you need?"

"Is that what we've come to, Tess?" He sounded sad. "Do I only call you when I need something?"

I looked at my watch. Could he be in his feel-sorry-for-me stage of drunkenness already? It was barely three o'clock in the afternoon.

"How's this, then? What do you want?"

I heard him clear his throat. "It's a lovely day, isn't it, Tess? Summers in Madison can be so wonderful. I remember many a sunny stroll with you when you were little. Do you remember that?"

I wanted to tell him, *No, Dad. I don't. Unless you count the times I'd walk with you to the corner after dinner. You'd go off to work and I'd hurry home and lock myself back into the empty house.*

"It is a nice day," I said instead. I tried to remember the last time I spoke to my father on the phone. I couldn't come up with anything in the past year.

"I'd like to invite you over for dinner, Tess. It won't be much. Maybe a frozen pizza. If you swing by Michael's and get us a pint of frozen custard, we can have a nice dessert. Would you like that?"

His voice was shaky.

"What's the occasion, Dad?"

It took him a while to answer.

"I've come to realize I was short with you at your last visit. When you were asking about what I was doing the day you were born."

I looked over at Mimi. She was rereading the letter from Webster-Englehart Labs.

"I remember."

"I've been thinking about your questions," my father continued. "It's difficult, I'm sure you understand, for me to talk about your mother. In the end she was so . . . so . . . so . . ."

"I know what she was in the end, Dad." How could I forget? In the end, she was the one who left us.

"But she wasn't always like that. And I have to set aside my own pain for you." My dad's voice was soft. "I realize little girls would of course be curious about what happened the day they came into this world. You're my little girl, Tess. No matter how big you get. No matter how much you try to take care of your old man, you're always going to be my little girl. So come on over. We'll have pizza and custard, and I'll tell you all about that special day Tess Kincaid arrived on the planet."

I held the phone, wondering what to say. Mimi set the letter down. The smile she gave me was warm and encouraging. She'd heard my side of the phone conversation. If she was right, it was her birthday, too. Would it be worth dredging up my father's painful memories to provide her with answers?

"Please, Tess. Forgive me one more time. After all, how many times have I had to forgive you? It's what we do for one another, isn't it? Let your old dad make up for his rude behavior of the other night. Come to dinner."

I sighed. "What flavor custard goes with frozen pizza, do you think?"

It was five o'clock straight up when I parked in front of my father's apartment. Mimi said she'd head back to the Hotel Red and get herself a room. She made me promise to call her the moment I left my father's and gave me a list of questions to be sure to ask him. I made her promise to go straight to the hotel. No stopping at the library. I also reminded her to never impersonate me again.

"Things are starting to happen now," she told me before she left. "Nothing's going to be the same again."

I knocked on my father's door and waited. I held the two pints of frozen vanilla custard away from my body. I figured I had two additional ignored knocks before I dug for my key to let myself in, and I didn't want the treats to melt.

You could have blown me over with a whistle when my father opened the door before I had to knock a second time.

"There's my Tess." He held the door wide and waved me in. He followed me on wobbly legs and braced himself against the kitchen counter as I put the custard in the freezer. I looked over at his chair.

There was no glass of liquor on the side table.

The television was turned off.

I took a good look at my father. He'd showered. His hair was brushed straight back and tucked behind his ears, like he was making an effort to corral his curly mane. His jeans were worn at the knees and frayed at the hem, but they were clean. I couldn't recall the last time I saw him in anything other than sweatpants or pajamas.

"Do you want me to put the pizza in now, Tess?" He had to clear his throat twice to get the sentence out. His hands shook as he pointed to the oven. "Or maybe you'd rather sit and talk before we eat. An easy chat on a lazy summer evening."

My father was sober. At least as sober as a man who drank all day, every day, for the past twenty years or so could get after laying off the booze for an entire day. Beads of sweat dotted his brow. His Adam's apple bobbed as if his throat were set on auto-pilot, programmed to swallow a beloved liquid that was painfully absent. His eyes had a filmy look despite his best efforts to focus on the daughter standing in front of him.

"Let's sit for a bit, Dad." I slipped my arm in his and walked him to his chair. "It's been quite a day for me. A nice visit sounds exactly like what I need right now."

He sat and smoothed a hand over the front of his red-and-white-striped polo shirt. It was too big for his skeletal frame, a relic reclaimed from some bottom drawer after being abandoned years earlier by a healthier, younger version of himself.

"You look good." I settled onto the couch across from him. "Is this all for me?"

"Dinner with my best gal." His smile begged my approval. "Nothing wrong with your old man wanting to let you know how important you are to him, is there? I don't tell you that enough, Tessie."

You don't tell me that at all, I wanted to say. But I didn't. I knew how rapidly his moods could shift. And worn-down drunk that he was, that could still be dangerous.

"Well, you clean up pretty good."

He pointed a finger at me and winked. "You may not realize it, but I wasn't always this old and feeble."

"Fifty-eight's not old, Dad."

"There was a time your dad could turn some heads," he continued. "I remember more than a few coeds back in my teaching days who let me know in no uncertain terms they'd be interested in a little extra attention from the professor."

I could have told him there was a daughter interested in that, too, but I kept that to myself.

"Your heart belonged to Mom, didn't it? She was always your number one girl."

His smile was softer. "Your mother was the damnedest woman I'd ever laid eyes on. Her beauty was unconventional. Like yours, Tess. The kind of beauty a man might not notice at first. But if he looked twice, he'd see how her features worked in harmony with an intelligence and humor that lifted her up and drew people to her. And if he dared to look a third time, well, he'd be spoiled off the flouncing floozies the rest of his life."

Those were the first tender words I'd heard my father say about my mother since she left us. He'd always remind me, on our annual trek to Picnic Point to mark her birthday, that my mother hadn't always been bad. It seemed important to him that I remember to keep some warmth in my heart for her. But his yearly pronouncements were always more directive than genuine. Once delivered, my father would not speak my mother's name for another 364 days. But on this night, when he was as clear of alcohol's haze as my adult eyes had ever seen, my father gave me a glimpse into the love he once felt for her.

I wondered if he still felt it. After all these years. After her betrayal and abandonment. Did he still love the woman she once was? Did he hold that separate from the woman she became?

"Tell me how to do it, Dad. How do you stop loving a person you once were so certain you'd adore forever?"

He looked away for a long time. Then he lowered his gaze to his lap. When he finally looked back up I got the feeling he was returning from a bittersweet memory.

"You were born on a Tuesday evening," he said. "Which means yesterday you were exactly some huge number of weeks old, doesn't it? Happy Tuesday, Tess."

I smiled at my father's unexpected whimsy. Was this a glimpse into what my mother found so attractive?

"Would you like to know more about that particular Tuesday night?"

"If it isn't too painful."

He looked away again. This time it only took a heartbeat or two before he returned his attention to me.

"You are my daughter. I'm afraid in my desperate desire to avoid any thought of your mother, I've deprived you of so much you were entitled to. You deserved better than your mother and I gave you, Tess. We've both hurt you beyond measure, haven't we? Me in my way, your mother in hers. You asked me about the day you were born. Such a simple request. Forgive me. I'm going to try to do better."

My breathing was shallow. I was glad I was sitting down.

"You were born the morning of October eleventh. But your mother went in to labor a little past noon the day before. You came two weeks before we expected you. Your mother had gone off to work that morning. When she realized she was going into labor she called the dean's secretary at the law school. There were no cell phones in those days. I'll never forget. I was in the middle of a lecture introducing the concept of federal sovereignty over state law. Bernice . . . that was the secretary's name . . . a sturdy woman with a face that always reminded me of a young pony. I wonder what ever became of her. At any rate, Bernice stepped into the back of the room and stood there, saying not a word, glaring at me with such determination I could do nothing but stop lecturing and look her way. I asked her if she needed something. Every student in the class turned around to see to whom I was speaking. Still, Bernice didn't say anything. Instead, she pantomimed. Perhaps she didn't want to break some professional boundary I might have with my students. So there she stood, in the back of the classroom, arcing her hands in front of her. From her ample bosom to her hips. Up and down. Again and again. I realize now she was trying to mimic a pregnancy. However, my mind was on federalist precedent, and I didn't seem to be able to shift gears fast enough to catch her meaning. Bernice must have sensed my confusion. She switched her actions. She locked her hands on her elbows and rocked them back and forth. Still I didn't get what she was signaling. It wasn't until a student in the third row called out *I think someone's having a baby* that I realized what Bernice was trying to tell me. I asked if Audra was in labor. Bernice finally spoke. She said yes. I was to get home as rapidly as possible and take her to the hospital." My father laughed at the charming story. "I left that instant. Lecture notes strewn about. Briefcase and books on the table. Any professorial decorum I had disappeared, and I ran out of the room. Whereupon I promptly forgot where my car was parked. Tess, in that moment I don't think I even could have told you what kind of car I had."

"What did you do?" This was the first time I'd heard this tale.

"Tesselly Brathorne came across me pacing in the hall, muttering to myself. I wish you could have met him. Brathorne was a brilliant scholar on English common law. A lion in the department. He was well past seventy at the time, yet no one in the law school could ever imagine a man of his stature considering retirement. He took one look at me, grabbed me by both shoulders, and said in that rumbling British accent of his, *Someone's either dying or being born. Which is it, Kincaid?* I told him my wife was in labor. Without missing a beat Brathorne demanded I follow him. He led me straight to his car. Of course a man of his position had a parking spot not twenty feet from the building. He buckled me into the front seat, and I directed him as he drove me to our house on Lathrop Street. Do you remember that house, Tess?"

I could have told him where the floorboards creaked. I could describe the secret place in the backyard where I buried that awful ballerina doll the neighbor girl brought me for my fifth birthday. I could have asked him if he recalled how Mom loved the shade of green she painted the dining room.

"Yeah, I remember."

"So Brathorne delivers me home. Your mother is standing there, on the front porch, suitcase beside her." My father laughed again. "And there in the driveway was my car! Turns out I'd walked to work that sunny autumn morning. Brathorne takes charge. Your mother, in the midst of early labor, looks magnificent. Like she's lit from within by a thousand golden candles. I remember wanting to hold her. To kiss her and tell her how lovely she was. Instead, she and Brathorne begin directing my every move. Audra hands me the car keys. Brathorne grabs her suitcase, tosses it in the backseat of my car, and demands I follow him. Off he leads us. Straight across the isthmus in midday traffic. Speeding and leaning on his horn the entire way. All British detachment tossed aside. Straight to the emergency room. He was out of his car and calling for medical support as your mother and I pulled up. As soon as they had your mother in a wheelchair, the old Brit grabbed my hands, squeezed them. *By bloody hell, Kincaid. You'll be a father by sundown. Everything's different now.* Then he told me to get inside and follow your mother." He fell silent for a few seconds. "I never saw him again. That old lion went to bed the next evening and never woke up. I am eternally grateful that one of his last acts of kindness on this earth was to get me where I needed to be when it was time for you to be born. Your mother insisted we recognize his contribution to your arrival. She named you after him."

"I never knew that." A feeling tugged in my chest. I couldn't identify it. It was foreign to me. But it was pleasant. I made mental note to research Tesselly Brathorne as soon as I got home. "Were you there, Dad? When I was born, I mean. Were you there? In the room?"

His voice was barely a whisper. "Brathorne was wrong about one thing. I wasn't a father by sundown. Your mother's labor was hard and long. She was so brave. I don't know how she stood the pain. Hour after hour. In that sterile room with all those machines. Nurses coming and going. Measuring. Poking. Prodding. Audra would be calm for relatively long periods. She and I would talk about what we'd name you. We'd call you Brathorne if you were a boy. Brathorne Kincaid! Can you imagine a more glorious name? Tess, of course, if you were a girl. Your mother told me she hoped you'd be a girl. I asked her why. I mean, back in those days I simply assumed everyone in this society dreamed of having a son as their firstborn. But your mother had a different desire. She said she wanted a girl so she could watch what you'd become. She wanted to see the opportunities for women expand and watch you take advantage of every one of them. All through her labor, your mother lay in that hospital bed and spun dreams for your future."

I reflected on how she'd be as disappointed as my father was in me. Had she seen something all those years ago that made her predict my shortcomings? Is that why she chose Mimi? Dr. Mimi with her first faculty job! How proud our mother will be.

"Then a contraction would hit," my father continued, "and all the calm discussion would turn into screaming pain. Her entire body would writhe in misery and I'd beg her to breathe. Then she'd be calm again. Exhausted and drenched in sweat, but calm. Of course, as the labor continued, the periods of calm grew shorter. Sometime after midnight on the eleventh of October the doctor came in, examined your mother, and pronounced her ready to deliver. They wheeled her off to the delivery room."

"Did you follow her?"

My father shook his head. "Your mother didn't want me there. She wanted to focus entirely on experiencing your birth. Without having to worry about how I was doing. I've wrapped myself up in nobility over the years, lying to myself that I sacrificed witnessing your birth in order to honor my wife's request. But truth told, after being with your mother all those hours . . . seeing her in that kind of pain . . . the coward in me took over. I was pleased to be spared the experience of watching the next chapter of Audra's torture. No, Tess. I wasn't there the moment you were born. I was in a waiting room down the hall and around the corner."

"How long did it take? I mean, how long were the two of you separated while Mom was in the delivery room?"

My father considered the question. "It wasn't that long, I imagine. But to a husband who was about to become a first-time father, it seemed like I sat in that waiting room for days. I remember I kept going back to the nurses' station . . . asking if they'd heard anything. They were used to dealing with anxious fathers, I assume. They offered me tea and promised to come get me the moment you were born. I remember being jealous of the two other expectant fathers waiting along with me. Especially the fellow who arrived at least an hour after I did. The nurses came and got them both before it was finally my turn to be escorted to your mother's room."

"How long, Dad? Can you estimate?"

He seemed bewildered by the request. "There were no complications with your delivery, if that's what you're concerned about. The doctor told me you were hale and healthy."

"Maybe I'm trying to get a picture of what it must have been like for you," I lied. I was trying to see how he might explain the hours my mother spent birthing. "How long were you in that waiting room?"

He looked away, as though searching for milestones that might inform him. "I'd say it was somewhere around six or seven hours between the time they wheeled your mother into the delivery room and the moment I was able to see her again. I walked in to see her holding you. Tears were in her eyes as I held you for the first time."

He didn't seem perplexed that an allegedly uncomplicated delivery would take seven hours.

"How was Mom?"

He shook his head. "She clung to you in such a way that I'll never doubt the instinct of maternal bonding. Wouldn't let you out of her sight. It was almost as though she were afraid you'd disappear from the planet if she didn't keep both eyes on you at all times."

I wondered if that was because she sensed, or perhaps even knew, she'd given birth to two daughters that long and painful day.

"Was there a lot of paperwork?"

His smile was curious. "Tess Kincaid! What an odd question. What do you imagine is the bureaucracy involved with birthing a child?"

A whole lot of time was unaccounted for on the day I was born. If Mimi was right and we were, indeed, twins, I needed to know my father's involvement with what happened to the second daughter born that day.

"I don't know. I mean, suddenly there's this new person on the planet. What's involved with registering her?"

My father laughed, and I realized the sound was foreign to my ears. "*Registering her?* Oh, Tess. You're a lawyer's daughter after all, aren't you? Oh, if only you'd applied yourself. Well, Miss By-the-Book. I recall being issued a birth certificate. And I needed to request a social security number for you. The hospital took care of all that. It seemed painless and efficient. I was busy focusing on you and your mother." He paused. "I wish I could have done a better job."

"What do you mean?"

"Your mother, despite enjoying her pregnancy, and in spite of her excitement while in labor, fell into profound despair following your birth. Postpartum depression was the diagnosis her obstetrician gave her. For that first year, your mother was lost to everyone but you. She'd stay in bed for days, getting up only to see to your needs. She was completely disinterested in visitors. She showed no interest in me, either. Thinking back on it, I realize I could have been kinder. I imagine what they say is true, isn't it? There's never only one person who destroys a relationship. But your mother was so distant in those months. Cut herself off entirely from the outside world. Her boss at the time—you remember Phillip Jasper, don't you? This was long before he was famous. Jasper was loyal to your mother. He kept extending her maternity leave. Told me to tell Audra to take all the time she needed. Her job would be waiting for her whenever she was ready. Your mother wanted nothing of it. Even forbade me from speaking Jasper's name for a while, insisting she had no plans to ever leave the house again. Eventually she seemed to get over her sadness. I remember coming home one day. You were about eight or nine months old. I was stunned to see your mother showered and dressed, standing behind the stove making our dinner. A few months later, after more and steady progress, she asked me to invite Jasper over for drinks one evening. He came. I excused myself and left them alone in the parlor." My father's face flushed. He used the back of his hand to wipe a sudden glistening of sweat from his forehead. "They had . . . they had a long talk. And she went back to work the next Monday."

"Who took care of me? While she was at work, I mean?"

"We had help. Undergrads mostly, looking to make some money between classes. They came and they went. Your mother was okay with that. In fact, I think she preferred not having one steady nanny care for you. She never wanted you to form a stronger bond with any caregiver than the one you had with her. And it worked, too. You and your mother had a special circle of light surrounding you whenever you were together. Oh, you missed her so much when she had to be away. Like you'd been robbed of your favorite toy. And whenever she'd return, whether she'd been gone a few hours or a few days, you'd lift up your arms to her." He chuckled. "You'd reach for her and say 'me . . . me . . . me' over and over until she picked you up in a wild embrace. That's how you got your nickname."

"What nickname? I don't have a nickname."

My father sighed. "Ah, kiddo. I imagine you've forgotten all about that. Your mother took to calling you Mimi, her clever reference to how you'd lift your arms and call for her to pick you up. I suspect you haven't heard that since she's been gone."

I had to force myself to breathe. I summoned enough air to whisper a question. "She called me Mimi?"

"I don't think I ever heard her call you anything else from the time you were a year or so old. She loved calling you that. Like the two of you were sharing an inside joke. Why, she even had a small charm made for herself. A tiny gold rectangle. Engraved *Mimi*. She wore it around her neck. Never took it off. Not even to shower."

My body shook with chills despite the warm evening. My mouth went dry. For a moment my field of vision careened out of focus. But there was no time for any of that. I needed to learn more and struggled to reorient myself to the conversation at hand.

"All was good when Mom went back to work?" It was as

innocuous a question as I could manage. "Things got back to normal?"

It took a while for my father to answer. "I don't think I'm the right person to judge what normal is, Tess. Your mother and I were passionate people. Sometimes the passion was glorious. Other times it ignited a far more sinister fire. But even with all that, I thought things were good. Until they weren't, of course."

"Tell me about that, Dad. Talk to me about how things got bad."

My father's hands began to tremble again. They were soon joined by his shoulders and legs. Within a few seconds his entire body was shaking.

"No, Tess. We made a promise, you and I. Didn't we? We won't talk about the bad stuff. Your mother left. The only way we'll make it through is to remember the good. Your mother wasn't always bad. Don't I tell you to remember that?"

I didn't know what to say, so I sat there. Silent. Wishing he'd resume his story about the day I was born.

He looked toward the half-empty bottle of whiskey sitting on top of the refrigerator. His eyes filled with a longing typically reserved for grooms on their wedding night.

I wanted to pull him back from whatever cave of imagined safety he was retreating toward. He'd been there. In the room with me. Talking. Remembering. Being kind. I wanted more of that.

"You want me to put that pizza in the oven, Dad?"

My mind was filled with words I knew I'd never say: *I'll stop my questions, Dad. Please. Let's have that dinner. There's plenty of custard, too. Let's watch the History Channel. You can tell me everything you know about the Nazis. I'll listen this time. I promise.*

My father ran his hand through his hair. He shrugged and sighed. "You know, Tess, all this talking has worn me out. Let's save the pizza for another night."

He picked up the remote and turned on the television before I could object.

Don't do this, Dad. Tell me more. Please. Did my mother have a special lullaby for me? Was there a way she liked to brush my hair? Please don't disappear, Dad.

I sat there for a minute or so. My father didn't look at me again. I finally stood, stepped over to him, and kissed the top of his head. I lingered for a moment, wondering how long it would be before I smelled again the soft scent of his freshly shampooed hair.

"Don't forget the custard in the freezer. I'll be over in a couple of days with groceries. Call me if you think of something special you need."

He didn't respond. I collected my purse and car keys, and I left. I stood outside his apartment door and listened to the sound of his footsteps shuffling toward the kitchen.

I was home by six-thirty to throw a leftover lasagna in the microwave and check my phone messages. There were three. The first was from Brian.

"Mildred left me a message to contact her immediately. I need to hear from you before I do, Tess. Call me and let me know *exactly* what you said to her. I mean it. You're on thin ice with me. Call me as soon as you get this."

I hit the delete key.

The second was from Rosie.

"Tess, what's going on? Brian's on a rampage here. He's suddenly Mr. Micromanager, and it's driving us all bonkers. We need a plan to push him back into hands-off land."

I saved that message and made myself a promise to call her first thing in the morning.

The third message was from John.

"Listen, Tess. I don't know what happened. What I did to screw things up. But obviously it was something. I'd like to know what it was. I miss you, Tess. I hope everything's okay on your end. Please call or text me, okay? Even if it's to give me the heave-ho."

I played his message two more times. He sounded sincere.

Mimi's words rang through my memory. She told me I was making up stories and acting as though they were true. She said I had nothing other than my fear and paranoia cementing me into a cycle of mistrust. Perhaps I should feel bad for leaving him stranded at Graze. But another part of me buzzed with the warnings that had kept me relatively safe for a good many years. I deleted his message.

I ate my lasagna while I scribbled notes about my conversation with my father. Mimi would want to know all the details. There appeared to be an ever-growing body of evidence to suggest my birth story was also hers. My mind kept coming back to the seven-hour gap when my mother and her newborn child . . . children? . . . were out of his sight. I jotted down *postpartum depression . . . clung to me . . .* and *home for a year*. I had no idea why, but the phrases seemed important. I couldn't bring myself to write down the one word that haunted me most. *Nickname.*

Mentally and emotionally exhausted, I took a long bubble bath, listening to an oldies station while I soaked. At some point Barry Manilow started singing about a weekend in New England, and a soft melancholy pulled at me. I listened to every word. I could see the rocky beaches he sang about. I could feel his yearning for what he couldn't have.

I was in bed by nine, falling into one of those hard and deep sleeps that feels like giant hands are pressing you down into the bed. My next awareness was of sunshine streaming into my bedroom. Bright, golden light that did nothing to dispel the darkness clouding my mood.

CHAPTER 20

"So, what do you make of the tale of my birth?" I asked Mimi as I poured myself a second cup of coffee. True to her promise, she'd arrived on my doorstep not long after I'd showered and dressed for the day. She told me she'd been too curious to sleep and had already had her breakfast, but she sat with me while I had mine. I pulled out the notes I'd made the night before, but I didn't need to refer to them. My conversation with my father was fresh in my mind, and she had been uncharacteristically quiet while I filled her in on all the details.

"I think your father ... our father ... whatever ... doesn't know two of us were born that day. Even if he didn't want to tell you, for whatever dumb-ass reason, I think you would have caught on to his cover-up."

"I agree. But why the need for a cover-up in the first place? Why the need to separate us? There has to be some other explanation. Maybe we aren't twins and all these coincidences are enough to get us our own display in Ripley's Believe It or Not. Or maybe we *are* twins but our mother was just as ignorant as our father that she'd given birth to two daughters. Maybe we were part of some kind of baby-selling operation."

"No. I'm convinced more than ever that's not the case. Our mother knew. There's no doubt in my mind."

"Explain that."

"I dated this guy once. Bradley. Handsome, handsome, handsome."

"What's that got to do with anything?"

"Let me finish. Bradley looked like a young Harrison Ford. I mean a dead ringer for the guy. I dated him longer than I should have just because he was so good looking that he made me feel prettier standing next to him. I say longer than I should have because Bradley was dumb as a box of rocks. Not cognitively impaired or anything like that. Just dumb. Didn't read books . . . or newspapers for that matter. Didn't wonder about the world. Didn't feel curiosity about anything, really. It was enough for Bradley simply to be handsome."

"I'm waiting for this to connect to our situation."

"He called me *babe*. Never anything else. From the day I met him. Never anything but *babe*. One day Bradley and I were at a café in South Beach. A woman walks up. Chats to Bradley for a bit. I smile and introduce myself. She tells me her name is Cecilia. She seemed pleasant enough. When she said she had to go, Bradley said, 'See you later, babe.' That's when I realized his name for me wasn't special. Bradley called every woman he ever dated *babe*. Probably made it easier for him and his unchallenged little brain. He never had to worry about a mix-up if he called every woman the same thing. See what I mean?"

I didn't and told her so.

Mimi reached across the breakfast nook table and laid her hand on mine. "According to your father, our mother was in bed, depressed and despondent, for almost a year. Clinging to you. That means I had to be somewhere. Probably Colorado. I have memories from there. We don't know why. Not yet, at least. When your mother gets better, she resumes her travels. And around the same time she takes to calling *you* by *my* name."

"My father said it was because I always said 'me, me, me' to get her to pick me up."

"Then maybe she named *me* after the nickname she'd given *you*. It's a chicken–egg thing. The timing doesn't really matter, but I'm convinced she called us each the same name so as not to inadvertently betray her role in the cover-up by mentioning the wrong name in the wrong place."

She must have read the hesitancy on my face.

"She left you, Tess. Why are you so hell-bent on protecting her?"

I didn't have an answer for that. As is typical, anger stepped in to replace the discomfort of uncertainty. It grew, demanding release. "So now what? We wait for your mother to get back and confront her?"

Mimi shook her head. "We need hard proof. Your dad said our mother went back to work. Traveling again. That must have been how she kept up the ruse of raising both of us. You in Madison and me in Colorado. We need to talk to the one person who knows about that traveling."

"Who?"

"Phillip Jasper."

CHAPTER 21

Detective Andy Anderson ran a hand over the bristly fuzz on his head. "Listen, I don't like to think of myself as a particularly impatient man. But I don't see the need for any more details." He leaned forward and counted off on his fingers. "I've got a dead body. I've got officers interviewing so many people the overtime's gonna send everybody to Cancun this winter. And I've got a security tape of you breaking into Jasper's office."

My heart seemed to stop beating for several seconds. Then it took off running, banging against my ribs so hard I was sure anyone watching would see my shirt heaving. A security tape?

"Andy, calm down." Sally Normandy reached out and laid her hand on my arm again. "Tess is walking us straight through what happened. She's been totally cooperative."

"Yeah?" Anderson asked. "Well, if this is your idea of cooperation, we got different dictionaries working. I'm the one with the badge. How about we do things my way for a while? See how far we get."

I turned to Sally Normandy. "You're not a police officer? Who are you?" I shifted my attention to Andy Anderson. "Who is she?"

Anderson smirked. "Some idea the chief had. You ask me, a homicide investigation is no time to be working experiments. I work things the tried and true way. Every interview room in this station is filled right now. We're gonna wrap this up before sunrise. No more strolling down the twists and turns of memory lane."

Sally stood and nodded toward the door. "Let's work out our differences on the other side of that wall."

Anderson scoffed. "I don't take orders from you."

Sally's voice remained calm despite Anderson's agitation. "You're correct. But I believe you *do* from the man who called me at home and asked me to come in to interview Tess. He's your boss's boss's boss. Do I have that chain of command correct? I can leave right now and allow you to conduct this line of questioning any way you deem fit, but I'm going to tell the chief the truth when he asks me how things went."

Anderson's jaw churned. He shot me a look that, if I weren't already scared out of my wits, would have pushed me there.

Sally's smile seemed sincere as she followed Anderson out the door. "We'll be right back, Tess. Can I get you anything?"

My mouth was a sandbox. Anderson was right. I'd been talking for what seemed like hours. "Some more water would be great. Thanks."

She nodded and left me alone in the room. My mind was an unattended fire hose with thoughts flailing aimlessly like some sort of giant, spitting snake hopped up on Red Bull, spurting fears in every direction.

What did they know about Mimi and me breaking into Jasper's office? Who did they have in those interview rooms? Who was saying what about me? Was I ever getting out of here?

Images flooded my mind. My apartment. Favorite patrons from the library. Rosie making a face behind Brian's back before her shoulders shook with silent giggles. Innocent and Agnes. Walking to my favorite coffee shop on Sunday mornings. Bringing groceries to my father.

Oh, God! What was going to become of my father?

And then I thought of John. Kind, sweet, funny, sexy John Rappaport.

I looked at the wall opposite me, knowing people were watching behind the one-way mirror. I imagined they were looking for some sort of behavior that would let them know if I was innocent or guilty.

I was both, I supposed. How was I supposed to act? What did they expect of me as I sat waiting for my interrogators to return?

Anderson and Sally came back in the room less than five minutes after they left. The detective's face was carved from cold granite. Like he had something he wanted to say but knew the cost would be too high. Sally, on the other hand, looked as if she'd arrived that very minute to start her shift. She seemed calm, rested, and relaxed as she handed me a fresh glass of water and returned to her seat beside me at the table.

"You were telling us what happened after Mimi suggested it was time to go see Phillip Jasper," she said.

That line from the movie *Alice in Wonderland* came to me: *Curiouser and curiouser.* It was bizarre enough for me to be sitting in the police station answering questions in a murder case.

But I still didn't know who was on the other side of that mirror or in those interview rooms.

"Tess?" Sally asked. "Are you all right?"

"You haven't answered my question," I said.

"Which question is that?" she asked.

"Who are you?" I nodded toward Anderson. "He's the detective. Yet here you are, asking me questions, waiting for me to say . . . what? The wrong thing? The right thing? What you need to hear to send me to jail?"

"We're looking for answers," Anderson said.

"I'm not talking to you right now." I realized I was in no position to snap and apologized. "It's been a long string of days. I'm afraid my nerves are shot. There's no reason for me to speak to you like that."

Sally's voice was as smooth as it had been all night. "I think we have a good idea how shot those nerves of yours are. In fact, that's why I'm here. I'm a psychologist, Tess. The officers who came to your apartment saw your distress."

"Cops knocking on my door telling me to come with them? Yeah. I'll bet I sounded distressed. Anybody would be. I don't see where that calls for a shrink." I forced myself to ease up. That kind of attitude would get me nowhere.

"You told the officers what happened when you first got here. Do you remember that?"

"Of course I do," I said. "But I wasn't ready for what they had to tell me. About the kid finding that body."

"So you were confused?" Sally asked.

"Still am, I guess."

"That makes sense to me. Maybe that's why I got the call."

"I've seen psychologists before," I said. "That didn't work out too well."

Sally nodded. "Did your father stop you from continuing in therapy?"

I didn't answer her.

"Were you upset about that? About your dad deciding not to let you talk to someone about your anger? About what was bothering you?"

"What is it you think you understand about my father and his parenting decisions? Tell me. Slowly. Don't leave out any details." I know I sounded bitter, mocking her like that. But I didn't really care.

Sally remained calm despite my attack. "I've been in this line of work a long time. I know how difficult it is for some parents to accept that their child may need help beyond what they are able to provide."

"My father was all I had after my mother . . . after my mother left us." I struggled to keep my voice civil. The two were quiet while I composed myself. I appreciated their kindness. After a while it was Detective Anderson who spoke. This time he kept his irritation out of his voice.

"So you decided to go see Jasper."

I nodded.

"It was Mimi's idea?" Sally asked.

"Yeah. But don't think I was some gullible lamb in all this. I wanted to figure this out as much as she did."

"What was she proposing, exactly?" Anderson asked.

"Just that we go talk to him. Find out what he knew about my mother's travels."

"So how'd we get to the breaking in part?"

"That came after we couldn't get in to see him. The first time, I mean. When we got turned away. But we knew we still needed to get our hands on travel records that would prove our mother was living two lives."

"Mimi suggested that, too?"

"Yes. Mimi's the PhD. The researcher. She said there's no way in hell any scientist worth their salt wouldn't keep meticulous records. Since our mother worked so closely with him, those notes would document *her* movements as well. Mimi said Jasper would have logs of the wheres and whens of her absences that would help us piece this whole thing together. If we got our hands on those files, we'd have the proof we needed to confront our mother."

"Phillip Jasper's office is in one of the most state-of-the-art buildings on campus. How did Mimi propose you were going to break in?"

"She said we should keep it simple. And she was right. It worked."

"What worked?" Anderson asked.

"We didn't break into the building," I said. "We never left."

I could sense Anderson's struggle to keep his irritation in check.

"Mimi and I didn't leave the biogenetics building after we were turned away from seeing him. We stayed. For the rest of the afternoon we sat in the atrium, reading magazines. We watched the students and faculty leave. When the folks at the information desk starting closing down, we scooted into a lobby restroom we'd watched being cleaned earlier. Then it was a matter of waiting another couple of hours. We talked. We played games on my cell phone. When we left the bathroom, the entire building was empty. We didn't run into a soul when we went up to Jasper's office."

"But surely his suite was secured," Sally Normandy said.

"Not the outer waiting room. The door was closed, but it wasn't locked. In fact, the door to Jasper's office wasn't even closed. Mimi assured me that was the way academia was. The only locks we encountered were on his file cabinets."

"How'd you break those?" Anderson asked.

"We didn't. Like I said, Mimi knows her way around faculty offices. She scouted Jasper's. He had a few pottery pieces on his shelves. The keys to the file cabinets were in a little blue jug. Took us about three minutes from the time we entered his office to have every file drawer opened."

"Did you find what you were looking for?" Sally asked.

"No." A heavy wave of sadness replaced my anger. It was magnetic, pulling the steely vault of my fearful soul down . . . down . . . deeper with each beat of my sorry heart. "But we did find something. Something I wish to God we never had."

CHAPTER 22

Sally and Anderson exchanged a look I couldn't read.

"Tell us about that, Tess," Sally said. "And again, step by step. Walk us through everything."

So I told them Mimi walked me to work that morning after I finished breakfast. We made our plans to go see Jasper later in the day. She promised me everything would work out fine. We'd have our proof before the day was out. Then she said she was going back to her hotel until it was time to go over to the bio-genetics building.

Once I got to work, I went about my preopening rituals. I looked at the log from the previous night's closing team and built my to-do list. Then, without reading Brian's scribbled demands, I peeled off four Post-it notes that he had stuck on my computer screen and logged into my library account. The blessed routine of it all helped me regain a bit of my internal footing.

A familiar coded knock sounded at the front door. Three long, two short, three long. I pulled my hands away from my keyboard and listened in silence. John Rappaport knocked again, this time more gently but with the same convention. I sat still. A few moments later I heard the metallic rattle of the night deposit box followed by the thud of books dropping. I sat, hands in my lap, second-guessing myself until I was sure he'd be well past the wide windows of the library. Then I forced the memory of his rumpled good looks out of my mind and went back to work.

Rosie came in to start her shift an hour after I opened the doors for business.

"Is he here?" she whispered, and stepped behind the circulation desk as I was checking out two cookbooks to a middle-aged woman who had applied for her first library card.

"If you mean Brian, I haven't seen him." I handed the woman her books and waved the next person in line forward. It was Connie Millaley, a longtime regular checking out the latest from her favorite romance author. I processed her and wished her a good day.

"He's getting on everybody's last nerve, Tess." Rosie started loading a cart with the books in the night deposit box. I saw her pick up the two John brought back that morning. I didn't see any note attached to either and felt a flicker of disappointment. "It's like he's bucking for Librarian of the Year one minute, all sweetness and *Can I help you?* The next he's a crew boss on a prison chain gang, pointing out our mistakes and warning us any monkey could do our job so we better shape up or get ready to file unemployment papers. Can't you get rid of him? At least during my shift? I mean, isn't there a board member somewhere he could be sucking up to and leaving us alone?"

I didn't bother to tell her I was numero uno on Brian's hit list. Maybe I'd have a job here next week, maybe I wouldn't. On that particular morning it didn't seem to matter.

"Innocent and Agnes are due in at eleven. I've got their project all set up on the side table. Afternoon crew checks in at four. You okay if I take my lunch break away from the library?"

Rosie's smile filled with conspiracy. "You and John meeting somewhere? A little al fresco flirting over sandwiches and chips?"

"No." I realized my tone was more severe than necessary when her smile vanished. "It's something personal. On campus. Is that okay?"

If Rosie was concerned about my harsh response, she didn't let on. "Sure. Innocent and Agnes can operate on their own. Clifford's coming in. He's got sixteen more hours to work off, and he wants them done before school starts. I thought I'd keep him busy repainting the backdrop for story hour. It'll put his artistic skills to better use than spray-painting cop cars."

I thanked her and got on about the morning. Brian didn't make an appearance. I figured he was either meeting with Mildred or back to his old no-show habits. It didn't seem important at the time, so I didn't dwell on it. Shortly before noon I said good-bye to Rosie, Innocent, and Agnes and headed to campus. Mimi and I had planned to meet outside the biogenetics building. We didn't have an appointment. If the great Phillip Jasper was, indeed, somehow aware of our mother's three-decade-old secret, we didn't want to give him time to come up with a cover story. As I hurried to meet Mimi, I was so focused on what we were determined to do I nearly plowed into Carl Crittens, my former classmate turned local pharmacist.

"Whoa there, Tess." He laid a hand on my shoulder to keep me from barreling into him. "What's got your mind in outer space today?"

"I'm sorry, Carl. I didn't see you there."

His chuckle hadn't changed since he was twelve. Shrill, but laced with enough humor to keep it from irritating. "That I can see. How's the world treating you?"

"Fine. But I'm in a bit of a rush. You know how it goes. Places to go, things to do . . ."

"People to see," he said in unison with me. "This doesn't have anything to do with your mystery, does it?"

He suddenly had my full attention. "My mystery, Carl?"

He lowered his voice and looked up and down the street, as if he wanted to make sure the folks hurrying to complete their lunch hour errands weren't eavesdropping. "The DNA kit. The one you picked up last week. I remember thinking when I rang you up, *What's good old Tess doing tracing her roots? She's Madison way back. Ask anybody in town and they'll tell you who she is from first breath.* I wanted to ask you what you were up to at the time, but you were moving faster than a tornado in May. Kind of like now, to tell you the truth." He gave me another one of his chuckles.

Mimi! I thought. *She didn't buy that kit in Boston.*

"It's no mystery at all." My irritation fueled an instant lie. "It's for a show-and-tell down at the library. We're thinking about doing a display on all the recent advances brought about by the human genome project. You know, get the kids interested in science by appealing to their own self-involvement."

Carl pursed his lips and nodded, as though he was thinking a great thought. "You know, I might be able to offer some assistance. As a medical professional I'm up-to-date on the latest literature. You know, I've subscribed to *Popular Science* for years now. Maybe I can buy you a cup of coffee real soon and we can work together on this project. What d'ya say?"

I say I've got to get to Mimi fast. If I don't wring her neck for yet another instance of posing as me, we've got a busy couple of hours ahead of us.

"Let me think about that, Carl." I forced a smile and pointed in front of me. "But right now I've got to be somewhere. It was great running into you."

Again with the chuckle. "Ah! I stopped you before you could, didn't I?"

"You okay?" Mimi was right where she said she'd be. I was impressed at how fast she was getting used to the sprawling campus. "You look like seven miles of bad road."

I stopped midstep. My father often used those same words when he was describing someone who had seen better days. It startled me for a moment to hear it come out of Mimi's mouth.

It must be my mother's phrase. She probably taught it to both my father and her Florida daughter.

"I've been better." I wanted to let her have it about lying about the DNA kit, but our time was limited and we had things to do. "You?"

"I'm fine. Excited a little, even. I spent the morning wandering around all these buildings. And of course I had to step into the history building to see where my office is going to be. Was that a dumb thing to do, you think?"

If she noticed my irritation she didn't react. Still, it kept me from any small talk. "Let's get going. The sooner we start, the sooner we'll have our answers."

"You remember our plan?"

I told her I did. Mimi was one step behind me as I headed into the glass and stone biogenetics building.

The reception lobby was as sleek and polished as an intergalactic spaceship. People walked in every direction across shiny tile floors. Most were casually dressed. A few wore white lab coats. One woman wearing a smartly tailored suit pulled a wheeled carryall as she clicked her high heels across the cavernous space. I figured her for some kind of sales rep . . . pharmaceuticals . . . books . . . lab equipment . . . I had no idea of the particulars. But she looked like someone who was focused on where she needed to be. Like her time was money. It was different with the others milling about. None of them seemed to be in a hurry to be anywhere else. Like this imperial hall dedicated to future-changing science was the one and only place they ever wanted to be. They looked ready to think great thoughts, test new ideas, earn their Nobels, and reshape the world.

Mimi and I crossed to the information desk. A pretty young woman greeted us with perfect teeth gleaming from behind shiny pink lips. She asked how she could help us.

"We're here to see Phillip Jasper," I said.

The woman's big blue eyes blinked a startled staccato. She looked to her right and left, as though hoping someone would ride in on a wheeled office chair to rescue her from two people who obviously didn't belong there.

"Dr. Jasper?" she asked. "That Phillip Jasper?"

"If you've got more than one, I'm here to see the guy who built this place." I think my irritation with Mimi was spilling over to this poor woman. "The one who's been on the cover of *Time* at least three times. You know the guy I'm talking about?"

"Dr. Jasper usually greets his guests personally." The receptionist looked me up and down. Her face suggested I wasn't in the same league as the people who typically came to visit the big boss. "I didn't get a list from his people today. Do you have an appointment?"

The woman's eyebrow arched when I said we didn't.

"I'm not even sure he's in the building," she said. "Dr. Jasper is a very, very busy man."

"He's here." I don't know where that assurance came from, but somehow I was certain Jasper was in his office, doing whatever it was very, very busy men do. Likewise, I don't know where I got the moxie to press the issue. Maybe it was the fatigue. Or desperation. Perhaps it was Mimi standing at my elbow. Whatever the reason, I plowed on. "He'll want to see us. Call his office and let him know we're here."

The receptionist again looked around for backup. I felt a little sorry for her. She couldn't have been more than nineteen or twenty. But I didn't feel sorry enough to let her keep us from getting where we needed to get. So I put on my best don't-mess-with-me voice when she told us she didn't think it was wise to call upstairs.

"What's your name?" I asked.

"I'm the receptionist."

"What's your name?"

She looked like someone struggling to remember the level of security clearance a person might need in order to receive the sort of information I was requesting.

"How about your first name," I asked. "What's that?"

"Skylar." She bit her bottom lip.

I turned toward Mimi. "There can't be more than one Skylar behind the desk, right? I'm sure when Phil hears we were turned away by someone named Skylar his people will be able to figure out right away who denied us entry to his inner sanctum." I shifted my attention back to the girl. "You like working here, Skylar?"

Skylar directed her gaze across the wide lobby toward the security guard explaining a building site map to a trio of Japanese girls in dark blue uniforms. I realized I must have frightened her and softened my tone.

"You don't need security. We come in peace. I promise you, Dr. Jasper will be glad to see us. Call up to his office and tell him we're here. You'll see."

She looked unsure, but no one was coming to her assistance, and I'm certain she understood we weren't going anywhere. She lowered the microphone on her headset to lip level, entered three numbers into her keyboard, and waited for someone on the other end to answer.

"I have someone here to see Dr. Jasper." Skylar glanced up at me as she spoke. "No. No appointment." She nodded as though the person she heard through her earpiece was verifying what she had already told us: The great man did not see anyone without an appointment. "That's what I thought . . . Um-hm . . . Um-hm . . . Thanks, Vicki. Sorry to bother you."

Skylar pressed a button on her keyboard before turning to us with a smug just-as-I-thought look.

"Dr. Jasper sends his regrets. He asks that I relay his gratitude for you stopping by today, but his schedule is tight and he has no room for drop-ins."

"We're not drop-ins, dammit." Mimi's voice was shrill. I shot her a look. We'd get nowhere if both of us ganged up on the poor girl.

"Listen, Skylar," I said. "It's really important we see Dr. Jasper. Like, so important I don't even have the words to tell you. Understand?"

"I understand Dr. Jasper has many people who'd like to meet him. But we have procedures here." She reached toward a tray on her desk, then pulled out a trifold brochure and a green sheet of paper. She laid them both on the counter in front of me. "This brochure gives an overview of what we do here in Bio-genetics. Teaching, research, community outreach. Stuff like that." She pointed to the green sheet. "And this is the schedule for this month's public lectures. Times, topics, and presenters are listed. There's no fee. You should come check 'em out. They're really kind of interesting."

"We don't want to hear a lecture." I struggled to keep the impatience out of my voice. "We want to see Dr. Jasper."

"For that you'll need an appointment."

I sighed and looked at Mimi. It was obvious she understood what I did. There was no way we were getting past Skylar.

"Fine," I said. "How do we get on his calendar?"

"You call his appointment secretary."

"May I have the number of his appointment secretary? Please?"

Skylar dialed her smug level up several notches. "If Dr. Jasper wanted you to have an appointment, his people would have provided you with that number. Now, it's time for you to leave. You gonna be cool with that? Or do I call security?"

CHAPTER 23

"But you didn't leave." Detective Anderson looked toward that mirror on the back of the interview room's wall. *Who's standing behind that glass?* I asked myself. *Who are you performing for?*

"Like I said, it was Mimi's idea. When we couldn't get in to see Jasper, we were both pretty shaken up. I mean, we had been so sure it was the next logical step to take. But we weren't getting anywhere without an appointment. So I told Mimi we were going to have to find another way."

"And that didn't satisfy her?" Sally asked.

"No. She insisted that at the very least Jasper had to know about our mother's travels. And given how closely our mother worked with him, we figured it was possible he might know even more than that. That's when she brought up how scientists keep files and records on everything they do. She said if there wasn't a way for Jasper to answer our questions directly, we'd have to get into his files."

"And that's when you cooked up the plan to hide in the bathroom?" Anderson asked.

"It worked, didn't it? Like I said, the building itself might be secure, but once Mimi and I went up to the seventh floor after it emptied out, the only things that were locked were his cabinets."

Anderson took another look over his shoulder toward the mirror. I ignored him and continued to relay the events, as best as I could remember them, to Sally. She seemed to be the only person in the room who seemed to care.

I'll give him this much, the man was organized. Not only was every file labeled, but he seemed to have entire cabinets dedicated to certain topics. The drawers under his desk held files dealing with the administration of the department—budgets, personnel files, stuff like that. Mimi and I looked at those only long enough to make sure they didn't contain anything about our mother's travels. Then we looked in the cabinets along his back wall. Those were dedicated to his research files. Applications, authorization letters, and budgets for grants. Flash drives labeled RAW DATA. Dozens of binders filled with papers. Mimi looked at those. She told me they were step-by-step instructions for how to run Jasper's various experiments.

"You mean *protocols?*" I asked her.

"Yeah. How'd you know that?" Mimi whispered despite our being alone in Jasper's darkened office.

"I don't know." Then suddenly I did. "I think I heard my mother use that word. I remember thinking it sounded important. Probably any word with more than two syllables would sound important to a kid."

"Yeah? Well, keep checking in with that little kid, okay? We've got to find proof Jasper can't explain away. Proof that he and Audra had something cooking that involved separating infant twins the moment they were born."

"*Audra?*" I asked. "You're calling your mother Audra now?"

A flash of regret skimmed Mimi's face. It quickly morphed into a mask of firm resolve. "I don't know what else to call her. *Duplicitous coconspirator* doesn't trip off the tongue. Now get back at it. Find us what we need. It's the only way we're going to solve this thing."

The protocols were arranged by date. Each drawer held an entire year of Jasper's work. It made it easy for the two of us to walk back in time, as if we were unwinding the spool of the renowned scientist's brilliant career. Flash drives devolved into floppy discs. By the time we opened the drawers containing data from twenty-five years ago, we discovered carousel rings, the kind used on old slide projectors, jammed into the backs of drawers. Files became thicker, packed tight with papers.

"This is old stuff," Mimi said. "I'm surprised he hasn't had these transferred to digital. Man, things were positively stone-age. Look at this." She pulled a stack of wire-bound notebooks out of the drawer. "Handwritten notes. I mean, how'd they get anything done?"

The top drawer of the next cabinet was marked with the year Mimi and I would have been twelve years old. The year my mother fled. I knew now that she had gone to Florida to raise her other twin, but in that year I only knew she'd abandoned my father and me with no explanation.

I took a deep breath, opened the drawer with a shaking hand, pulled out the top file, and saw my mother's signature on the first page.

My knees buckled. I took the file to Jasper's desk and flopped into his chair.

"What do you have?" Mimi asked.

It took me a while to answer. I had no interest in the letters that formed words that formed sentences that formed communication. My eyes traced the broad strokes she used. Her handwriting, something I had no memory of ever seeing before, was confident and efficient. Tall, bold capital letters. No fancy flourishes or wide, loopy curves.

My mother wrote this, I thought. *My mother's hand touched this paper.*

I held the sheet to my nose, hoping to catch a whiff of her. Then I laid my hand flat over the page, willing our essences to merge.

"What does it say, Tess?"

I forced myself to read the words my mother had written so many years before. "It's a summary. She's reminding Jasper what needs to be done to close out a funding request for a grad student they'd accepted into their lab." My eyes scanned the entire file. "This is all about who's assigned to what project. Looks like my mother ran herd on everyone associated with Jasper's work."

"Anything specific about the work itself? This is why things need to be digitized. We ought to be able to simply search on the word *Florida* or *twin* and get to what we need. Sifting through tons of paper files is not efficient at all."

I didn't care about efficiency at that moment. After so many years of treating my mother as a forbidden topic of conversation or thought, I was holding paper she held. It was as close to a real connection I'd had in seventeen years. I could have stopped our snooping right there and then and been content with the treasure I'd found.

If only I had.

"There's no drawer marked any earlier than when we'd have been five years old." Mimi shoved the last drawer closed with her foot. She sounded disappointed. "The bastard's only got his legit research stuff here. I should have known. But we're onto something, Tess. Look at all this. Jasper's an organized scientist. He's got records about his involvement with this stored somewhere, and we have to find them. Do you know where he lives?"

Mimi was looking for something that no longer held my interest. I left Jasper's desk and started opening file drawers at random, looking for anything that might hold another piece of my mother. I saw her face on a newsletter from the year I would have been four. There she was, smiling in a black-and-white photograph as she stood behind Phillip Jasper, who was holding a giant mock-up of a check. The headline read UNIVERSITY SCHOLAR RECEIVES MILLION-DOLLAR GRANT. In the drawer dedicated to the year I would have been six, there was a framed photograph of Jasper and several other men in suits, each holding a symbolic shovel of dirt. My mother stood next to a sign announcing the expansion of the old genetics laboratory. I studied her face. She looked so prim and professional, wearing a plaid jacket over a gray flannel skirt. Something like a memory pulled at me. She liked a certain green sweater with that jacket, didn't she? But the memory faded before I could be certain.

What I *was* certain of was the look on her face. She wasn't smiling in this photograph as she was in the newsletter.

I laid the framed photo back where I'd found it, closed the drawer, and opened the one beneath it. That drawer documented Jasper's career the year I would have been five. It was filled with files and folders similar to the ones I'd already seen. I was about to close it when I noticed something different wedged in the back. It was a container, approximately the size of a standard shoe box but made of hard plastic. Opaque white with a blue lid. It took some maneuvering to free it from the overstuffed drawer.

"What's that?" Mimi asked.

I set the container on Jasper's desk and lifted the lid. My gasp brought Mimi to my side.

A photograph of my mother, perched on the hood of a car, wearing a wide-brimmed straw hat, mouth frozen mid-laugh and eyes glistening with joy, looked up at me.

"That's Audra." Mimi lifted the photograph from the box. "And obviously not in business clothes. What's it doing here?"

"That's *my* mother." I heard the bitterness in my voice. "From her time here. Before she made the decision to go raise you."

"Wow. She really does look like us, doesn't she?"

"Yes, Mimi. That's the thing about mothers and daughters."

I sifted through the stack of cards, letters, photographs, and souvenirs. I found birthday cards meant for Phillip Jasper, signed in my mother's hand. A few were humorous. The rest were signed with love. There were several programs, most for academic dinners honoring various faculty. Each had the date scribbled across the top in writing I didn't recognize but assumed was Jasper's. Under each handwritten date was a brief sentence.

Our first kiss
Blue satin frock with full skirt
She loves me!

Almost caught in parking lot . . . this reminder was punctuated with a drawing of a smiling face.

Mimi stood behind me while I prowled through matchbooks from Chicago restaurants; postcards from Las Vegas, Sheboygan, and Atlanta; keys from seven hotels. There was a paper napkin with a blotted, fossilized kiss in deep pink lipstick. I picked up a folder made of creamy vellum card stock. The front carried an embossed outline of a grand building with the words *Stanley Hotel, Estes Park* stamped underneath in gold. I opened the folder and saw Phillip Jasper and my mother huddled together. Smiling for the camera. Separated only by the grinning toddler they held between them.

"Hey!" Mimi reached for the folder. "That's me. What's Jasper doing in Colorado holding me when I was a baby?"

I snatched the photograph back from her. "That's not you, Mimi. That's me. My father may have burned all the pictures of my mother, but he kept the ones of me. I know what I looked like as a kid."

"Why were you in Colorado?" she asked.

"Look at the picture. I was, what? Two . . . three maybe when this picture was taken? Forgive me for not knowing what took me to the Rocky Mountains."

"We're identical twins. Let's face it. It could be either of us. But look at how happy the two of them look with whichever one of us it is they're holding."

I studied the photo in my hand. I zeroed in on my mother. Her eyes glowed with an inner light beautifully captured by the camera. Her smile was relaxed and easy. She seemed so at ease. So happy.

I shoved the folder back in the box, snapped the lid tight, and tucked it under my arm. "Let's go."

Mimi hesitated. "But we haven't found what we need yet."

I shook my head. "Audra and Phillip Jasper were lovers. Probably for years. I'm keeping this box. It's leverage to get Jasper to talk if we can't find the rest of his notes."

"Don't you see what this means?" she asked.

A ball of acid rolled in my stomach. Maybe it was an example of that twin talk Mimi liked to yap about, but I knew what she was planning on saying next and I was in no mood to hear it.

"We don't know anything, Mimi. Nothing beyond the fact they were lovers."

"Who conspired to keep twins apart? Face it, Tess. Do the math. Your mother and father were married how long before you came along? In all those years she never got pregnant? Then she gets involved with Phillip Jasper and the next thing you know she's laughing with her arms around her big pregnant belly while he takes secret photos?"

I would have given her every penny in my savings account to keep her from saying the words she uttered next.

"Face it, Tess. Sanford Kincaid isn't our father. Phillip Jasper is."

"I'm too exhausted to handle any more of your stories, Mimi."

"You know I'm right." Excitement sang in her words. Nancy Drew had solved her mystery. "That may be why they separated us. We'll learn more about their motivation when we confront our mother. Maybe she had made the decision to end the relationship and stay with your father. Jasper could have threatened to reveal everything if Audra didn't give him one daughter to raise . . . a piece of his lover he could keep forever. She could have been desperate to keep the affair secret and in a moment of postdelivery vulnerability would have agreed to anything to keep your father from learning of her betrayal. That would explain her immediate and long depression, wouldn't it? Why she wouldn't allow your father to even mention Jasper's name?"

"You're starting with your stories again, Mimi."

"But it's the only thing that makes sense!"

"Then why would she go back to work with a man who'd coerced her into such an arrangement?"

"Maybe she thought it was the only way she could have both of us in her life. If Jasper was lovesick enough to keep these mementos all these years, he'd agree to let her have time with both twins so long as she came back to him."

"Then how do you explain her departure to full-time life in Florida? Did you have an Uncle Phillip who came to see you while you grew up? Why would he let her take off and raise you all by herself?"

Mimi thought for a moment. "Maybe *she* threatened *him* once his career took flight. If he didn't back away from both of us she'd let the world know he'd had a sexual relationship with an employee. That he'd spent grant dollars on hotels and trips to support what was, by definition, sexual harassment. He'd be a big-enough name to know that kind of scandal would stop the federal money spigot from raining down limitless supplies of research dollars. He probably thought he needed to stay away from both of us." Her eyes went wide. "Think, Tess. He'd *have* to keep her quiet. Why, I'll bet it was *his* money that kept my mother and me financially secure all those years."

I didn't have the energy to reply. Once Mimi got started on her illogical train of logic, there was no stopping her. All I knew was that I was finished for the night. I picked up the shoe box and walked out of Jasper's office. Mimi hurried to catch up with me.

"Don't worry," she said as we waited for the elevator. "We're getting closer. I'm sure of it. Everything's going to turn out just fine."

I remember thinking how comforting that sounded at the time.

I hope I'm never as wrong about anything else ever again.

CHAPTER 24

I was surprised at how well I slept that night after we prowled through Jasper's office. Mimi walked me home. I asked her if she wanted to spend the night, but she begged off. I considered pressing her on it. It was past ten and full-on dark, after all. But the discovery that our mother was having an affair with Phillip Jasper and the speculation that he may very well be our father must have stirred up emotions in her that were as heavy as the ones tormenting me. She probably needed the same time alone that I did to process it all. So I told her there was plenty of time to go through the box I'd taken from Jasper's office, wished her a good night, and watched her walk off toward her hotel.

I went straight to bed, leaving that plastic shoe box filled with evidence on my breakfast nook table. I fell asleep fast. I don't remember dreaming. All I know is that when I woke up I knew exactly what my next step needed to be. I called Rosie, asked her to open the library for me, and told her I needed to take a few days off. There must have been something in my voice. She didn't question me about why, but told me not to worry about a thing. She'd see me when I got back.

Then I headed to my car and hoped I was early enough to catch my father in good shape to answer my questions.

* * *

"There's my Tess." My father answered his apartment door before I had to use my key. For a moment I felt a flutter of optimism. Maybe the sobriety he'd so obviously wanted me to see during my last visit was holding. Then I noticed he was wearing the same clothes he had on when he had me over for that pizza dinner. A glance in the direction of the kitchen showed me that the half-empty bottle of whiskey I'd seen on my last visit was gone. On the counter, next to my father's coffee mug, stood an opened bottle of rye with what looked to be only an inch of liquid remaining.

"You not working today?" His gait was wobbly as he headed back to his chair.

I picked up the remote from the side table and turned off the TV set. "I'm taking a few days for myself. Want me to make a pot of coffee?"

A shadow crossed his face. "Fresh out. Best I can do is a glass of water."

"You gotta tell me when you're running low on things, Dad. I can't read your mind, you know. What else do you need?"

He waved my question away. "Stop barking orders. If you've come for a visit, take a seat. If you've come to be disrespectful, take a hike."

I sat on the arm of the sofa. I had no intention to shock him with what I'd learned about my mother and Jasper's affair, but despite his mood I needed to take advantage of whatever focus my father had before the liquor wiped him out for the day. Looking back, I probably could have eased into the topic a bit more gently.

"What do you know about Mom's relationship with Phillip Jasper?"

His eyes fluttered. His hands stayed on his lap, but I saw his fingers reach out and curl. Not into a fist. I'd seen that move hundreds of times. This time his hands moved differently. Like they were trying to grip on to something that wasn't there. When he spoke, his voice was firm. He sounded like the old

Sanford Kincaid, the legal scholar who could shut down any challenge from a daring student.

"Your mother worked for Jasper for many years. You know that."

I nodded. "Did you guys talk about her work? I mean, would she share with you what was going on down at his lab?"

"Where's this going, Tess?"

I was violating our age-old rule. Today was not my mother's birthday. My father's tone told me he recognized the breach and didn't appreciate it.

"Jasper's quite the guy now, isn't he? Big shot scientist and all. What was it like in those early days? It must have been pretty exciting for Mom to be a part of it."

My father took a long sip of the rye inside his coffee mug. "I don't follow Jasper's work."

"But Mom had to have been excited about it, right? His stuff is pretty cutting edge from what I understand."

He shot me a look that should have warned me off.

You know about the affair, don't you, I thought. *It's not only me you're protecting by not talking about my mother. It's you, too, isn't it? The memory of your wife's infidelity. That's what made her a forbidden topic.*

"I have a new friend. Met her last week. She's landed a one-year teaching assignment at the university. History. Tells me it's murder getting tenure. Long hours. All consuming. What was it like for Mom to work with someone at that phase of his career?"

He focused on the squirrel running in circles outside his living room window.

"And I remember all the traveling Mom had to do. Conferences . . . symposiums. Did that ever bother you?"

My father wiped a trembling hand over his mouth. "Sometimes, I guess. At the time, I had my own work. The university had placed *me* on the faculty as well, you know."

You're trying to figure out why she did it. You're wondering what Jasper had that you didn't.

It was cruel of me to press on. I see that now. But on that day all I wanted was answers.

"I'll bet it was kind of fun for her. Especially before I came along, I mean. You building your position. Jasper building his. Mom right there with both of you."

"I don't want to talk about this."

"You told me Mom had a difficult time getting back into the swing of things after I was born. That she didn't even want you to mention Jasper's name. But she *did* go back. Did she ever explain why? Not to mention the fact it must have been hard on her, what with what you told me about her being so bonded to me and all. I mean, who took care of me when Mom was at work?"

"We managed, I guess. Like all young couples do."

"But most new mothers aren't working for an up-and-comer like Phillip Jasper. What about when I was a baby? Who took care of me while Mom traveled?"

I watched my father's jaw churn. Something in my internal guidance system told me to back off. But like everybody else telling a dark tale in hindsight, I didn't listen.

"Did Mom ever take me on any of her trips?"

My father didn't answer me.

"Did Mom ever go to Colorado? With Jasper, I mean. Did she take me with her?"

My father made a move to stand, but I beat him to it. I rose and stood over him, blocking any escape he may have been planning.

"Is it so wrong to want to know my story, Dad? What my parents' lives were like before I was born? What about my early years, before I could remember things myself? Stuff was going on, right? I never hear stories about what it was like back then. Was I funny? What were my first words? Did I have an imaginary friend? Did I badger you and Mom for a puppy? How long did I spend in diapers? What did I do on my first day of school? Who in the hell were my parents? What did they do for a living? Who were their friends? How'd they have fun?"

"Let it be." My father wasn't commanding anymore. There wasn't a hint of threat in his tone.

"I deserve to know. It's like an entire chunk of me is missing. We've spent so many years blocking out this part of my life . . . this part of *your* life."

"Stop, Tess." My father was pleading. "It hasn't been so bad, has it? We've made do. You have your good memories of your mother. Before she was bad. Can't you let it be enough?"

On instinct, I stepped back, allowing the fearful child I'd been trained to be pull me away from where my father sat. My chest was suddenly heavy with shame. Each breath a leaden struggle. A searing headache pounced on me without warning. I put a hand to my temple and closed my eyes. The image of the photograph I had seen the night before came to me. My mother's radiant smile as she and Jasper held her beloved daughter. A smile forever denied to me without explanation or regret. The image unleashed my anger before I had time to rein the monster in. My shame disappeared, clearing space that was instantly replaced with rage. For the first time it was directed at the man I'd spent my entire life calling father.

"I'm sick to death of *enough!*" I was shouting. "I'm tired of begging for scraps when other people feast! I won't apologize for wanting more. I deserve to know my history. I won't pretend it doesn't matter!" My voice stabbed my ears. I saw spit flying from my mouth as I screamed. "My mother left me. Me! And not talking about it *isn't* enough. Not anymore. You can drink yourself to oblivion every night if that's your plan, but I need to know! Why? Why did she leave? You know! And you're going to tell me! Everything! I know about the affair she had with Phillip Jasper. Tell me what you know! I deserve this!"

My father jumped out of his chair and slapped me hard across the face. He hadn't hit me like that since I was a teenager. I stood, stunned and silent. Feeling a trickle of blood seep from my lower lip. My anger scurried back into its hole, vacating the premises to let shame move in. I'd driven my father to this. This man of letters and loss. This man who'd suffered as much at the hands of my mother as I had. He'd promised me the day I left for college that he'd never hit me again, and he hadn't. Not until that day. Not until I drove him to violence.

"I'm so sorry, Daddy." Tears spilled from my eyes.

"You made me do it." His voice was small and faraway. "You made me do this. Look at what you've forced me to do."

I reached out to touch his shoulder, but he recoiled. Then he hit me again.

"I did all this for you. All the pain and hardship. I went through it all for you." He looked at me, his eyes radiating his anguish. "We had a promise, Tess. I kept my end."

I coughed my voice clear of my tears. "I know, Daddy. I'm sorry." I reached out again. This time he let me touch him. "It's all right. It doesn't even hurt, really. I'm so sorry." I led him back to his chair, keeping my hand on his shoulder until he was seated. Then I took his mug to the kitchen and emptied the bottle of rye into it. I bowed my head as I handed him his cup of salvation.

"I'll be back later, okay? I'll bring some coffee. And a special treat for dessert. How would that be?"

My father focused again on the squirrel outside the window.

I turned the television on and handed him the remote.

"I'll see you later, Daddy." I looked back one last time before I walked out the door. "I'm sorry. Can you forgive me?"

His silence escorted me out the door.

CHAPTER 25

I don't remember how I got back to my place after that. I must have driven for a while, trying to calm down, but I couldn't tell you where I went. I do know I left his apartment around ten-thirty and it was past noon when I pulled into my driveway.

"Were you alone?" Sally Normandy asked.

"Yes. Why?" Now that I knew she was a psychologist, I heard every question with a different ear.

"Can you please just answer?" Andy Anderson still sounded frustrated, but his aggressive edge was gone. Now he sounded tired.

"Yes. I was alone."

"Was there anything in the car that might help us understand where you drove during that time you can't recall?" Sally asked. "Groceries? A bag from the mall?"

"Souvenir from the zoo, maybe?" Anderson suggested.

"Is that supposed to be funny?" I asked. "No. There was nothing in the car. I probably cruised the streets. I've lived in Madison my entire life. I could drive the west side blindfolded."

Sally's smile was soft. "Then what happened?"

"He was there. John, I mean."

"John Rappaport?" Anderson jotted something on his notepad. "Your boyfriend?"

"No. Yes. I mean, no. John's not my boyfriend. But yes, he was there. He told me he went by the library on his lunch hour. Rosie told him I was out for the rest of the week, so he came by my apartment. Wanted to check on me."

"Sounds like something a boyfriend would do," Sally offered. "Was he upset?"

"No. At least I don't think so. More concerned, I'd say. I'm not a rude person. But abandoning him at the restaurant . . ."

"There's that word again," Sally interrupted. "*Abandoning*. Comes up a lot."

I felt the rumble of my anger monster. "Please don't psychoanalyze me."

"I'm just making note," she said.

"Please don't." I caught myself and softened my bitter tone. "It was a difficult encounter."

"I'd love to hear about it."

I wouldn't have thought twice about it if I'd pulled up in front of my apartment and seen Mimi waiting for me on my front porch. But seeing John there . . . waiting . . . I wasn't prepared for that. I had made quite the scene when I accused him of being in league with Mimi, warning him to stay away from me, calling him names. I was surprised he'd ever want to speak to me again. Yet there he was. I got out of my car and tried to think of some kind of acceptable opening remark as I approached him. As it turned out, I didn't need one.

"My God, Tess!" John's eyes went wide when he saw my face. "What happened to you?"

I realized he was looking at the bruises from where my father hit me. My hand instinctively went to my cheek. I felt cakes of dried blood and realized it must have looked far worse than it actually was.

"I fell." I maneuvered my way around him to take my place on the porch while he stood two steps lower on the sidewalk. "This morning. I slipped getting out of the shower and hit my face on the side of the tub."

"The hell you did." Despite his swearing and the urgency in his voice, I knew he meant me no harm. "I can see the handprint from here. Someone hit you. Tell me who."

"I said I fell, John. This morning. I've always bruised easily. I can't do a thing about what you think you see."

"Is there someone else? Is that why you've not been returning my calls? Tess, are you in danger from this guy? I'll go with you to the police right now. You don't have to be afraid."

I gave him a long look. I wanted to fill my eyes with the sight of him. Fill my memory banks with the knowledge that there once was a man who acted as though he cared for me. Of course, he didn't know me. Not really. If he did, he'd be running as fast as those muscular legs would carry him. Far away from the messed-up woman locked in a messed-up vortex of secrets and lies. The one who no longer even knew where she belonged. Or who she was, for that matter.

John came from normal. His mother and father still lived in the Green Bay home where they raised their children. I hadn't laid eyes on my mother in seventeen years. And have I mentioned the guy whose name I carry is, in all likelihood, *not* my father? John had loving memories of a lifetime spent growing up with his brothers. There'd be inside jokes between them. Entire messages conveyed with a certain smirk or roll of the eyes. How could I explain I met my twin sister about a week ago? That we share nothing other than our appearance. There's no memories. No history. Not even any real trust.

That was precisely the kind of crazy John Rappaport didn't need in his life. Crazy begets crazy and devours any morsel of normal lying in its path. In that moment, standing there on the porch, the memory of the advice John's grandfather had given him came back to me.

Figure out where you're going, Johnny. Then find the person you want to take with you.

John had a future filled with promise, status, and prestige ahead of him. He'd be a loving husband and father, an ethical attorney who'd make strong contributions to his profession and his community. He was the type of man who, once he loved someone, would hold her ferociously close. Her pain would be his to soothe. Her problems his to resolve. I'd be, at best, an anchor slowing John's forward movement to the life he deserved. With me, he'd spend so much time and toil helping sort out my screwed-up history he'd never be able to focus on what he needed to in order to become the magnificent piece of upstanding he was destined to be. He'd have to warn his family not to bring up my shattered family as they passed the mashed potatoes at Thanksgiving. He'd spend years apologizing to colleagues for his dropout wife, the one still earning hourly wages at the corner library while their own wives were building their case for tenure or designing franchise opportunities to expand their bistro business. Whatever initial affection he might feel for me would decay, replaced with disappointment that would morph first into pity, then resentment, before it made the final transmutation into disgust.

A sense of calming clarity overcame me. For the first time since I saw Mimi walking down Regent Street, all confusion disappeared long enough for me to understand my next step.

"I need you to leave, John."

He shook his head. "I'm not going anywhere, Tess. Look, I get we're walking on some weird and bumpy road right now. But I'm willing to see it through if you are." His eyes were soft, promising a gentle place to land if I was willing to take a leap. "I don't know what all that was back at the restaurant, but I swear to you I've never met Mimi. Never spoken to her. Wouldn't know her if she passed me in the streets." He offered a small smile. "Well, if what you tell me is true, I'd probably recognize her. But I'd think she was you."

He'd given me an opening.

"Now you're calling me a liar?"

"What? No! I'm making a joke. Lighten this tension that's real enough to slap a coat of paint on."

"You think this is funny? I walk away from you. Tell you I never want to see you again. Don't respond to your texts, your phone calls. And you come here to call me a liar. First about how I got my bruise, then a second time about what Mimi looks like. To top it off you decide to go for a laugh with some sort of sicko stand-up routine right here in front of my porch? How am I supposed to respond to that?"

"I . . . what . . . I thought . . . Look, Tess, can we start over? You're clearly upset. I can see that. I want to help . . ."

"With what?" I raised my voice. "With you? Because from where I stand you're what's upsetting me."

"I came by to see if you were all right."

"I don't believe that for one minute. You're like all men. A woman tells you what she wants and, heaven forbid, if it doesn't fit with *your* plans, you disregard it and plow straight ahead with your own agenda."

"I don't get how that . . ."

"You don't get what? What I'm talking about? Well, Mr. Fancy Wine Blogger Law Student, let me spell it out for you. I don't want to see you anymore. I told you that. Both with my words and with my actions. But you've decided to keep calling and texting. When that doesn't get you what you want, you show up uninvited on my front lawn. Now, you might think that's a romantic gesture. You may even think it's mighty great of you to grant me a second shot at the wonderful John Rappaport given the scene I made at Graze. But think for a minute and tell me how else could anyone interpret all you're doing other than *Fuck you, Tess Kincaid. I don't care one thing about what YOU want. I'm not going anywhere.*"

"That's not what I meant!"

"Well, that's exactly what your actions have said!"

We stood there in silence. My guess is, he was trying to figure a way out of the hole I'd dug for him. I was hoping for nothing more than his acceptance that I was one piece of piled-up mess way too hot for him to even think about picking up.

"You're right," he finally said. "I have put my desires ahead of what you've been telling me you want. I'm sorry for that." He kept his eyes on mine. I had the feeling he wanted to plead his case but realized anything he said would only make my position stronger. "I hear you. You want nothing to do with me. I'm leaving now. Sad. Sorry. Confused. But I'm leaving. And I want you to know . . . I won't change my phone number, Tess. If you ever feel the desire to use it, I promise I'll pick up."

Then he turned and went back to his car.

Anderson and Sally finished scribbling the notes they'd taken while I told them the story. When they were done writing, they looked at one another as if they were deciding who would ask the next question. Sally turned up the winner.

"How'd you feel after he left?"

"You want me to say I felt like shit? That I'd lied to a good man? Maybe even broke his heart a little? Or am I supposed to break down in tears because maybe I broke mine, too? What is it you want from me?"

Neither of them reacted to my anger.

"We want to know how you felt telling John to leave you," Sally said.

"I haven't thought much about it," I lied. "I had bigger issues at the time."

"So what happened next?" Anderson asked as he scribbled again in his notepad.

I didn't say anything for a few seconds. I got the feeling they both knew the answer to that question, but they wanted me to say it. Wanted to see if my account of what happened gelled with their time line. With what those other people . . . the ones Anderson's officers had in other interview rooms . . . were saying.

"Tess?" Sally asked in that gentle voice of hers. "What happened next?"

I wiped my palms against my jeans.

"Mimi showed up. Not long after John left. I'd say a few minutes before one. I'd gone inside. For a moment I thought it was John knocking. Coming back to take one more stab at things. But it was Mimi. I opened the door and there she was, smiling and excited, like she always was. Said she couldn't wait to go through the box I'd taken from Jasper's office."

"Were you happy to see her?" Sally asked.

"She could be annoying, and I for sure had learned that I couldn't trust her. But there was something about her confidence, her way of looking at life like it was one big adventure."

Sally nodded. "Did it make you imagine her way of looking at the world . . . her success . . . her confidence . . . might have been yours if you'd been raised as sisters down in Florida?"

The water I was in was hot enough already, so I opted for the truth. "That would be a fantasy, wouldn't it? And there's no sense in dwelling on what can never be." I knew what this sounded like and wondered if my honesty might push me a step or two closer to being locked away.

"What did you and Mimi do?" Sally asked.

"We went through the box. All those things Jasper kept from his time with our mother. Photographs. Ticket stubs. Mimi said it was the scientist in him that made him make notes about the when and where of each thing. To me he was like some lovesick teenager. But his notes did make for a full picture of what was going on between them."

"And that was?" Anderson asked.

It was hard for me to get the words out. "They were in love. For a long time. There were letters from my mother promising to leave my father from way back. Before I was born, even. Other letters said she had doubts. That she was torn up inside, what with being in love with both my father and Jasper. Birthday cards. Valentine's. That box was crammed full."

"What did you make of all that?" Sally asked.

"It made me sick. I thought of everything my dad's gone through since she aband . . . since she left us. She was playing him for a sucker. It turned my stomach."

"And Mimi?" Sally wondered.

I huffed out my disgust. "All she saw was the romance. How she couldn't wait to talk to Audra about how her heart must have been torn in two. Remember, she had a very different relationship with our mother than I did. Mimi was the daughter my mother chose. She was all about how tough it must have been for poor Mommy. I wanted to strangle her." I regretted the words the moment I spoke them. "That's a figure of speech, you understand."

Anderson jotted another entry.

"Anyway," I continued. "Turns out Mimi's focus on the romance got us to our next step. If it hadn't been for her I would have overlooked the obvious."

"Which was?" Sally asked.

"She looked at all the stuff in the box. I mean, there was a lot of it. All spread across my breakfast nook table. I was so hell-bent on being angry at my mother that I couldn't see what Mimi did. But after we'd read all the notes and cards, after we looked at every photograph and souvenir, she leaned back in the chair and asked the key question."

"And that was?" Anderson had his pen ready for another scribble.

"Regardless of whether he was our father or not, if our mother and Jasper were so much in love, why weren't they together?"

CHAPTER 26

"We need to hear this straight from the horse's mouth," Mimi said after she'd had her fill of Jasper's photographs and letters. "When Mom gets back I'm going to tell her about my job offer here. I'll ask her to help me go apartment hunting."

"Do you think she'd dare?" Until that moment I don't think I realized there was a very strong possibility I'd see my mother again. "Would she risk running into my father? Or Phillip Jasper?"

Funny how I didn't even consider she might be afraid to run into me.

"Are you kidding? She'll come running. If only to get me as far away from Madison as possible. She'll come."

"Then what?"

"We arrange a showdown. I'll take my mother on a tour of the campus. Introduce her to my new colleagues. We'll spend a day looking at places to live. Get her good and edgy. Then it'll be time for dinner. My mother and I will be at . . . what's your favorite restaurant?"

"Would you do that? Betray your own mother? Set her up for that kind of humiliation?"

Mimi stepped toward me as if she was hoping for a hug, but I stepped back.

"She owes us this, Tess. And she owes you so much more. My heart breaks when I think of how crippled you are from the loss of her. You have a sister now. And I'm not going to let anyone bring you pain ever again. Can't you see? This is the only way to resolve this. For the first time, everything will be out in the open. Now, pick a restaurant. My mother and I will be there at a predetermined time. You walk in a few minutes later. She'll have no choice but to tell us everything."

Detective Anderson interrupted my recollection.

"How'd that sit with you? Mimi suggesting you make up a story, I mean. Hell, let's call it what it was. How'd you feel about the two of you planning to lie?"

He looked like a cat ready to pounce on an injured bird.

"I . . . I didn't know what to think. I didn't like the idea. But at the time it seemed like the only thing we could do."

"So the two of you were, what? Planning on hanging out 'til Mimi's mother arrived on the scene?" he asked. "Develop your bond as sisters? Learn to braid one another's hair?"

"Easy now." Sally Normandy turned to me. "Let me see if my time line is correct." She flipped through several pages in her notebook. "Your confrontation with your father, when he slapped you, was yesterday morning. Do I have that right?"

I reached my hand to the side of my face. It was still tender. The bruise must have been at its purple-and-green peak. "Yes."

"Then John Rappaport came by your house to check on you. You said he was on his lunch hour? About what time would he have arrived at your apartment?"

They were laying out the time line. Looking for a slip. Trying to find a way to trap me.

"Probably close to one o'clock. Maybe a bit after."

"You said Mimi came by a little before one." Anderson tapped his finger on the page where he'd made note of what I'd said. "Were they both there at the same time?"

"No. John was gone when Mimi arrived. But only by a few minutes." I looked toward Sally. "I didn't check the clock. It was all around the middle of the day."

She nodded. "I understand. Mimi came by a short time after John left. The two of you came up with the plan for Audra to see her two daughters together."

"Mimi said it was best if our first encounter was in a public place. She said her mother would have to keep it together. Not make a scene. She thought we'd be more likely to get what we needed that way."

"Sounds reasonable," Sally said. "And Mimi had no idea at that time when her mother might be coming back, is that right?"

"That's what she said. Her . . . our . . . Audra was in the Amazon. She wasn't able to reach her by phone. We had to wait."

"What happened after that?"

For a moment it seemed like the room fell away. In a flash and for only an instant. Like everything in my entire field of vision got sucked into some cosmic vacuum cleaner, leaving me nothing to see but a milky expanse of emptiness. Then the next second everything was right back where it was before. Anderson had his pen poised over his notepad. Sally smiled that calm way she did. The clock on the wall was still behind that cage.

Anderson and Sally exchanged a look that told me this was why they'd invested all these hours with me.

"Go on," Sally said. "What happened with the rest of yesterday afternoon?"

I took a deep breath. Then I dived into the answer they already knew.

"Mimi left my apartment. Said she had some papers to fill out about her new job. We were going to meet the next day—today—for lunch. After she left I felt . . . I don't know. Scared, maybe. Alone. My father had been so brutal. I'd forced John away. I probably didn't even have my job anymore, not if Brian had anything to say about it. Everything in my life was disappearing and there wasn't one damned thing I could do about any of it. I tried to take a nap, but my mind was swirling with the realization that I'd soon be seeing my mother. What if she rejected me again? The thoughts came flying at me, and I couldn't shut

them off. I remember turning on the television, flipping through
the channels, hoping something would catch my attention and
help me focus on something else. I mean, who was I really? I
wasn't Sanford Kincaid's daughter. My mother sure didn't want
me, did she? I wasn't stupid enough to think Jasper would welcome me with open arms. It was like in all the world, I only had
me to rely on. And I didn't feel up to the job. There'd been so
many lies. And I had no control over what might happen next. I
was stuck in the middle of something that was enough to make
a person crazy."

"Or drive them to murder," Anderson offered.

"I told you, I don't know anything about that. Why don't
you believe me?"

Sally smiled that Cheshire cat smile of hers. The one that was
supposed to make me think all I had to do was tell my story and
everything would end well. "Let's keep going, Tess. What happened when all those thoughts were racing in your mind?"

I gave Anderson a tentative glance. I remember thinking there
were few things more futile than making a case in front of someone who already had their mind made up. I focused on Sally as
I spoke, hoping her steadiness would keep me from freaking out
long enough to let them hear my whole story.

"My head started to pound," I said. "I felt cold all over despite it being so damned hot in that apartment. I had to get out
of there. So I left. I walked out of my apartment. I don't think I
even turned off the television."

"Did you know where you were going?" Sally asked.

"I don't know. I don't think I did. Seems to me I just started
walking. Next thing I knew I was on campus."

"Did it feel like one continuous passage of time?" Sally in-
quired. "Were you aware of putting one foot in front of the
other? Or was it like the time you were driving and had no concept of how long you'd been out?"

I tried to imagine which option would hold me in better
stead.

"It wasn't like when I left my father's. I didn't lose any time.

But my body was on autopilot. My feet took me on the same walk I've taken hundreds of times. Maybe it was all done subconsciously, but once I realized I was on the campus, I figured I'd go talk to the one person who could relate to what I was going through. It takes one to know one, and all that. I imagined Mimi, despite that perky can-do attitude of hers, might be going through the same torture as me. So I went to the History Department looking for her."

"Did you find her?" Anderson asked.

"No. I didn't." I heard the tremble in my voice. My hands balled into fists on their own accord. I tucked them under my legs, but not fast enough for Anderson and Sally not to notice. My heart drummed so hard I was afraid it would bruise the inside of my chest.

"What *did* you find?" Anderson asked.

I looked him in the eye. This was it. If I could be brave enough to tell him what came next, I deserved to see his full reaction.

"They'd never heard of her." My heart pounded even harder once I spoke the words. "Not the person behind the information desk. Not the three people I encountered coming out of the faculty mailroom. Not even the dean's own assistant when I stormed into his office demanding to know what was going on. There was no professor taking a sabbatical. There'd been no job search. No one there had heard of Mimi Winslow, or any other PhD out of Tufts who studied the cultural impact of Barry Manilow."

"That must have been quite a blow," Sally said. "What did you do?"

"I couldn't believe it! Mimi came to Madison specifically to interview for the job. How could no one in the entire department not know her?"

"You're telling me what you were thinking, Tess." Sally's voice was firmer now. "Tell me what you did. What did you do after you realized Mimi's connection to the History Department was nonexistent?"

"Things came to my mind. The knife going missing in my kitchen. The commotion I heard behind the library. John disappearing from our lunch table and coming back a few seconds after I saw Mimi leave. Her posing as me with so many different people."

"*Do,* Tess. What did you *do?*"

Were they trying to pin me into a corner? Did they know something they weren't telling me?

"I don't remember what I did after that."

"That's bullshit!" Anderson yelled.

"Detective!" Sally yelled right back. "Simmer down."

He pointed a finger at me while he made his case to her. "Any three-year-old can put together their last twenty-four hours. I don't see any reason Tess here can't do the same."

"Because she's been traumatized, Detective!"

"Not as much as that body in the morgue!" Anderson showed no sign of backing down this time.

Sally held his gaze and said nothing. My own tension decreased as I watched her wait him out. Finally, he shook his head. When he spoke, his tone was calmer, but there was no mistaking his continued frustration.

"Tess," he said. "What *do* you remember after you learned Mimi hadn't come to Madison for a job interview?"

I looked at Sally. Her gentle eyes were encouraging as she nodded for me to continue.

"I remember walking. I had no idea what time it was. I walked down to University Avenue. A kid on a skateboard zoomed by me. I almost fell."

"When did you see Mimi next?" Sally asked.

"Everything was so crowded. Students standing on the corners, waiting for buses. Cars bumper to bumper. People talking and laughing. It was like I was there but wasn't. Like I was watching it all happening, and I was aware it was *my* ears hearing the noise. *My* eyes seeing the scene. But I felt apart from it all. Like it wasn't really happening. Does that make any sense?"

"It does."

"All I could think about was Mimi. She'd had so many details. Her office. Her plans to wow everyone so they'd ask her to stay on. Why would she do that?"

"So you kept walking?" Anderson asked.

I nodded. "Until I got to the Chazen Museum. That concrete patio in front of it seemed so clean. Quiet. Peaceful. I went over to one of the benches. I guess you could say I sat down, but it felt more like I collapsed. My legs didn't want to carry me anymore. I don't know how long I sat there. I was numb. After a while, there she was."

"Mimi?" Sally asked.

"Yes. Sitting next to me. Asking if I'd been by the History Department."

"She knew she'd been found out?" Anderson asked.

"She said she could tell from the look on my face. Started right in telling me she could explain everything. Begging me not to be pissed at her. Said she'd learned about my existence about a month earlier and needed to come find me."

"You didn't think it was weird?" Anderson asked. "Her showing up like that? It's a big campus. Even bigger town. It didn't dawn on you that something else might be happening to lead her to the very bench you decided to take a rest on?"

"No. It didn't. I was so lost. And Mimi always made a habit of showing up. So, no. I didn't think it was odd. I didn't think anything."

"How did she explain herself?" Sally asked. "How had she learned about you?"

"She said she'd been down at her mother's house in Coral Gables, looking for a faculty position. Working on her tan. Relaxing after finishing her dissertation and keeping an eye on the house while her mom was in the Amazon. She told me she spent one evening going through old photo albums. You know, pictures of her as a kid and stuff. She was putting the albums away and she saw a box deep in the back of her mom's closet. She looked through it and saw love letters from some guy she knew wasn't her father."

"From Jasper?" Anderson asked.

I nodded. "She told me she knew now, after all we'd learned, that the letters were from Jasper. According to her, the letters she found in her mother's closet were simply signed *Love, Me.* There were photos, too, she said. Pictures of her mother with a man. Mimi was in some of them, too. When she was a toddler. She said there was one photo where Jasper and her mother were playing with *two* toddlers. Two toddlers who looked to be about the same age. Mimi read the letters. Apparently Madison was mentioned. You know, *Love, Me* saying he can't wait to get down to Florida. How frigid it was in Madison and how nice the ocean breezes and palm trees must be. Stuff like that."

"She show you any of these letters?" Anderson asked. "Any of the photographs?"

"No, but she said a couple of times the guy wrote about his plans for when she was free. Mimi said one letter in particular talked about making a new life in Coral Gables with *both girls.*"

"Now I'm confused," Anderson said. "You're telling us Mimi knew who you were when she ran into you? Back in that bathroom at the hotel. She knew who you were?"

"No. She figured whoever wrote those letters had a kid of his own. That maybe there were plans to blend the families together. Mimi didn't know the details, but she said the more she read the letters and looked at the photographs, the more she became convinced that her mother was keeping a secret. But her mother was out in the jungle. There was no way to contact her."

"So she hops on a plane and goes to the town she read about in a thirty-year-old letter?" Anderson asked.

"If you knew Mimi the way I do, you'd have no problem believing that. She's the kind of person who seems to always know things are going to turn out fine for her. All she needs to do is take that first step. According to her, she didn't know what she should look for. She only knew she'd find it in Madison. Said she was as surprised as I was when she came out of that bathroom stall and saw me face-to-face. But to Mimi, it was proof that she was doing exactly what the universe wanted her to be doing."

"And her story about the faculty position?" Sally asked. "How did she explain that?"

"Like I said, she was surprised to find me standing right in front of her. Said she had no idea what kind of person I was, but she wondered if I was the other toddler in that picture of her mother and the man. So she lied. Made up the story on the spot, hoping to buy some time to get to know me. After a while she was in it too deep and had to keep the lie alive."

Detective Anderson kept his eyes on his notepad. I would have paid big money to know what he was thinking. I knew how preposterous the story sounded, and I was the one telling it.

"When did you decide to go back to Phillip Jasper's office?" Sally Normandy seemed to have no problem following my story. "I thought the original plan was to wait until her mother came to Madison and confront her together."

"I told Mimi I was sick of this whole thing. I was upset with her lying to me. I felt the pain of my mother's abandonment like it just happened. I was worried about Brian firing me because of Mimi's shenanigans. I'd been torturing my father . . . well, the man I've always thought of as my father . . . all to dig deeper into this chaos. I had broken John's heart. I wanted it all to end. I wanted the entire time since I met her to disappear, to erase itself from my memory banks so I could go back to my safe little life."

"But your life isn't safe, is it?" Sally was looking at my bruised face. "What did you and Mimi do next?"

I took a look around. I was in an interview room at the police station. I was answering questions about a murder. There was no other option but to press forward.

"We went to see Phillip Jasper."

CHAPTER 27

"Like I said, I wanted this whole flaming pile of crap to be done. Mimi said if I didn't want to wait and pull off the plan to confront Audra, the only other choice was to talk to Jasper. I told her I wouldn't. I was done and I meant it. But she took hold of my arm, held on tight, and told me I had no right. I couldn't walk away. We'd both been deceived. There was no way forward, at least in Mimi's mind, until all the cards were on the table and all the lies were ended. I argued with her, insisting the facts of my parentage meant nothing to me. But that was a lie and she knew it. She kept it up. Apologizing for her ruse. Swearing there'd be nothing but the truth between us from now on. She said she was going to see Jasper without me. I told her that was a mistake. That if it was going to happen, it was best if I went to see Jasper alone. We didn't know how he might handle the fact that the secret daughters of his affair now knew one another. Until we did, it was best for me to continue with what people in Madison knew me to be: a woman wanting to learn more about her mother. Keep everything simple. It took some convincing, but in the end she waited on a bench outside the biogenetics building and I went in alone."

"What time was this?" Anderson asked.

"It was a little before five o'clock," I said. "The same receptionist was on duty. I think I pissed her off, showing up so close to quitting time."

*   *   *

"Don't even bother unless you have an appointment," she said when I stood in front of her desk.

"My name is Tess Kincaid," I told her. "Call upstairs and tell whoever answers that Audra Kincaid's daughter is here to see Jasper. Tell them if Dr. Jasper finds out Audra's daughter was turned away at the gate, he'll be sorely disappointed."

I was counting on Jasper freaking when he learned one of Audra's twins was downstairs. He'd see me. If only to assess what kind of threat I was to him. I forced a smile as the receptionist reluctantly called upstairs.

"I have a Tess Kincaid here again to see Dr. Jasper." She shot me the evil eye and shifted her tone. "This time she says I'm supposed to tell you she's Audra Kincaid's daughter. Like that's supposed to mean something." Three seconds later the receptionist's face changed. She looked over my shoulder. "No," she said to whoever was on the other end of the line. "She's here by herself. Hold on, I'll ask." The receptionist gave me a pleasant look this time. "Is your mother with you?"

"No."

"Because your mother's name is on Dr. Jasper's Full Access list. That means if she was here you could go straight on up without needing to stop here."

I held on to the side of her desk to steady myself. My mother was on Jasper's list? Full Access? Was she still in contact with him after all these years? Was their affair continuing?

"No. Mom's not here with me today." The tone I was going for was nonchalance. "But she wanted me to talk to Phillip about something."

The receptionist hesitated for a moment, then repeated my lie into her mouthpiece. I held my breath and glanced over my shoulder at where a beefy security guard stood.

"Okay. You want to come down here and escort?" I heard the receptionist ask before she thanked whoever was listening and disconnected the call.

"Dr. Jasper will meet you on his floor." Skylar pointed to the bank of elevators across from her information station. "He's on seven."

I thanked her and made my way on wobbly legs to the bank of elevators. I pressed the call button, and sleek glass doors opened to reveal an empty car before I had time to speculate what it all meant that my mother's name was on Phillip Jasper's approved visitors' list. I stepped in and tapped the button that would take me to my destination. My stomach rumbled and my knees shook as the gleaming copper box lifting me upward slowed to a halt. A woman's soft voice, tinged with an aristo-cratic air, came over the cabin's speakers.

Floor seven. Have a wonderful day of discovery.

I smoothed a hand over the front of my white cotton sundress and suddenly wished I'd taken more care that morning. But I didn't have time to dwell on that particular self-criticism once the elevator doors opened. One man stood there. I watched the color drain from his face as I stepped forward.

"My God," he whispered. "You look exactly like her."

Phillip Jasper didn't need to introduce himself. Anyone who'd lived in Madison longer than a year would have seen his chiseled face in the paper at least a dozen times. Probably would have commented he was too handsome to be a scientist. His hair, graying in just the right spots, was too thick for him to have stressed over endless grant applications. His shoulders were too broad, his back too straight, to have spent a lifetime bent over a microscope. This man, wearing a tailored gray suit, blue dress shirt, and rose-colored tie, looked more corporate titan than bookish academic.

Jasper reached for my hand and scanned me from head to toe. "It's like a step back in time. Your hair . . ." He stopped himself and blinked . . . many times, as if his mind was facing input too overwhelming to handle. A moment later he must have realized he was a famous guy standing in an elevator foyer. He dropped my hand and pointed to his right.

"Please." He motioned down the sun-drenched hallway. "Let's talk in my office. We'll have some privacy there."

Jasper led me through his outer office, past a lovely-looking middle-aged woman seated behind a gleaming maple desk. I figured her for Jasper's executive assistant and wondered how long she'd been with him. Had she been my mother's immediate replacement? Did she adore the genius she worked for as much as my mother had?

Did she know all his secrets?

Jasper's personal space seemed larger in the daylight than it had when Mimi and I were there snooping through his files with only a desk lamp to light the room. Floor-to-ceiling windows formed the east and south walls, flooding the room with natural light and offering a postcard view of central campus and the capitol building in the distance. The remaining two walls were faced with granite. Each hosted an oversized abstract painting. One, at least six feet high and ten feet wide, was an explosion of reds and purples swirling in a chaotic dance that heightened my already significant anxiety. The other, slightly smaller but still of impressive size, was at least two dozen shades of green. It reminded me of a rain forest, or at least pictures I've seen of rain forests. It made me think of Mimi's mother . . . our mother . . . Audra . . . and the Amazon adventure she was currently enjoying, blissfully ignorant that her two daughters were about to expose her and her lover.

Jasper closed the door behind me and pointed toward the paintings.

"Do you remember these?" he asked.

What did he mean? Did he know Mimi and I had been there?

"Tell me what you see," he suggested.

I wasn't sure how to begin the conversation I was there to have and, in that instant, was grateful for the diversion. I stepped toward the smaller of the two gigantic paintings and gave it a second look. I liked the way the various greens shimmered and flowed into one another. The shadings were so subtle. The emphasis on texture rather than form.

A sensation tugged deep within me. First in my stomach, then at my throat. It was followed by a mental image. More flash than fully formed representation. Paint dripping over a large canvas spread across a concrete floor. Before my heart could beat again the image scattered like the blown-away sand of a mandala. It was replaced by a teasing snippet of music. A few notes. My brain screamed at me to name the song. But like the earlier image, the music slipped into oblivion before I could grab it.

Frustrated, I shifted my attention to the violent red and purple painting. The colors twisted into one another like a cyclone called forth by Satan himself. I felt an encroaching presence of rage, yet despite that emotion being my near constant companion, I knew the anger I felt didn't belong to me. It was the artist's alone. I wondered if Jasper, a scientist of global importance, mounted the two paintings as a type of experiment. One designed to provoke whoever visited his offices. Did he use them to gain a fuller understanding of his guests' psyches, thereby giving him an upper hand?

I turned back to the green painting, and my sense of the artist's rage disappeared. As my eyes traced the gentle melting of colors, the music teasing my memory came back to me. This time it was a piano crescendo. Nearly enough to make me think I knew what note came next. A melodic tease hinting that I'd know the song if I would only start singing.

Then, once again, it disappeared, replaced by a visual flash in my mind. A thin figure, viewed from behind. Wearing shorts. Tanned legs streaked with paint. Feet dancing to music I could no longer hear. Then laughter. Not mine, but somehow offered for my enjoyment.

Then that vanished, too.

"My mother." I pointed to the large green abstract. "My mother painted this."

"She did. As a present for my birthday." A sadness came over Jasper's handsome face, and he suddenly looked a decade older than the urbane man who'd escorted me into his office. "It couldn't have been more than a year after she came to work with me. That was a very long time ago. Before you were even born."

I nodded toward the larger painting. "Did she paint that one, too?"

He nodded. "Years later. This one wasn't a gift. I commissioned it. Your mother had tremendous artistic promise. I always feared she'd leave our work here to pursue formal training in New York or Chicago." He paused. "As it turned out, she left for a totally different reason, didn't she?"

Jasper turned to stare at the red and purple extravaganza. He appeared to be lost in painful reminiscence. For a moment I almost felt sorry for him.

He snapped out of his reverie and addressed me in a kind tone. "I've often wondered what became of you. You were such a charming little girl." He pointed toward the large green canvas. "And even as a child, you always admired that painting. I remember once you told me you wanted to go there, to whatever place your mother's painting conjured in your mind. You said you were going to visit all the pretty birds living there."

I had spent so many years actively trying to forget anything associated with my mother. But for the sake of my mission, I forced myself into that long-abandoned territory.

"She brought me to the office sometimes," I said. "Not here. The old place."

"Yes," Jasper said. "We were in the building on old University when your mother and I worked together. There'd been so many long days and weekends that I needed your mother's help, and she was always kind enough to indulge me. Your father was often away from home. Building his own career at the law school. She never seemed to mind the time away from home until after you were born. She made it clear if I wanted her here extended hours, she'd be bringing you. I never minded. You would play or read so sweetly while your mother and I worked. Audra hated the travel our work demanded. She never wanted to be away from her child one moment longer than absolutely necessary."

His words were crumbs of bread dropping from a table to a starving dog below. I'd spent so long pretending I didn't need the woman who'd abandoned me. After so many years fighting to forget, I now ached to remember.

An object took shape in my mind. A small pink suitcase with bright orange flowers. Filled with dolls and coloring books.

"I had a toy kit," I whispered.

"Indeed, you did. A small rolling thing. We'd set you up at a desk, supply you with sandwiches and, if I'm recalling correctly, a bottle of orange soda. I remember being quite impressed at your ability to focus. You were so bright. I had you tested here in our lab. Your IQ was nearly two standard deviations above the mean. You were reading chapter books by your fifth birthday."

"You and my mother were friends. More than coworkers."

Once again Jasper's eyes took on the look of someone lost in another time. "I considered Audra the dearest of companions. She believed in me. If it weren't for her, this building wouldn't exist. All the advancements we've made over the past decades were born from the work she and I did when I was a young researcher. She encouraged me. Stood shoulder to shoulder with me when more senior faculty branded my research as nothing more than fantasy." He was quiet for nearly a minute. I heard the pain in his voice when he spoke again. "I've missed her terribly."

I recognized an opening. "Tell me about that. Your work with my mother, I mean."

"She doesn't speak of our time together?"

"I haven't seen my mother since the day she left."

Phillip Jasper stutter-stepped back. "She didn't take you with her? All these years . . . I thought . . . I assumed . . . Where is she?"

"I don't have a clue," I lied. I didn't feel the need to tell him my mother was off to the Amazon. Still interested in science. Still looking for adventure. "That's why I'm here. I appreciate you taking the time to meet. It's been me and my dad alone all this time. As you can imagine, he doesn't like to talk about her much. I'd love to know more about what my mother was like before . . . before she left."

"How is Sandy?" Jasper's voice took on a chilled edge. "I must say I wasn't surprised when he lost his position at the law school. Your mother told me often how hard he worked. But endless hours of mediocre work is still mediocre work. Your mother was deserving of a better future than your father could ever offer her."

"Neither one of us deserved to be tossed aside like yesterday's garbage."

Jasper took one step toward me. His eyes were pools of remorse. "Of course, of course. Forgive my crude remark. I don't for one moment underestimate the pain you've experienced. Leaving your father is one thing. It happens in adult relationships. But to leave you. That was something I would never have predicted."

"Tell me what you were working on back in those days." I dug my fingers into my palms to keep from raging against Jasper's pompous evaluations of my family. "I'd love to know more about my mother's time here."

"She was the soul of my work. My muse. My inspiration."

I clenched my fists tighter. I needed him to keep talking. Mimi and I had to get some sort of hard evidence of Jasper's involvement with all this. Where it would lead, I had no idea at that moment. The whole mess was like a rotten onion revealing itself one stinking layer at a time.

Jasper went to his desk and pulled a black velvet pouch from the back of the bottom drawer. Mimi had checked there. I don't know how she missed the pouch. "I can't tell you how many times I've told myself to throw these away. I never seem to be able to do it." He shook the pouch's contents free. Dozens of photographs rained down onto the shiny surface. "Here. Think of these as a small chronicle of your mother's and my time together."

Jasper stepped away and took a seat on a low, black leather sofa across the room. I got the impression he was inviting me to take time with the photographs. He settled in. Like the only thing he had to do in the world was to look at me and answer whatever questions I had.

Until the day before, I hadn't seen a picture of my mother in over fifteen years. It seemed now I was surrounded by them. The woman in the first photo I picked up, striking a pose beside what was obviously a laboratory table, could have been me in my early twenties. Her hair, her face, the way her eyes crinkled as she smiled and laid a hand identical to mine on the eyepiece of a microscope. All were near mirror images of myself.

I watched my mother age as I sifted through the photographs. Her hairstyle changed. Her clothing became more tailored. I wondered if her mode of dress became more sophisticated as Jasper's position changed. An assistant working in a newly hired assistant professor's lab could get away with jeans and T-shirts, but a colleague to a faculty member bringing in millions of dollars in grant money would need to present herself in a more professional manner. I even felt the stir of memory with one of her ensembles. A form-fitting knit skirt and sweater combination. Pale blue with white accents at collar and cuffs. I held it up toward Jasper.

"I remember this outfit," I said. "I thought she looked so pretty in it."

I laid the photo aside and scanned the pile. There were several images of my mother, looking to be the age she was when she left us, smiling for the camera. I picked up one that riveted my attention. In it, my mother leaned against the fender of a car. She wore a heavy winter coat. Snow was piled on the car's hood. I could almost feel the chilled air as I looked into my mother's laughing eyes.

And I was there, too. In the picture, about two years old, wearing a bright pink snowsuit with bunny ears, nestled in my mother's arms.

"You took photographs of my mother and me?" I asked.

"She brought you to work often."

I looked back to the two giant abstracts on Jasper's wall.

"Why would I come to work with her so much? Why did you take all these pictures?"

"Your mother was very special to me," Jasper explained. "It was a wonderful time in my life."

"I don't know what to say." I stared at the man who held secrets Mimi and I had every right to know.

"Ask me anything, Tess. You're a grown woman now. You deserve however much of the truth you want to handle."

"You and my mother were close."

He looked away, like he was shocked at my bluntness. Maybe he was choosing his words.

"We were," he finally said. "As were you and I, Tess."

Snippets came to my consciousness. Sitting at my mother's desk, printing out my spelling words while she and Jasper worked.

"You taught me how to use a microscope," I said.

He smiled. "You remember that? You told me a certain fungus slide looked like a fairyland tree. I'll never forget that." He paused. When he spoke again, there was a sadness in his voice. "And you say you never hear from your mother?"

"No. Not since she left."

"No idea where she might be living?"

"No." I hoped I was a convincing liar. "No idea at all."

"I'm sorry I made the assumption Audra had taken you with her. Had I known you were here, I would have . . . I don't know what I would have done. Or could have done, for that matter."

"You and my mother had an affair."

Phillip Jasper's face drained of color. He leaned back against the sofa, his breath shallow and rapid. "Your father told you that?"

"No. I've recently discovered letters. Photographs. Souvenirs from your travels." I didn't tell him they were from his own stash. "The two of you were in love."

He stayed silent for several minutes.

"The strain of life with your father had become unbearable," Jasper finally said. "His drinking, his anger, his total yet ineffective focus on work. Audra was miserable. We grew closer. Soon we were in love. We tried to hide it, of course, but there came the point when we no longer wanted to hide what we'd become to one another. I'd been awarded a sizeable grant. Several universities contacted me about relocating. It was a perfect time for us to break free and forge a new life. It was your mother who chose our new home. We planned to accept the very generous offer the University of Colorado made us."

"She planned to leave my father?"

"She did. We'd build a life together in Boulder." His voice was low and soft, as though he was describing a dream he wished would come to him every night.

"What happened?"

His expression changed. The muscles around his jaw tightened. "She discovered she was pregnant." He looked toward the giant red and purple canvas, staring at it for several long moments. "Timing is everything, isn't it, Tess? Had we been living in today's world, no one would bat an eye at the sight of a divorced pregnant woman. But thirty years ago? That was quite another story. Despite my pleas, your mother refused to leave your father while she was carrying you."

"Did you ever question the paternity of that pregnancy?"

The question tripped something in Jasper. He looked at me with an appraising eye.

"No, Tess, I didn't."

"Why not?" I pressed on despite my concerns. "I mean, the affair, it could be possible, right?"

He again held my gaze for several heartbeats before speaking. "There's no need to get into the details of my certainty."

I nodded and moved on.

"Did the two of you maintain your relationship? Do you still? Does she come to Madison to visit? Is that why you have her on some special no-questions-asked list?"

"Your mother's always been on that list. I want her to be free to return to me at any moment."

"Maybe this is too painful for you to discuss."

He took a deep breath. "The thought of your mother is always with me. Painful? Sometimes. But not at the moment. I never thought I'd ever speak of her again. At least not of the special tenderness we had for one another. Now you're here. Someone who loved her as much as I. In a way it's quite lovely to be able to speak openly about her."

"So you two *did* continue to be together after she became pregnant. Despite her decision to stay in her marriage." I could feel my rage rising. Like a wave far offshore. A surging swell threatening to build to a tsunami. Destroying everything in its path. Jasper and Audra used my father. Allowed him to become excited about a pregnancy he thought was conceived with a woman who loved only him. Never allowing him the opportunity to agree or disagree with his wife's decision to carry her lover's twins. Never granting him input as they foisted onto him the responsibility of raising one of their bastard daughters. I pushed my back deep into the cushions of the chair and focused on keeping my body calm.

"Our love was as strong as ever," Jasper continued. "And we were involved in laying the groundwork of research that would change. . . ." He seemed to struggle for the right word. "Well, it would change everything, wouldn't it? Your mother was a full partner here. I don't want you to think for one moment, Tess, that I've forgotten all your mother has done for science."

"I don't think I'll *ever* be able to forget what she's done."

Jasper gave me a look. Like he was waiting for me to say something else. I put on my best poker face. Maybe he was satisfied as he sized me up. Maybe he was playing with me. Whatever he was thinking, he didn't press the issue.

"Your mother was in the lab when she discovered she was going into labor. I was as excited as she. Hoping that once she'd given birth she'd feel strong enough to leave your father. I grabbed my keys, ready to stand beside her every step of the way." His eyes got that faraway look again. "But she insisted I have nothing to do with the birth. Asked me to drive her home. Sandy would be the one to take her to the hospital."

"And after I was born, was it back to normal for you two lovebirds?"

"Please don't do that, Tess. Don't let bitterness or anger infiltrate your memory. This wasn't a tawdry office dalliance. What your mother and I had was strong and real."

"Then why aren't you my stepfather?"

Jasper stood. He crossed the room and pulled a bottle of water from a small refrigerator hidden behind a cabinet door, then offered me one. When I declined, he stepped to the window overlooking campus. He stayed there, his back to me for several minutes while he sipped his water and focused on the activities seven stories below. Then he turned and resumed his spot on the sofa.

"Your birth changed your mother. She stayed away from the lab. I tried repeatedly to contact her. But she seemed interested only in you. She demanded I stay away. Told me she was done with our research, despite our having still so much to learn. She said she wanted to make a go of it as a mother. Try to salvage what she could of her marriage. I suggested the strain of fatherhood might make Sandy even less available to her. I went so far as to question whether she and her child could ever be truly safe with a man like him." He paused. "Your father's temper was well known. I'm sure it's one of the reasons he was never considered for tenure." Jasper pointed toward my cheek. "And the evidence suggests time hasn't mellowed the bastard."

"Don't speak of my father. You have no knowledge of what he's experienced. You and my mother made decisions that changed his life. Broke his heart. That wasn't fair. I'll not have you disparage him."

Jasper's eyes softened. "I understand. I apologize."

"Tell me what happened next."

"I didn't see your mother for nearly a year. I was driven frantic at the idea I'd lost her. Then one day your father dropped by. Invited me to your home. He, of course, had no idea of how Audra and I felt about one another. I can see now how cruel that was. But I accepted his invitation. Not to humiliate your father, but to see Audra again. And I was eager to see you, too. I went to your home, thrilled to be in her presence again. Ecstatic to finally meet you. Your mother and I talked. Alone. Away from your father. She agreed to come back. At first it was for the work. We had important projects to continue. She told me she wanted to be part of it all again. But her return would be predicated on the work alone. She insisted there could be no further personal relationship. I was devastated by that condition. But I'd have agreed to anything she asked. To be able to see her daily. Hear her voice. I was ready to settle for whatever dust she was willing to provide."

"That boundary didn't last long, did it?"

"No. Not long at all. She came back to work and we discovered the bond we shared was too powerful. She was back in my life. My arms. My heart. I was happy again. Watching you grow was a large part of that happiness. Those were the most jubilant years of my life."

"But it ended."

Jasper shook his head. "For reasons I will never understand, everything collapsed. In one heartbeat all my joy evaporated. Your mother came to me one afternoon, more upset than I'd ever seen her. Marks across her face very similar to the ones you're wearing now. Sandy had learned of our affair. Audra announced she was leaving me. Leaving our work. I tried to convince her, of course. I urged her to go to the police. I told her we'd face Sandy's anger together. She refused. That's when your mother informed me she was leaving your father as well. She was determined to build a new life. Despite all my pleadings, she stood firm, insisting I'd never see her again."

"And you haven't?" I asked.

"Audra turned her back to me and walked out of my office." Jasper's voice was a soft whisper. "I haven't seen her since."

"What did you do then?" I asked.

"My career was all I had left. I buried myself in my work. I became successful, the leader in my field. But every accolade, every honor, is cold comfort for the loss of your mother. If abandoning my work would have kept Audra in my life, I would have gladly made that trade."

He was lying. I don't know how I knew it, but I was certain. After all these years he was clinging to whatever sham he and my mother had put in place so long ago. All in the name of saving his precious career. I wanted to hit him. Wipe that smug veil of academic superiority right off his face. He'd manipulated my mother. The two of them had conspired to humiliate my father. At that moment I wanted nothing more than to make Phillip Jasper hurt. As my rage intensified, I wasn't sure I'd be able to control it.

So I did what Jasper said my mother had done all those years ago. It was either that or lose myself to my wrath. I struggled to keep my voice steady, thanked him for his time, turned my back to him, and walked out.

My heart was racing from retelling what had happened in Jasper's office, but Sally and Detective Anderson looked calm and collected in their government-issued chairs.

"Then what happened?" Sally asked.

"I needed to be alone. To get rid of all the fury that was pounding in me."

"Where did you go?" Anderson asked.

"I don't remember."

"Did you meet up with Mimi?"

"I don't know. Maybe."

"Did the two of you get together to debrief?"

"I don't remember!"

I started to shake. First my shoulders. Then my legs. I was suddenly quite cold. "I don't know what happened next!" I turned toward Sally. "It was like you asked me before. About losing time, I mean. One moment I was walking out of Jasper's office and the next I was sitting in the living room of my apartment. Today. Wearing different clothes. Feeling hungry. Hearing loud knocking at my front door."

"Those would be the police officers who brought you here?" Anderson asked.

I nodded.

"So Mimi just shows up in your life one day, practically moves in with you. But you can't tell us what you know about this murder?"

"I don't know anything! I've told you a hundred times! I don't know anything!" I fought back tears of frustration and turned to Sally. "I've been doing exactly what you've asked of me. Telling you the whole story. Details. Every tiny one of them. Step by step. Just like you wanted."

Sally Normandy reached across the table and put a gentle hand on my arm. "It's okay, Tess. I think we have a pretty good idea of what's happening here."

"And it all adds up to you knowing exactly how that body got in that marsh," Anderson said.

"No!" I pounded my fist on the table hard enough that Sally and Anderson reared back.

"Quite the temper you've got there, Tess," Anderson said.

My hands shook. I buried them in my lap and looked away.

"You mind if we bring someone in here for a minute?" Anderson asked. "I could do it behind the mirror, but it might speed things along if you hear for yourself what this person has to say."

Was this someone they had in one of the other rooms? Someone saying things about what happened? Trying to trip me up?

"Who is it?" I asked.

"Do you have any objection to someone coming in?" Anderson asked again. "Yes or no."

Sally turned toward me. "It can't hurt, Tess. In fact, I think Andy's right. I think this will help things."

"If it gets me home sooner, I'm all for it."

Anderson opened the door, leaned out, and waved. "You wanna come in here? Please?"

He stood aside and a young woman entered. She looked tired and maybe a bit afraid. It took a second for me to recognize her under the harsh lights of the interrogation room. She was the receptionist from Phillip Jasper's building. A moment later her name popped into my brain. Skylar. She looked at me, then away.

"Is this the woman you helped?" Anderson asked.

Skylar nodded. "It's her."

"How many times did you see her come into your building?"

"Twice. First a couple of days ago. Then again yesterday. Right as I was about to head home for the day."

"You notice anything out of the ordinary when you spoke to her?" Anderson asked.

She hesitated. "Well, it's awfully hard to get an appointment with Dr. Jasper. She didn't have one." Skylar looked on the verge of tears. "But she came in all bossy. Forced me to call upstairs."

"I didn't force anyone," I said.

"Not *forced*," Skylar amended. "She didn't touch me or anything like that. But she wasn't going to leave unless I called. I could tell that much."

"What happened?" Anderson asked.

"The first time, you mean? I called upstairs. Of course she wasn't cleared to see Dr. Jasper. I told her, then I sent her home. But the second time she came in really demanding. She made me . . . well, she didn't *make* me . . . she told me to call upstairs and tell them who she was. I guess she was right. It worked. Dr. Jasper's people said to send her on up."

"You told an officer earlier that you kept an eye out for security when Ms. Kincaid came by that first time. Why's that?"

Skylar alternated pained glances between Anderson and Sally. "Well . . ."

"Go ahead," Sally said. "Say what you need to."

Skylar looked at me with apologetic eyes. "Well, she talked about herself in plural. Using the word *we*. I thought that was pretty odd. She waited before answering me sometimes. Looking at something. I don't know how else to describe it."

"I was looking at Mimi! And of course I used the term *we*. *We* were standing right there."

Skylar took a step back. "Can I go?"

Anderson escorted her to the door. "Thank you for your statement, Skylar. And your patience. If we need anything more, we'll call you."

He closed the door behind her.

"Is there anything you'd like to change about your story?" Anderson asked.

Skylar did nothing more than confirm what I'd already told them. "No."

Anderson and Sally exchanged another one of their cryptic looks. Then she reached for the laptop.

"You said you and Mimi broke into Jasper's office. You found the cache of letters and photos proving their long affair." She keyed instructions while she spoke.

"We didn't technically break in. I told you we hid in the restroom until everyone went home."

"That's right," she said. "That was probably your best move. Security in that building is state of the art."

"I can give back all the stuff if you want."

Sally turned the laptop around so I could view the screen. "We called for copies of the security cameras' digital recordings. Here's your first visit." She pressed a key, and the screen displayed the interior of the biogenetics building. The angle suggested that the camera was mounted high. The scene was an overhead shot of the reception desk. There was no audio. I first saw Skylar smiling and handing identification badges to three men in suits. Then she pointed to her left. The men walked off in the direction she indicated. She busied herself with something on her desk.

A few seconds later I saw myself walk up to her desk, wearing the clothes I wore on Mimi's and my first visit. I watched an image of myself lean against the reception desk. I saw Skyler shake her head. Then I saw a quizzical look on her face, followed by her looking over my shoulder. Finally, she picked up the phone. I saw on the screen the same assured facial expression when whoever was on the other end of the line told her to send us away.

Then I saw myself turn around and walk out of the camera's range.

"Where's Mimi?" Anderson asked.

"Out of the frame, I guess."

Sally spun the laptop around and entered another series of commands before turning the screen back for my review.

"Here's later that same day. Different camera. Tell me what you see."

I saw again the interior of the biogenetics lobby but without the hustle and bustle of a busy academic arena that was present in the first scene. This time the camera gave an overhead shot of a long, empty corridor. A few seconds later I saw myself emerge from a door.

"That's me coming out of the bathroom. Just like I told you."

"Keep watching," Anderson said.

I leaned forward. I saw myself stand next to the closed door, looking up and down the wide hallway. I watched myself take a few hesitant steps forward, stop, then look back over my shoulder before hurrying out of the frame.

"I'll ask you again," Anderson said. "Where's Mimi?"

I opened my mouth and gulped in air. "This is a trick. You've done something to the picture. Photoshop or something. She was right there. You can tell. When I stopped. I was waiting for her."

"The bathroom door didn't open again," Anderson said. "Mimi, what? Walked through the wall?"

"She was right there!" I pounded my fist against the table again. This time neither of them flinched. "You've done something. I don't know what or how. You're making this look like something it wasn't!"

"Calm down, Tess." Sally pulled the computer toward her again. "Take a few deep breaths for me, will you?"

I tried, but still my breathing came in gasps.

"Slower." Sally's suggestion was silky calm. "I know this is difficult, but what you need to do right now is relax. Breathe . . . Steady . . . Easy."

With each word I felt more of my tension subside. Sally was a woman who knew how to use her voice. Moments later my chest rose and fell in a gentle and even pattern.

"That's much better." Sally's words were a warm blanket. "You have nothing to worry about, Tess. Everyone here is trying to understand the best way to help you. Do you believe that?"

In that moment I did. That's how convincing she was.

"Can you do something else for me?" she asked. "Can you close your eyes?"

I shook my head.

"You need to relax, Tess. The best way to do that is to shut out all distractions and focus your full attention on the sound of my voice. Can you do that?"

My entire body grew warm from the gentleness of her words. I decided to trust, closed my eyes, and concentrated on Sally. I felt myself being pulled away from the fear and tension I'd carried since I entered the police station. Her words directed me. Starting at the top of my head, she bid my body to relax. First my face. Then my shoulders. With soft words delivered at a steady cadence, she urged my muscles to smooth out and grow heavy. She moved on to my arms and my legs. In less than five minutes, Sally transformed me from a taut bundle of apprehension and fear into someone who had nothing better to do in all the world but float along and enjoy the very pleasant sensation of my warm and heavy body.

"Now, Tess. I want you to continue to breathe. Let your breath find and maintain its own natural rhythm. If your mind wanders, that's okay. That's what minds do. Don't judge your thoughts. Don't filter or stop them. Follow wherever your mind and memory lead you. Be like a curious puppy. Follow the trail of images, feelings, and thoughts with an open sense of wonder."

At that moment I would have been perfectly fine with whatever she suggested. It felt that good to finally be at peace.

"I'm going to play some music now, Tess. As you sit there so relaxed, so calm, I want you to listen. Focus your full attention on the sounds."

I heard the tapping of keys on her laptop. A few seconds later

I heard whistling come through the speakers. It was a pleasant tune. Vaguely familiar. Then I heard a man singing. Midrange and agreeable.

You know I can't smile without you.

"Follow the tune, Tess." Sally continued to use that gentle, hypnotic cadence. "Tell me where this music is taking you."

"I know the words," I said.

"Because you know the song," she said. "Are any images coming to mind?"

My brain floated along with the tune. Quick glimpses of visions I couldn't bring into focus came and went.

"I can't catch them."

"That's okay, Tess. You're doing great. Continue listening to the music."

I can't laugh and I can't sing. I'm finding it hard to do anything.

That line brought another sound to my mind. A woman's laughter. Then another image. This one lingered.

"I'm with my mother. We're wrapping a present. A Valentine's Day gift for my teacher."

"Very good, Tess." The song kept playing. "Is your mother saying anything?"

"She's joking about how many heart-covered mugs my teacher will get." My own voice sounded different to me. Younger somehow. "Mom's saying my gift will be different."

"What did you give your teacher? What present are you wrapping?"

I strained to pull the mental image closer. "I don't know. I can't . . . It's a pair of mittens. We got my teacher a pair of pink mittens."

"Good job." The song disappeared, and I again heard keyboard keys click. "Let's try another one. Focus on this tune and tell me where it takes you."

I heard a piano playing a classical piece. Deep and brooding. My shoulders tightened. My hands squeezed the arms of the chair. The piano lumbered on. My breathing accelerated. Rapid and shallow. After a while a man's voice accompanied the instrument.

Spirit move me . . .

The man kept singing. I rocked back and forth in my seat.

. . . Whirling like a cyclone in my mind.

My eyes shot open. "Turn it off! Stop it!" I jumped out of my chair. "Stop it!"

Anderson was on his feet, moving toward me. I lurched back, knocking over my chair and nearly falling. I stumbled into the corner, sliding down the wall into a crouch.

Hot tears spilled down my cheeks. "Stop it! Stop hurting Mommy . . ."

CHAPTER 28

"You're okay, Tess." Sally Normandy hurried over to kneel beside me. "You're safe." She wrapped her arms around me, rocking back and forth, murmuring I had nothing to fear. "Take deep breaths. You're going to be all right."

My gasps were short and frantic. I wondered if anyone had ever choked on their own tears. Sally's hair brushed my cheek. She smelled like a vanilla cupcake fresh out of the oven. I heaved a giant sigh, then let my lungs fill with air. I wanted to freeze that moment. Let this kind woman wrap me in her assurance that all would be well. But I knew this night wasn't over. In a very real sense the interview was only beginning. I looked up past Sally's shoulder and saw Detective Anderson standing over us, hands on his hips. The harsh overhead light made the scowl on his face all the more sinister.

"What's wrong with me? Am I . . . *crazy?*" I asked that same question several times before I pushed myself away from Sally's embrace, edged farther back into the corner, and wiped the tears off my face with shaking hands. "Is . . . is that what's happening to me?"

Sally laid her warm hand on mine. "No, Tess. You're not crazy."

I looked up at Anderson. "Do . . . do you think I am?"

He stared down at me for too long. He gave Sally a tired look, then glanced at the wall with the one-way mirror before bringing his attention back to me. "I deal with crimes and clues. I leave crazy for people with alphabet soup after their names."

"Come on, Tess." Sally stood and reached out to me. "Stand up. Let's get you back in a chair. You'll be more comfortable."

I shook my head, pulled my knees up to my chest, locked my arms around them, and jammed myself as tightly as I could into that corner. I swayed, tapping each shoulder to the wall. First my right, then my left. Again and again. I stared out into the room, not allowing my eyes to focus on any one object. I brought all my attention to the moment each shoulder touched the wall.

"Stop!" I yelled out each time my flesh met cinder block. "Stop! Stop! Stop!"

"What now?" Anderson asked Sally. "You got her locked into some kind of mental breakdown or something?"

"Stop . . . Stop . . ." I wasn't yelling anymore, but I stayed fixated on my command. My voice sounded so very far away. My mind seemed shattered. Part of it was dedicated to my incessant chant. Another part wondered how long I could last. Still another was detached from the entire scene, monitoring what was going on with an aloof lack of concern.

"Tess! Listen to me." Sally's voice was firm now. "I'm going to touch you. Tell me where you feel me touching you."

She bent down and laid her hand on me.

"Come back to your body, Tess. Come back to this moment," Sally commanded. "Focus. Tell me where you feel my hand."

My chest burned with the strain of breathing. "M . . . my . . . my arm."

"Where on your arm?"

My head lolled back against the wall. I closed my eyes.

"Where on your arm, Tess? Focus. Where am I touching you?"

"By my wrist," I whispered.

"Very good. Keep breathing. Stay in your body, Tess. Tell me where you are right now."

I couldn't grasp what she wanted. Should I tell her I was in the corner, protecting myself from whatever might come next? Or did she want to know my memories? Did she mean for me to inform her of all the images flooding into my consciousness? I opened my eyes, blinked away the tears, and looked at her.

"I'm in the police station. You're a psychologist." I looked up at Andy Anderson. "And you're a detective. You want to blame me for something I didn't do." A fresh wave of tears dripped down my cheeks. I didn't bother to wipe them away. "You want to trip me up. Lock me away."

"No one's here to hurt you, Tess." Sally stood, again offering me her hand. "I understand what's going on, and I promise you no harm will come to you. Can you come sit? Fill us in on what's left for us to understand?"

Her voice was gentle. But it inspired the kind of confidence that made me want to please her. I remember thinking she was probably very good at what she did. I stumbled to my feet. Sally was there to steady me as I walked to my chair. Anderson had already resumed his position across the table.

"We finally got preliminary DNA testing back," he said. "You want to confirm whose body it is the boy found under those rocks?"

I wanted to scream. Tell him again it was all Mimi's fault. But I didn't have the energy. Besides, it would do me no good. They didn't believe in Mimi.

I started rocking again. I ran my hands up and down my arms, shivering as though I was stranded in a snowstorm. I started humming an old Barry Manilow tune. The one about how he was the guy who wrote all the songs.

"Is she going off again?" Anderson asked Sally. "Should you maybe give her some medication or something?"

"She's protecting herself." Sally kept her eyes on me while she answered him. "Give her time."

"I've given her all damned night. Maybe it's time to admit this isn't working."

"There's no *working* here, Detective. Tess has spent years

shielding herself from something unspeakable. Her defenses have kept her safe for a long time. Now they're crumbling. She's terrified."

Anderson ran a hand over his buzz cut and sighed. I expected him to start yelling, but when he spoke he sounded resigned.

"You seem to have all the answers," he said. "You ask her. See how far you get."

Sally gave me a subtle smile. As if she was letting me know it was okay to tell her whatever it was I wanted to say.

"It must have been very upsetting to hear the body had been found." She reached to the side and picked up a small evidence bag. She held it for me to see. "Can you tell me now who this necklace belongs to?"

I stared at the golden chain with the small engraved charm. I reached out, withdrawing my hand before it could touch the plastic encasing it.

"You know who this belongs to, don't you?"

I sucked my lower lip into my mouth. A sound, high pitched and piercing, escaped me. Like an overfilled balloon slowly leaking air. I pulled my eyes away from the necklace and looked into Sally's.

"Tell me, Tess. Whose necklace is this?"

My mouth opened and the piercing wail stopped. My lips smacked open a few times, but no sound emerged. Until, finally, I heard my own voice.

"That's my mother's necklace." I huffed out another sound, this one short and primal. "My mother wore that always. To keep me near her."

"For the record, are you telling us the body recovered from the marsh is that of your mother?" Anderson's tone was all business. "Audra Winslow Kincaid?"

I kept my eyes on Sally. She nodded her encouragement.

"Yes," I whimpered after I uttered the word. Then my shoulders heaved and my left leg began to bounce.

"How do you know that?" Anderson asked.

I looked away. My legs calmed. My breathing settled.

THE WRONG SISTER   239

"Stay with us, Tess," Sally directed. "Don't go away. You have nothing to fear. I'm right here beside you."

I brought my attention back to her. Her face was soft. She looked like one of those pictures you see of Princess Grace. Where her face is so filled with love, you know she's got to be one of the kindest people who ever lived. That's how Sally Normandy looked.

I shook my head and said nothing.

"Were you there, Tess?" Sally asked. "Were you there when your mother was put under those rocks?"

I moved. It was slight, more tic than full nod, but they were each watching me so closely it was enough.

CHAPTER 29

"I'm afraid I have to ask you more questions." The kindness remained in Sally's voice. She pushed the box of tissues toward me and waited while I wiped an ugly mixture of tears, saliva, and snot off my face. "I know it's hard. I'm hoping you'll trust me when I tell you everything is going to be all right. No one can hurt you anymore."

I tightened my grip on the arms of my chair and looked toward Anderson. "He wants to hurt me. He wants to blame me for something I didn't do."

"For the love of . . ." Anderson sounded exhausted.

"You're frightening her," Sally told him. "Maybe it's better if you stand against the wall. You might not seem so looming a presence."

I could tell he wanted to be the one pressing me for details. But he sighed, waved his hands in an exasperated *whatever* way, and walked over to the corner. Sally waited a few moments. I focused on calming my breathing.

"You said Phillip Jasper saw a bruise across your mother's face the last time he saw her."

I looked down at my hands. "When my mother was at his office to tell him she was leaving."

"Do you know how your mother came to have that bruise?" Sally asked.

I kept my focus on a small red blotch on my right thumb. Where did that come from? Was it a pimple? A cut?

"Tess, stay with me. Do you know how your mother got her bruise?"

I forced my mouth to open. One tiny aperture. "He hit her," I whispered.

"Who?"

I traced my left thumb over the red spot. Was it ink? Had I been making a sign at work?

"Don't drift away, Tess. Who hit your mother?"

I raised my face to meet hers. "My father." The encouragement her eyes telegraphed gave volume to my voice. "My father hit my mother. Many times. Not just that day. But on that day I was afraid he'd never stop."

"You saw it?"

I nodded. My voice was barely a whisper. "It was my fault."

"What was?"

"He was doing it for me. My father was beating my mother because of what I told him."

Sally looked over to where Anderson stood. I turned my attention toward him as well. "He hurt her because of me. Is *that* what you're waiting for? You win! You tripped me up! My father hurt my mother, and it was all my fault."

I began to sob. I choked on my own tears and gasped for air. Anderson and Sally remained silent. Eventually my fury exhausted itself. I felt hot and weak. I swallowed hard and shivered despite feeling as if the temperature in the room had been raised twenty degrees.

"You were twelve years old." Sally waited until my last tear fell before speaking. "Help us understand how you could have made your father beat your mother."

I took a tissue and swiped it across my face in three rough moves. I was surprised at how coarse my voice sounded when I spoke.

"I saw them."

"Your father and mother?" Sally asked. "You saw them fighting?"

I shook my head. "My mother and Phillip Jasper. I saw them together."

Sally remained in her pose of understanding. "In an embrace?"

I nodded.

"Was this the first you knew of their relationship?"

I nodded again.

"Did they see you?"

"No." My voice was louder than it should have been. I forced it to a lower volume. "No, they didn't. I was supposed to be at school. But there had been a fire drill. All the students were out on the lawn. Fire trucks came. Kids started walking away from the schoolyard in all the commotion. I left, too. I was hungry. My lunch box was in my locker, and those firemen weren't letting anybody back in."

"So you headed home? Your mother and Jasper were there?"

I shook my head. "The weather was warm. I don't know the exact day, but it was late spring. I remember there were only a few days left of school. I figured I'd go to my mom's office. Maybe she'd take me to lunch. Maybe she'd give me money to buy a sandwich down on State Street."

"You went to the biogenetics building?"

"No. It wasn't built then. I went to the old place. Where my mother used to work. I knew the back staircase. Tucked in the corner. The one that always smelled wet no matter what the day was like outside. It was the fastest way to get to the lab where her office was. I remember passing a couple of students when I got to her floor. They were heading out. Probably to grab their own sandwiches. Maybe they'd sit in the grass. Like I said, it was a really warm day."

Sally tapped her hand on the table. Like she was trying to grab my attention. "Stay focused, Tess. Can you do that for me? You climbed the musty staircase, passed some students, then what?"

My chest heaved. My hands shook. "The door to my mother's office was open. I went in, but she wasn't there. Then

I heard her laugh. Just a little. Like a giggle maybe. I walked toward the sound. It was coming from a small room off my mother's space. The room where the copiers and worktables were. They didn't see me."

"Who's *they*, Tess? We need to hear it from you."

I looked to the corner. Anderson was standing with his arms crossed over his chest, listening to every word. I turned back to Sally.

"My mother was there with Phillip Jasper. She was leaning against a cabinet. Her arms were around his neck and he was . . . he was . . ."

"You're doing great, Tess. What was Phillip Jasper doing?"

A brief sob escaped in an angry choke. "He was unbuttoning her blouse! His fingers were working their way down the front, and my mother was letting him! She wasn't stopping him! She was smiling!"

"That must have been hard for you to see."

I slammed both hands on the table. "She was my *mother!* She had a *husband!* You're not supposed to be doing that if you have a husband! And you're not supposed to be doing that while you're at work and your husband is trying so hard to make everything right for the family!"

"Relax, Tess. Take a deep breath. Calm down." Sally gave me a minute to settle. "What did you do then?"

"I backed away. I remember walking on my tiptoes, trying to be quiet. I was afraid of what might happen if they caught me."

"Did you go back to school? Back to the fire drill?"

I shook my head. "I ran home. The house was empty. I went straight to my room. I don't know how long I was there. All I remember was my rage. Then hearing my father's footsteps coming up the stairs. He was calling for us. First my mother's name, then mine. He opened my bedroom door, took one look at the disaster my anger monster had made, and demanded to know what was going on. He started picking up the pillows and blankets I'd yanked off my bed. Yelling at me for making such a mess. Shouting how I needed to gather all the books off the floor and return them to their shelves. Warning me I'd be punished for the mess I'd made."

"Did that make you mad?" Anderson asked. "Madder even than you were before?"

I bit my lower lip and looked at him through tear-swollen eyes. "It wasn't fair," I whispered.

Sally tapped her hand on the table again, and I turned to face her. "What happened then?"

I rocked back and forth. I weighed how much to tell her and decided I had nothing to lose by explaining it all. "I told him it wasn't my fault. That my mother had made me so mad I couldn't control what I was doing. I told him everything. What I saw. My mother kissing her boss. Letting him do all sorts of things to her and smiling while he did them. He didn't believe me at first, but I kept talking. Describing. He didn't seem mad at me anymore. He stood there. In my wrecked bedroom. Holding on to a stuffed Hello Kitty. He didn't move one bit. Then my mother came home. I heard the front door open. She called out my name. I opened my mouth to respond to her, but my father held up his hand, signaling me to be quiet."

"Did he seem angry?"

"No. He looked sad. Sadder than I'd ever seen anybody look. But then there was something else, too. I couldn't describe it. He called out to her in a sweet voice. Told her the two of us were up in my room. Asked her to come on up. He sounded so nice and normal. But the look on his face scared me."

"What happened next?" Anderson asked.

"My father grabbed my mother as soon as she walked in my bedroom. First by the arm. Lifted her right up off the ground. I remember she looked like a rag doll the way he was shaking her. Like she didn't have any bones in her body. Then he grabbed her hair. He started slapping her. Calling her all kinds of names. My mother was struggling to get her feet under her. But he kept yelling and hitting. I screamed for him to stop. He was hurting her way more than he ever had before."

"Did he stop?" Sally asked.

"Kind of. He twisted his hand in her hair and pulled her so she could stand if she used her tippy toes. My father looked at me. He started screaming at *me* then. *Isn't this what you wanted? Isn't this why you told me? Look what you're making me do, Tess!* Then he hit her again. And again. *Look what you're making me do!*"

"Oh, Tess!" Sally reached out and laid a warm hand on my arm. "You were a little girl then. Can the grown-up you are now see that you had nothing to do with your father beating your mother?"

"But I did!" I jerked my arm away from her comfort. "I told him! I told him what I saw! If I would have kept my big mouth shut it never would have happened. None of this ever would have happened!"

"Did you see your father kill your mother?" Anderson stepped out of his corner and stood behind Sally. "Were you there?"

I shook my head. "I ran out of that room. I should have stayed and protected my mother, but I was so mad. At her for what I'd seen her doing with Jasper. And at my father for what he was doing to her. I was scared, too. I knew my dad. There was no telling what it would take to make him stop."

"Where'd you go?" Sally asked.

"I ran back to school. Classes were over for the day by then, but some of the kids had after-school stuff. I was done crying. I wasn't even mad anymore. But I was still plenty scared. I remember I went to my locker and got my lunch. My classroom was empty, so I went in there and ate."

"How long did you stay?" Anderson was all business.

"I don't know. But Mr. Finley, the gym teacher, walked past and saw me in there. He barked out at me, telling me it was way past time to go home. When I didn't move, he came in. He took one look at me and he wasn't barking anymore. He took me to the principal's office, but Mrs. Kohler wasn't in. I remember her secretary telling Mr. Finley it had something to do with the fire drill. So he asked her what he was supposed to do with me. Miss

Margie . . . that was Mrs. Kohler's secretary . . . Miss Margie. She told Mr. Finley she'd take care of things."

"That's a lot of details coming into focus," Anderson growled. "Would have been nice if you'd shared these with us hours ago."

Sally spoke to him before I had to. "This is par for the course, Andy. Tess has spent a lifetime protecting herself from memories of torture and agony. She built a fortress around what she experienced as though her life depended on it. To a twelve-year-old? Living through that kind of ongoing abuse? I'm sure she truly believed her life *did* depend on holding all those memories in a dark and deep place. And it worked. For a whole lot of years she was able to convince herself she hadn't experienced the murderous terror she, indeed, had. My hunch is that when Tess heard about the body being discovered, either on the radio or in the newspapers, a tiny sliver in her memory vault cracked open. It's taken us hours today, but we've been able to open the door to that vault—the one Mimi stood guard in front of to shield Tess from her pain. The details are going to spill out now. In an ironic way, the very memories she's been trying so hard to forget are the things that will protect her." Sally shifted her focus back to me. "That's why Mimi came to you, Tess."

"I'm losing my mind. That's what you're telling me."

Sally's face reflected her understanding and support. "No. Not at all. I know it all sounds crazy to you right now."

I flinched at the word *crazy.*

"Let me rephrase that. It must sound *unbelievable* to you right now. You experienced Mimi as a flesh-and-blood woman. An intriguing mystery. You described yourself as being distrustful of her at first. That was your terrified inner twelve-year-old. Mimi came to you to help you tell your truth. To let the world know what really happened to your mother. You came to trust Mimi, didn't you?"

I inhaled but said nothing.

"You said you admired Mimi's confidence. Her fearlessness. Remember how she encouraged you to speak with John?"

I nodded.

"*You* wanted to ask John out. But the protective shell you've been living in didn't allow for anything so bold. You needed Mimi to encourage you. That was your mind's first step toward trusting her. Toward you accepting what you needed to do."

"But she was real," I said. "I saw her. I heard her. She slept on my couch."

"That was your mind allowing you to become comfortable with her. Your subconscious mind brought Mimi into your conscious awareness in a way that seemed very normal. You first saw her walking down a familiar street. Then you spoke to her in a bar in a neighborhood you know like the back of your hand. You shared a drink on a hot summer evening. What could be more normal?"

"I don't know what to think. It can only be one of two things. Either Mimi exists and you're trying to trick me somehow, or Mimi doesn't exist and I'm insane. Either way sounds like trouble for me."

"Can you look at it from another angle? Can you see twelve-year-old Tess needing to save herself? She watched her mother die at the hands of her father . . ."

"I never said that!" My interruption was louder than necessary. "I never said my father killed my mother."

"Then who did?" Anderson asked.

Again, Sally intervened before I needed to speak. "Andy, please. You're going to have to let Tess tell her story as it reveals itself to her."

Anderson made a face as if he wasn't buying any of this. Sally clarified for him. "You have a son, correct? Five years old?"

"I don't see what Timmy has to do with this."

"Think of Timmy's devotion to you. That sparkle in his eyes he gets when he knows he's made you proud. It's a truism of human nature, Detective. Kids will do anything to please or protect their parents. Tess witnessed an unspeakable act. She saw the most powerful person in her life eliminate her own mother with his bare and bloody hands. She was alone. Terrorized.

Traumatized. And the very man who'd perpetrated her torture was telling her again and again he did it all for her. Is it really that difficult for you to understand that Tess wouldn't dare whisper one word against her father?"

Sally had pieced things together. I bowed my head and watched Anderson wrestle with what she had just described.

"So what do you suggest we do?" he asked. "And, I swear to God, if you tell me we have to listen to more details, I'm going to need my own Mimi to keep me sane."

Sally's eyes flared at the insensitivity of his remark. Anderson raised both hands in apology and stepped back to once again lean against the wall.

"Go on, Tess." Sally's voice returned to its therapeutic cadence and tone. "You said you recalled going to the principal's office and the secretary . . . Miss Margie, was it? You said she told the gym teacher she'd take care of things. What did she do?"

"She took me into the bathroom. Not the one the kids use, but the big one that's for teachers. She told me to wash my face and splash on some cold water to get rid of the puffiness."

"Did you follow her advice?"

I nodded. "While I was cleaning myself up she told me a story about her own dad." I shrugged. "Maybe Phillip Jasper was right. Maybe everyone in town really did know about my dad's temper. Anyway, she told me when she was a little girl, sometimes she needed to stay away from home for a night. She asked me if I wanted to go home with her."

"Did that seem strange to you?"

"Not at all. Miss Margie had a daughter a year older than me. Olivia. My grade and her grade got together twice a month for music appreciation. Olivia and I were assigned to the same group sometimes. She seemed nice. And since her mom was the principal's secretary, that made Olivia kind of a celebrity. Besides, my mother knew Miss Margie. I remember telling my mother once that some kids were making fun of Olivia because she never had a dad. They said her mom had done a bad thing. My mom told me to ignore what they were saying. She said there were lots of reasons little girls didn't have dads and I was always to treat Miss Margie with the respect she deserved. So when she asked if I wanted to go home with her, well, that sounded like a great idea to me."

"I'll bet."

"Miss Margie called my mother. Told her she and Olivia were going to have a pizza night and wanted to know if I could join them for a sleepover. Miss Margie even said my mom didn't have to worry about clothes for the next day. She'd look through Olivia's closet and find something for me."

"So your mother was alive at that point?" Anderson asked.

I would have bet good money I had no tears left, but when Anderson asked that, one last drop found its way down my cheek. "I remember being relieved."

Anderson nodded. "Go on."

"I went to school the next day. After the pizza night with Olivia and Miss Margie. I don't remember much of what went on, but when school was done I walked home like it was any other day."

"Did you see your mother?" Anderson asked.

"Yes." I bowed my head again. "Yes, I saw her."

"Did that frighten you, Tess?" Sally asked.

I brought my hands to my face, covering my eyes against the memory. "She was bruised. Not only her face, but her neck and arms. My father was there, too. He wasn't dressed for work. He was still in his bathrobe. They hadn't seen me come in. They were in the kitchen. I remember a big bottle of whiskey was sitting on the table. It was almost empty. My father looked so sad, so sorry for what he'd done. He was crying, begging her to forgive him. Promising this would be the last time he ever did those things. But she kept insisting." I jerked my head up. I looked at Sally, blinking my eyes. "She told my father *I'm done with all this. I don't want you.* She said it over and over, despite my father's pleas. My mother was telling *him* that. She was getting ready to leave *him!* Not me! All these years I . . ."

"All these years you thought she was saying those words to

you." Sally finished my thought for me. "All kids think everything is about them. Can you see how that childhood misconception formed the basis of the belief that your mother abandoned you?"

I didn't respond.

"Did your mother leave then?" Anderson asked.

"She tried. I remember she had her car keys in her hand. But my father blocked her way. Then he, he started yelling again. His hand was in a fist. He . . ."

"Did you see your father hit your mother again?" Anderson pressed.

Again I said nothing.

"What did you do then, Tess?" Sally asked.

"I went upstairs. To my bedroom."

"Did your mother come up to check on you?"

This time I looked straight at Detective Andy Anderson.

"I never saw my mother alive again."

CHAPTER 30

Someone knocked on the interview room door. Anderson answered it and stood in front of the opening, blocking me from seeing who was there.

"He's here," a disembodied voice said. "Room four. I don't know how much good he's gonna do ya. Guy's so drunk it was all he could do to walk in on his own."

"Okay. Let him sleep it off while I finish up here. How are the rest of the interviews going?"

"Check a clock, Anderson. It's tomorrow already. We got most everybody's statements. Sent 'em all home. The boss is coming in the morning."

"Thanks. Secure Sleeping Beauty's door, then go on home yourself. We'll review the statements tomorrow."

Anderson closed the door and returned to his spot behind Sally.

"Were you talking about my father?" I asked. "Is he here?"

"We have to hear what he has to say about all this," Anderson said.

"Don't hurt him. He's more fragile than he looks. He's sick."

"You still feel the need to protect him, don't you?" Sally asked.

"Does that make me crazy?"

"No. And I'm going to tell you again. You're not crazy."

"Nobody's going to hurt him?"

"You heard Detective Anderson. Your father's sleeping it off in an interview room. We didn't question him earlier. We needed to get to your truth before we brought him in. His rights will be protected. You need to take care of you."

I turned my head toward Anderson. He looked tired.

"Am I under arrest?"

"Not at all," Sally assured me. "A few more questions and we'll have an officer drive you home. I'll bet you're ready for a long shower and even longer sleep-in."

"I have to be at work."

"Let's not worry about that right now." She settled back in her chair. I wondered how she kept calm and relaxed after so many hours in this room. Anderson looked ready to drop, yet Sally had the appearance of someone who hadn't any need for a second wind. "You said you never saw your mother alive after she and your father argued in the kitchen."

"He wasn't arguing at first. My father was begging. It was my mother telling him she was leaving. She made him so angry. We were her family. You can't blame him. I was mad, too."

"You told us Phillip Jasper was surprised to learn your mother hadn't taken you with her when she left your father. He couldn't have known the reason was that she was dead. We have no evidence whatsoever that your mother was planning on leaving *you*. So I'm wondering if you can start challenging that notion when it pops into your mind."

I thought about that for a bit. "Maybe."

"Maybe, too, you can accept the idea that when you heard about the body being found, your subconscious realized it had to be your mother's body. Childhood fears returned. But this time combined with an adult's awareness of what truly happened. That tension between morbid fear and appetite for justice caused a split. You needed a way to bridge the two . . . to resolve things . . . to protect yourself while allowing room for truth. In that moment, Mimi appeared."

"I don't know. She's so real."

"You've seen the surveillance footage from Biogenetics," Anderson said. "No Mimi. You've heard from the folks in History. No Mimi. No faculty job. We have a statement from your friend, the pharmacist, stating he's certain it was you who purchased the DNA kit."

"Carl Crittens? You interviewed him?"

Anderson nodded toward the one-way mirror. "Every time you mentioned a name, we brought 'em in. Every place you said you and Mimi were, we pulled what evidence we could." He tapped an earpiece in his left ear I hadn't noticed before. "I'm getting updates after each interview. Nobody's seen Mimi. I could show you the recordings from Hotel Red's cameras. Your story checks out. You were sitting out on their patio having your gin and tonic. Right when you said. But you were sitting there alone."

"But I . . . she . . ." I turned to Sally and shook my head. "These memories I'm having of my mother now . . . Phillip Jasper kissing her . . . my father . . . my father . . ."

"Those memories have always been there," Sally said. "Too scary for a twelve-year-old to handle. Your mind created Mimi. It was her job to hold the memories of your terror."

"I don't . . ."

"You'd witnessed your father's murderous rage," Sally explained. "Mimi kept you one step removed from your terror. She allowed you to ignore your fear and keep your relationship with your father. To your eyes he was the only person left in your world. You were a kid. You needed a parent. Someone to protect you. You clung to the only one you had left. Can you see how Mimi and this entire experience allowed you to tell what you knew you needed to, yet still stay safe? When you saw your father kill your mother . . ."

"I never said that! How many times do I have to tell you?" My agitation rose despite my fatigue.

"Relax, Tess." Sally had gone back to the voice she used when she made me feel so tired and heavy. "You're as safe here as you've always been. Some memories are emerging. The rest will come in time. Don't fight them. Close your eyes again. Can you do that for me?"

I looked at Anderson. Then at the mirror where who-knows-how-many people were monitoring my every word. Checking them out and whispering into Anderson's ear.

"I won't let anyone harm you," Sally soothed. "Close your eyes."

I looked at her one more time, hoping she could read my plea for protection. She nodded her encouragement, and I did as she asked.

"It was a very scary night for you." Sally's voice came to me from the other side of my quivering eyelids. "You were a little girl. You'd seen horrific things. Heard vicious words. You went up to your bedroom. You needed to get away."

Sally stopped speaking. I kept my eyes closed. My breathing slowed. Once again, my body felt heavy and warm. Then she spoke again.

"What did you do up there in your room?"

"I don't remember."

"I'll bet you can. Call that childhood bedroom of yours to mind. Imagine how it was decorated. Was there a desk for you to do homework? Perhaps a tree outside your window. Color in the details."

It took me a while to respond. "My bedspread is chenille. White. With a ballerina dancing on her tiptoes."

"Very good. Think back to that day. Are you sitting on your bed?"

"No." My voice sounded as if I was hearing it through a long metal tube. "I was on the floor. By the window."

"What were you doing?"

"I don't remember."

"Try. Picture twelve-year-old Tess. She's scared. She's run to her bedroom to escape. What is she doing?"

"She's hiding."

"Of course she is. What a clever little girl."

"She's behind the drape. Curled up. No one can see her."

"You're doing fine. Tell me what happened next."

My breathing grew shallow and rapid. My hands tightened into fists. "It got dark. I had to go to the bathroom, but I was too afraid to move. I didn't want to pee my pants."

"I can understand that."

"Then he came in. My father. *Tess. Tess. Where are you?* He didn't sound angry anymore."

"And then?"

"I don't remember."

"Tell me what you see. What picture is your mind giving you?"

"He pulled back the drape. Looked down on me hugging my knees against my chest." I inhaled a loud, short burst of air.

"What's happening now, Tess?"

"He's pulling me up. Onto my feet. *Your mother's been bad. Very bad. You shouldn't have told me. You made me do it. Why did you tell me?*"

"And you believed him, didn't you?"

I ignored her question. "I asked my father if I could go to the bathroom. He looked so sad. He hugged me close and tight. Then he released me. *Go on. You don't have to be scared anymore, Tess. Mommy won't hurt you ever again. You're my little angel. I'd do anything for you.*"

"What came next?"

My forehead wrinkled in concentration.

"I see dark. Full-on."

"Where? Where was it dark?"

I shook my head. "I don't know. There's rumbling. Motion."

"Are you in a car?"

"Maybe."

"Is your father driving? Is your mother in the car with you?"

"I don't know." I rocked back and forth. "It's even darker now. Muddy. I'm scared. *Don't be frightened, Tess,* he said. *We'll go home soon. I have one last thing to do for you. Then we can forget all about the hurt Mommy caused.*"

"Where are you?"

"I hear splashing. My shoes are getting wet. I need these shoes for gym class. Daddy's going to be upset if they get ruined!"

"You're doing great, Tess. What's Daddy doing now? What's making the splash?"

I stopped rocking. My chest heaved with the rapidity of a machine gun.

"Tell me what you see, Tess. What do you hear?"

"Rocks. I hear rocks thudding against one another."

"What do you see?"

"A pile. Half in, half out of the water."

"Are you piling those rocks?"

I didn't answer.

"Is Daddy piling the rocks?"

"I don't know."

"Is Daddy forcing you to help?"

I banged my fists against my legs.

"Daddy's piling the rocks down by the water. What are you doing, Tess?"

"I don't remember." I opened my eyes and pushed my chair away from the table. "I don't remember!" I screamed.

Sally got up and came to me. She knelt and rested a comforting arm across the back of my chair. She rested her forehead against my shoulder. I remember thinking it seemed like a motherly thing for her to do.

"I want to go home."

Sally patted my arm, then stood to face Anderson.

"She's spent. We have a good idea of what happened. Let her go home," she suggested. "Let's all of us get a good night's rest. Tess can come to my office tomorrow. We can work more on the rest of what she's been repressing all these years."

I turned my own pleading eyes toward Anderson. It took him a while to answer.

"What time tomorrow?" he asked Sally.

She looked at me. "Does ten o'clock sound okay? Does that give you time enough to rest?"

"I have to go to work," I whispered.

"You let me handle that. Ten o'clock?" She reached into her pocket and pulled out a card. "My clinic's on Regent. Not far from you, actually."

I took her card and ran my thumb across the embossed lettering. "I don't know . . ."

"I can help you put all of this behind you," she said. "You can finally be free to grieve your mother. Free to live your own life. Without fear."

I kept my focus on her business card.

"Ten good for you, Tess?" Sally asked.

"What about Mimi?"

Sally gave my shoulder a gentle squeeze. "Mimi served a purpose. She gave you the courage to tell us the truth. She's giving you the courage now to heal."

Anderson shuffled in place, running a hand over his almost-there hair. "C'mon. Let's get an officer to drive you home."

CHAPTER 31

The officer who drove me home asked if I wanted her to go inside and check the place out. The look on her face told me she knew all about the crazy girl with the invisible friend. I told her I'd be fine. Still, she kept her squad car in the driveway until I was all the way into my apartment. A fleeting concern about what rumors the neighbors might manufacture to explain the police picking me up and returning me twelve-plus hours later was replaced with the realization that it didn't matter. I'd have to move anyway. This whole mess would be all over the newspapers in a matter of days. Maybe by tomorrow. My landlord would have no problem letting a lunatic out of her lease.

Everything in my apartment looked the same. I don't know what I was expecting, but I wasn't prepared for reentering my world and finding it exactly as I left it. I ran my hand over the back of my sofa. The upholstery was as nubby as it always had been. The hydrangeas and day lilies were still on my breakfast nook table. I'd picked them from Toni's garden on Monday, the day I wanted the place to look nice when John came to pick me up.

John. Surely he'd been one of the people Anderson's crew brought down to the station to interview. He'd seemed so hurt when I stopped returning his calls and texts. So concerned when he saw the bruises on my face. Still, my hunch was he, like my landlord, would be exhaling long and slow any time he remembered how close he came to hitching his wagon to a certifiable nutcase.

Live long and thrive, John Rappaport. Graduate from law school. Get yourself an office overlooking a gridiron. Then follow your grandpa's advice. Once you know where you're going, find yourself a nice girl to take the ride with you. Give yourself bonus points if she likes to read.

I should have gone straight to bed. My day had been long. Sally was expecting me in little more than nine hours. But after I washed my face and changed clothes, my insides hummed like an electrical cord that lost its insulation. I went into the kitchen and turned the gas on under the kettle. I reached for the box of chamomile tea, then changed my mind. I turned off the stove and pulled a bottle of Pinot Grigio from the fridge. It had been chilling since the day I'd picked the hydrangeas. I poured myself a glass and sat at my table built for two. The first sip was bracing. The second was smoother. I leaned back against the chair and allowed myself to relax.

It was over.

I was free.

My father always warned me that no one likes a braggart. He said the trait was especially distasteful in women. I'd always been a dutiful student of his teachings, hiding my light under a bushel anytime it threatened to illuminate the space where I stood. But, dammit, I'd done it. I'd planned my work and worked my plan.

I drained my glass with one long drink.

I was almost there.

There'd be a few details to wrap up, of course. If I still had a job, I'd need to quit. Once the story hit the newspapers about the "real" story of my mother's disappearance, even Brian would understand my need to take some time for myself. Rosie and Innocent and Agnes would probably want to stop by and offer their support and condolences. I'd probably have to do a session or two with Sally Normandy. By my estimates the acute phase of my plan needed to last no longer than a month. Six weeks at the outside. Then I could go.

Who would blame me for not wanting to stick around for my father's trial? After all, Sally will tell the court, he was the source of my trauma. The prosecution will explain how he killed my mother in front of me and led me to believe I drove him to it. They'll describe how he tortured me, a motherless child, with threats of violence. Created a situation where I was driven to a psychotic split and needed an imaginary double to save me.

Six weeks should do it, and then I was free.

But until my bags were packed and Madison, Wisconsin, was in the rearview mirror, I needed to keep myself well rested and alert. I walked to the sink, rinsed out my glass, and went down the hall. I could still get a good seven hours of sleep before I needed to visit Sally and convince her she was the greatest therapist this side of the Atlantic.

I set the alarm, pulled back the sheets, and turned out my bedside lamp. I settled my head on the pillow, allowed myself to relax, and dreamed of freedom.

My body grew heavy as I drifted toward sleep. It was not unlike the hypnotic state Sally tried to lead me into back in the police interview room. She was good. Staying focused on what I needed to do while she was trying to put me under took some work. This time I gave myself to it, allowing my fatigue to pull me deeper and deeper into the blissful abyss of sleep.

That's when I heard it.

Instantly awake, I opened my eyes and focused on the sounds in my dark apartment.

I heard it again.

A soft shuffling. Had I left a window open? Was a curtain blowing in the night breeze? But the weather was still stifling. Everything in the house was closed to accommodate the air conditioner.

I heard steps. Coming down the hall. Terror paralyzed me. I dared not turn on the light for fear of being seen.

Then another sound. Music.

I made it through the rain. I kept my world protected.

The footsteps came closer.

My body flushed with a surge of heat and fear.

"I love that song, don't you?"

That voice, so exactly like mine.

"You're not real," I whispered.

I'm drunk. Wine on an empty stomach.

"Tell yourself what you need to," she said.

My hands shook as I switched on the bedside light.

She was sitting on the edge of my bed. I pulled my feet up and away, not wanting to touch her.

"You did a great job with Sally and that ass of a police detective. I couldn't have done better myself. I'm proud of you, Tess."

For a long moment, I stared at her, and she looked right back at me. She was smiling.

"I . . . it was an accident," I said, my voice small and pleading. "I didn't mean to hurt her. I just wanted everything to go back to the way it was. I didn't mean for her to die."

"Oh, Tess. Who do you think you're talking to?"

I remembered sneaking out of the house all those years ago. I had no idea where I was going, but I hadn't gotten ten yards before my mother caught up with me. She grabbed me by the arm and pulled me into an embrace right there in the middle of Lathrop Street. Me flailing and her cooing.

"She tried to settle you down. But you weren't having any of it."

"How do you know that?"

Mimi's indulgent smile signaled she'd always know something I didn't. "Your mother suggested a long walk. Down by the willows behind Edgewood."

"It was my favorite place."

"She held your hand and led you to that spot the two of you had come to think of as your special hideaway. Down an overgrown lane by the marsh."

"Cattails brushed my legs. She told me we were moving. Far away."

"But you didn't care about your mother's plan. You kicked her. Screamed that you saw what she had done. She wanted to comfort you. Put her arms around you. Whisper she was so sorry her sweet Mimi had to see those things."

"Stop calling me that!" I screamed at Mimi the same way I'd screamed at my mother.

"You lunged at her as she stepped toward you with her arms open. Your anger monster was off its chain. It's amazing what a skinny preteen, all arms and legs and no more than seventy pounds, can do to a sad, exhausted, and bruised adult. Then again, while she may have been used to your father's beatings, your mother wasn't expecting a violent assault at the hands of her own daughter."

I felt again the rage I felt that day. "How dare she apologize! After all she'd done! I didn't want anything to do with her!"

"I think she got the message when you picked up that rock and smashed it down on her head. Remember?"

"Stop."

"She fell into the water. All you had to do was pull her free. Instead, you stood there and watched her drown."

"You're not real."

"Her body floated in front of you."

"I tried to push her down, but she wouldn't stay."

"But you're a clever girl. You gathered rocks. Chunks and slabs big enough to pile on top of her body."

"Stop."

"You buried her under those stones. Then ran back to Daddy."

"I could take care of him. I'd never leave him like she wanted to. We'd be fine. Just the two of us."

Mimi's eyes telegraphed her sympathy. "It was a big job for a little girl. All his drinking. All those moves. But now you're done. You've taken care of him."

I tightened my blanket around me. Like when I was little and thought I'd be safe from the monsters under my bed if only I stayed under the covers.

"You've duped them all. Your friends, the police, that psychologist. But you can't hide the truth from me."

"You can't be here," I whispered. "This is impossible."

Mimi scooted up the bed. She reached out and embraced me. I made a feeble attempt to push her away.

"Everything's going to be all right." Mimi's murmuring was a lifeline in a dark sea. "I'm your big sister. You're not alone anymore."

I leaned my head onto her shoulder. I felt her stroke my damp hair.

"I've got you, Tess," she cooed. "I've got you."

Connect with Us

Visit us online at
KensingtonBooks.com
to read more from your favorite authors, see books
by series, view reading group guides, and more.

Join us on social media

for sneak peeks, chances to win books and prize packs,
and to share your thoughts with other readers.

facebook.com/kensingtonpublishing
twitter.com/kensingtonbooks

Tell us what you think!

To share your thoughts, submit a review,
or sign up for our eNewsletters, please visit:
KensingtonBooks.com/TellUs.